Bury Me A G 3

Tranay Adams

Lock Down Publications
Presents
Bury Me A G 3
A Novel by *Tranay Adams*

Lock Down Publications

P.O. Box 1482

Pine Lake, Ga 30072-1482

Copyright 2015 by Tranay Adams Bury Me A G 3

First Edition September 2015
Printed in the United States of America

Lock Down Publications
Email: tranayadams@gmail.com
Facebook: Tranay Adams
Like our page on Facebook: Lock Down Publications
@www.facebook.com/lockdownpublications.ldp
Cover design and layout by: Dynasty's Cover Me
Book interior design by: Shawn Walker
Edited by: Tumika Cain

Tranay Adams

Chapter One

Wicked sat a worn brown leather bag down on a table against the wall that looked like it was made to carry a bowling ball. With latex-gloved hands, he unzipped the bag and began pulling out shiny silver tools that were made specifically for torture. One by one, he laid the tools on the old, rusty iron tabletop until he drew the last. *Snikt!* He turned around to Te'Qui, smiling devilishly. The illumination from the dim light bulb in the ceiling pounced off of the Instrument of Death and a glare swept up its length.

Te'Qui's ten-year-old eyes bulged and his mouth hung open. His heart raged inside of his chest, showing its impression on his left peck as it beat out of control. His head snapped from left to right. At this moment, he was wondering how the hell slinging a little crack to cop some chains for him and his best friend had left his right hand dead and his older brother ready to torture him because he wouldn't give up the cat that gave them the drugs. If he could go back and change the past couple of weeks he would, but unfortunately he couldn't, so he was left to deal with this mad man and his aunt.

Helen dropped the spent beer can at her feet, crushed it with her flat and kicked it aside. Wicked advanced in his direction with the tool in his hand and evil thoughts on his mind. With nothing to lose, Te'Qui decided to make a run for it. He made a mad dash for the steps, but something caught him while in motion. Suddenly propelled up into the air, he came down hard on his face, busting and bloodying his mouth. Licking his lips and swallowing, he tasted metal. His eyelids opened just in time to see his red tooth tumbling up. He felt around inside his mouth and came across the space between his teeth. When he looked to his fingers they were stained with blood.

He looked to his ankle and saw that it had been shackled to the wall. He'd been much too panicked to notice before. When he looked up, Wicked and Helen were approaching him, laughing like a couple of crazed maniacs.

Te'Qui squeezed his eyelids closed and mouthed a prayer to himself, hoping that God Almighty would pull his black ass out of this one.

"The Lord can't save you, lil' homie. Only you can," Wicked spoke honestly. "You either tell me who this cat is that gave you and bro bro that work, or I'm gonna make sure you get acquainted with each and every tool in that there bag behind me, ya dig?"

Te'Qui closed his eyes as he swallowed hard. He peeled them back open and stared up at his enemy with defiant eyes.

"Yeah, I dig and I still ain't telling you shit! Suck my dick!" He threw up both middle fingers, letting them linger.

Te'Qui was pissed off at Wicked for threatening to bring harm to him for not dropping dime on who it was that gave him and his brother the crack to sell, being that he was against snitching. In fact, Wicked was one of the main niggaz that drilled into his head that telling wasn't an option, under any circumstances. Te'Qui couldn't believe it. For as long as the maniac gang-banger had known him, he was about to slaughter him like a pig for not submitting to him.

Ain't this about a bitch? The young nigga thought, feeling flabbergasted. *Before I eat the cheese, they'll be bury me a g.*

"Oh, I'm gonna love this," Wicked stated with a fiendish smile. Kicking the youngster in the chin, he knocked him unconscious then pressed his sneaker against the little dude's chest, moving to perform surgery with the shiny instrument. He stopped himself short when his cell phone rang, intending to ignored it, but something told him that he should see who it was. Withdrawing his cellular, he flipped it open and glanced at the screen. His brows furrowed seeing the name, but he knew he'd best answer the call. Placing the device to his ear, he answered.

"What's brackin'?" His eyes wandered as he listened to what he was being told. He was hot as a firecracker, being that the call had interrupted him right when he was about to lay his torture game down on Te'Qui. "I'm in the middle of something right now. Let me wrap this up and..." He was cut short from the earful he received. "I know, I know, I know..." He blew hot air, feeling cheated, because he knew that the plans that he had for Te'Qui would have to wait until later. The call he had gotten was a very important one and the situation had to be addressed pronto. "I'll be there, two hunnit." He disconnected the call and slipped the cell into his pocket. "You one lucky lil' nigga, you know that?"

"Who was that?" His Aunt Helen frowned.

Ignoring her question, he simply said, "I got some business I gotta tend to." He sat the tool into the worn leather bag. "You babysit our friend here until I get back, alright?" He zipped the bag up and turned to her, pulling a compact handgun from the small of his back.

"Alright." She nodded and took the gun.

"Good." He hugged her affectionately and kissed her on the cheek. "I'll be back in a minute."

Wicked headed back up the staircase, leaving his aunt alone with Te'Qui. She planted a chair down before him and leaned forward, allowing the handgun to dangle between her legs as she watched him attentively.

***

Wicked hopped behind the wheel of his BMW and tucked his banger underneath the driver seat. After firing up the sexy machine and adjusting the rearview mirror, he pulled off, cranking up the volume on Dr. Dre's *Bang Bang* from The Chronic 2001.

Everyday it's the same thing,
L.A. ain't changed
Niggas still player hating,
but Dre ain't changed
I'm just a lot smarter now
'Cause these niggas is banging ten times harder now
Niggas bringing they ass up in the wrong part of town
Better turn they car around
Rollin' the window down (hey, can we talk it out?
Nah get the fuck out!)
Johnny got a shotgun
And he ain't even strong enough to cock one
Fuck tryin' to job hunt.

Wicked stared ahead watching the street and taking swigs from his flask. Face solemn, deadpan look in his eyes. The night's cool air blew in through the cracked open windows, disturbing the loose strands of hair sticking out of his cornrows, while the illumination of light posts flickered on and off his face as he drove the dark city streets. Taking a swallow of the dark liquor, his mind wandered back to the day he became indebted to one of the most ruthless Jamaicans Kingston had ever spawned.

Wicked disrobed and entered the shower in flip-flops. The room was humid and foggy. He stared straight ahead, but he could see all of the men surrounding him. Each of them were occupied, lathering themselves with soap, washing shampoo from out of their hair, or heading back into the locker room to dry off and dress. The inmates were minding their own business and paying him no mind. Seeing this, Wicked turned his back against the spray of the showerhead. When the hot liquid hit his head, it laid his hair down and coated his body. He made sure to keep an eye open while he lathered up. By no means was Wicked a stranger to prison, every time he went in, he left with a new set of enemies. He robbed, cheated, stole, and opened niggaz up with razors. He never knew when his dirt would come back to haunt him, so he had to grow an extra pair of eyes in the back of his head.

The hot water that poured over Wicked's form soothed and relaxed him, freeing him of his tension. It felt damn good. So good that he closed his eyes and soaked in that moment. That one moment was all it took for some shit to jump off. Wicked's eyelids snapped open hearing hurried flip-flopped feet slapping against the wet tile. He looked from left to right, identifying the four men closing in on him. He knew he had to react fast or that was going to be his ass.

"Ah, niggaz wanna pack me, Blood?"

Crack! Bwap! Pwap!

Wicked dropped one of the opposing men with ease and followed up with the next. He chopped him in his throat, causing him to gag then grabbed him by the back of his neck. With a grunt, he swung him into the white tiled wall. Thunk! He busted his nose and mouth, falling to the floor and leaving a smear of red behind. Wicked went to turn around and met with a solid right to the chin. His head slammed up against the wall and he fell to his palms and knees. He went to get up, but a kick in the ribs brought him back down on all fours. Before he knew it, he was swarmed. His body and head got real acquainted with fists and bare feet. The men assaulted him until they were left with flaring nostrils and heaving chests.

"Hold his ass, hold 'em right there!" The baldheaded convict gave the order, dropping the lock into a sock, causing it to go slack. He grasped the opposite end of it and spun it around

rapidly, twisting it up, setting the lock in place. "So, you like raping lil' girls, huh, mothafucka? Alright."

His eyebrows arched and his nose scrunched up, lips peeling back in a sneer. He threw his hand back, grunting and swinging the sock across his face. Crack! Thwhack! Bwap! Whack! The assault split open Wicked's forehead and right cheek, red webbing his eye. His nose fractured and burgundy blood flushed from his nasal cavity, tatting up the tiled floor and washing down the drain. His eyes were hooded and his vision was blurry. He moaned. His head throbbed like he had the worst migraine and his broken jaw was aching.

"Big brudda!" *The voice rang from the doorway.*

The bald con and his henchmen's heads snapped in the direction from which the voice came. They found a tall, skinny man with keloids and burns on his bony chest. His hair was a crop of wild dreads that were long and thick. They looked bigger than his head and heavier than his body. Standing on both sides of him were three Rastas. They were sporting shorter dreads, nappy heads, and fades. They wore menacing expressions and looked like they'd kill on their leader's command, like a couple of trained attack dogs. Beyond them were two C.O.'s masking the door so no one would be able to get out of the shower room unless they permitted it.

"Let da mon go now, he's takin' 'nuff of a beatin.'" *The dread spoke with an easy Jamaican drawl.*

"What? You betta raise yo punk ass up from outta here!" *Baldhead frowned, looking him up and down.*

"Me dunt 'spect nuttin' fa free, I'm willin' ta buy da man's debt from ya."

Baldhead's forehead wrinkled and he exchanged glances with his men. Turning back to the dread, he said, "Are you fuckin' serious?"

"As cansah."

"Nuh uh." He shook his head, *"Ain't 'bout the money, this cock sucka..."* He grabbed a fist full of Wicked's thick, nappy hair and pulled his head back. His eyes were peeled to their whites and he was groaning in pain. He was in bad shape. *"...likes sticking his grown ass dick in lil' babies, the slimy mothafucka that he is."*

"Me know of da man's sins and me have bigga plans fa him."

"Like what?"

"Dat's no business of yours, and I'm growin' impatient wit' ya chit chat."

"Nigga, fuck you!" He scrunched his face up, looking at him like *'who in the fuck do you think you are?'*

"Right." With that said, the dread and his men drew shanks from the waistlines of their towels. The blades were long and thick, looking like they'd cause major damage no matter what part of the human body they hit. *"Here's the deal, Mr. Big Shot..."* He twisted the knife in his long dirty fingernail as he talked. *"I'm gonna give ya ten boxes of cigarettes of ya choosin' and ya gon' take 'em or ya gon' take deez knives up ya ass."* His eyebrows slanted downward and he clenched his teeth hard, creating wrinkles around his gruffly face. *"The decision is yours, batty bwoi! Choose wisely."*

The baldheaded convict looked from the shanks the dreads were wielding to the weapons of his henchmen. They had two blades between them. If they bucked against the rude boys there wasn't any doubt in his mind that they'd be lying sprawled about on the wet floor of the shower room with their blood spiraling down the drain. He wanted to say fuck it and lock ass with the Rastas, but being the wise leader that he was, he couldn't jeopardize the lives of his men over his foolish pride.

"Alright," he submitted. *"You can take this piece of shit."* He looked to his men that were holding Wicked up. *"Let 'em*

go." They released him and he went face first, busting and bloodying his mouth, too weakened from the beating to hold himself up. The spray of the showerhead pelted his head and washed the blood from his bleeding wounds, sending it down the drain. His eyes were no more than slits as he continued his groans of pain.

Baldhead pointed a crooked and calloused finger at the dreads' leader. "But I want my ten boxes of Newports, tomorrow afternoon, soon as chow is over." He spoke with hostility trying to save face, knowing damn well that the opposition would have left him, and all of his crew, leaking something awful.

The dread nodded and said, "Ya got it, Mr. Big Shot, tomorrow afternoon." He turned to the C.O.'s that were watching the door for him. "Gentlemen, would ya be so kind as ta let these fine men through?" The correctional officers stepped from out of the doorway, allowing the men to exit.

Once baldhead and his men had made their departure, the dread kneeled down to Wicked, tapping his shoulder until he was sure that he had his attention. The battered man's eyes shifted to him and he kept right along groaning.

"Ya a proud mon, so I know ya won't wanna go into PC fa fear of lookin' like a sissy bwoi," he began. "Ya want ta stay in Gen Pop? Alright, ya eat and play dee yard wit' me and mine."

"Uuuhhhhh!" Wicked groaned in agony, he wanted to buck, but his pain left his mouth paralyzed.

"Exactly," he continued. "Anotha ting, I jus' bought ya ass, ya belong ta me now, ya my bitch. Ya debt is paid when I say so and notta time earlier. I'll see ya later, Sleepin' Beauty." He rose to his feet and stomped his head, leaving him in darkness. Wicked wouldn't wake up until sometime later the next day. From that day forth he ate and played the yard with the Jamaicans. They protected him from the other inmates looking

to tax his ass for the girl that he had raped. The dread got his walking papers a year before he got his. He figured that he must have been keeping tabs on him, because he had someone get into contact with him shortly after he left prison.

Wicked killed his vehicle and took another swig from the flask before screwing the cap back on it.

Wicked wasn't feeling being in Roots presence again, especially after what had happened. He had it in mind to lay the Kingston gangsta down, but had second thoughts. Giving homie that eternal sleep would definitely bring out some of the most ruthless criminals from his motherland. Now, by no means was Wicked afraid of these men, but he was far from stupid. His lone gun would be no match for all of theirs. So he had no choice but to push that suicide mission to the back of his mental.

He slid it into his back pocket and wiped his mouth with the back of his hand as he peered out through the driver side window. Across the street there was an old white house with a rusting metal fence and a dirt patch lawn. He wasn't sure that it was the place that he was looking for, so he checked the text message the caller had sent him with the address on the front of the house. Seeing that it was the home he was told to meet the caller, he stashed his cell in his pocket and slid his banger from beneath the driver seat. He tucked it on his waistline as he hopped out of the car and slammed the door behind him. He was about to jog across the street until a pickup truck sped past him, holding him up. Wicked looked up and down the block before hurriedly making his way across the street and into the yard of the white house.

He came upon the steps and froze where he was when he found a cat sitting on a chair facing him. The shade of darkness hid the man's features, but Wicked did make out his auburn dreadlocks and the automatic shotgun in his gloved hands. That mothafucka was trained on him, so if he tried to run then a hot one was going to swallow his back before he cleared the yard. Wicked made sure not to make any sudden movements. The last thing he wanted to do was to get murdered before he was able to exact his revenge.

"Raise ya hans real slow like." The man with the auburn locks spoke with authority.

"Punk ass mothafucka," Wicked said under his breath, doing as he was ordered. Being naturally rebellious, he hated being told what to do, but he wasn't a fool. The dread had a shotgun on him. Approaching cautiously, the Rasta recovered the steel on his waistline and a little pistol in a holster strapped to his ankle. Next, he stashed the guns on his person. He kept his shotgun on him as he leaned forward and pounded on the door with his fist. Someone shouted something to him in his native tongue and his shouted back, before opening the black iron door. He motioned toward the entrance by throwing his head to it and gesturing with his weapon. Wicked lowered his hands and crossed the threshold. As soon as he did, he was smacked in the face with the repugnant odor of some very potent weed. He narrowed his eyes, trying to peer through the fog ahead of him. His head snapped over his shoulders, hearing the door click shut behind him. He looked back ahead and made his way across the foyer and down the corridor, taking in the blaring noise that was Bob Marley's *I Shot the Sheriff.*

Wicked closed his eyes further and coughed, bringing a fist to his mouth. The weed was stronger than the hind legs of a donkey and smelled like diarrhea that had been heated up in the microwave. Stopping at the doorway of the den, he saw three Jamaicans sitting at a table wearing latex gloves. They bagged and chopped up work. Every so often they'd stop to indulge the biggest joint that he'd ever seen in his life. They laughed and talked shit amongst each other, carrying on like he wasn't even there. Or so he thought.

"Wiiickeeedd." The dread that had saved his ass back in prison greeted, with weed slanted eyes. A jovial expression was scrolled across his face as he passed the joint to the cat at his right. "Come heah." He motioned him over and rose to his feet, pulling the latex gloves from his bony hands. He scratched his gruffly cheek and embraced his guest with a hug that surprised him. He was always snickering and joyful when he was high. A far cry from the cutthroat dread he exhibited back in the joint.

"What's up with it? What chu need?" Wicked gave him a funny look.

"I needa tock."

"Talk?"

"Yeah, tock." He threw his arm around his shoulders and ushered him toward the bedroom. "Right dis way, ma friend."

Wicked's eyes latched on to the Jamaicans at the table as he was escorted toward the bedroom. They turned around in their chairs letting their eyes linger on him until he'd passed them. Their looks made him queasy and his stomach did somersaults. If the dread had his demise in mind then he was a mothafucking fool if he thought he was going down without a fight. Homeboy at the door may have relieved him of his guns, but he still had a box cutter wedged in his right sneaker. If the dread made the wrong move then that was his ass.

"Step into my office." Roots opened the door to a bedroom. He closed the door behind them when he entered. Wicked took in the bedroom as the dread locked the door. The space was fairly empty, save for the bed and the nightstand. When the Rasta turned around, he made sure to keep a close eye on his hands. He followed him over to the bed where they found a manila envelope. He opened the envelope and pulled out three photographs, passing them to him.

Wicked went through the photographs, feeling relieved that the Jamaican didn't try anything. Two of the photos were of a very tall and handsome dark-skinned man, while the last one was of him, a newborn baby and an attractive woman that looked like she may have been from Belize.

Wicked's brows furrowed and he looked up at the Rasta like *'Fuck you want me to do with these?'*

"Me want his fuckin' head on a platta." He eyes darkened and he scrunched his nose.

"This ain't 'bout shit. My murda game stay on point, Roots."

"Me know, me know." He patted his shoulder. "Ya skills wit dee gun is one of da reasons why me enlisted ya. I knew a mon wit' ya talents would be very useful ta my buddin' organization."

Wicked nodded his understanding. "So, if I do this for you, we square?"

"Yes. And just ta show ya dat it's not all dat bad wockin' fa me, I brought cha a gift." He pulled a joint from his shirt pocket and passed it to him. Wicked slid it beneath his nose, inhaling the loud aroma. A smile curled his lips.

"This that shit," he claimed. "You got this from the Motherland?"

"Yep, Jamaica, me home."

"Good looking out." He slapped hands with him.

"No problem. Me got somethin' else fa ya. Follow me." He opened the door and led him out into the living room, stopping at the basement door. After flipping on a switch, he unchained and unlocked the door. He stuck his hand out toward the doorway and nodded, signaling for him to go first. Wicked went on inside of the basement with Roots following closely behind, pulling the door shut.

The old wooden steps squeaked as Wicked descended them. He ran face first into a spider's web causing him to narrow his eyes and shake his head. He spat the web out that got in his mouth and pulled it loose from his face, letting it fall to the steps. Feeling something crawling up the back of his neck, he smacked it and took a gander at his palm. There wasn't anything there.

"Fucking spiders and shit, Blood, you needa getta exterminator." He glanced back at Roots and he was wearing a solemn expression. He went on down the staircase.

Woof! Woof! Woof! Woof!

He heard barking the further he got down the staircase. He looked to the left and saw a couple of Rottweilers standing around a naked, battered man who was tied to a rusting iron chair. His head was hung and he was shaking like one of those bitches on the pole at Magic City. His legs were chewed up and bloody and there was a puddle of piss between his bare, dirty feet.

Hearing the squeaking of the steps as the men descended them, the beasts snapped around and charged forth, barking. Wicked stopped where he was and instinctively went for the head bussa on his waistline, forgetting that it wasn't there. "Aww, shit!" He took a step back from the dogs, retreating from them.

"Say, Roots, you needa call off these mothafucking hounds!"

"Right." Roots rattled off some shit in his native language and the vicious animals dispersed. They went from angry beasts to a couple of fucking puppies. Wicked was surprised.

"Who is this?" He looked to the Jamaican and pointed a crooked finger to homeboy in the chair.

"Ya present." The Rasta smirked and gripped his shoulder, turning him toward the tortured man. "Unwrap 'em."

Wicked balled his face up. He looked from him to the beaten man, wondering what the hell was up. The way he saw it, if it was a trick, a hundred of them Jamaican niggaz with machetes would have come from everywhere ready to chop his ass up like a fucking coconut. Figuring that it wasn't a setup, he approached the poor bastard strapped to the chair, he placed his boot to his privates and mashed on them. He threw his head back, wailing at the top of his lungs. He screamed so loud that Wicked's and Roots' eardrums quaked. The men squinted their eyes and turned their heads, feeling the stinging of the noise in their ears. It felt like needles were jabbing them.

A light bulb of recognition came on inside of Wicked's head when he saw the man's face. The battered man was the cat that had led the pack of wolves back in prison that attacked him. This was the same cock sucka that had beaten his face with that lock in the sock in the shower room.

Wicked smiled maliciously and rubbed his hands together, like he had come up with the perfect master plan.

"My, oh my, how the tables have turned." He slid his wet tongue across his top row of gold teeth and sucked in his bottom lip, nodding his head. "Payback is a mothafucka, homeboy." He looked back at Roots. "G' looking, dread."

"Dun't mention it." He gave him a nod.

Wicked kneeled down and reached inside of his sneaker, snatching a box cutter free. Next, he grabbed baldhead by his neck, gripping it tightly, causing redness to form around his hand. He pushed the small square up the box cutter, extending the blade. Fear inhabited the man's eyes. The frightened man murmured and squirmed, trying to shake loose of the mad man's iron hold.

"No, arghhh!" His eyelids snapped open as wide as they could and he screamed aloud, spittle flying everywhere. Wicked smiled devilishly and his tongue curled at his top lip. He curved the box cutter around baldhead's forehead down along his hairline. Blood oozed out of the wound following the sharp razor's trail. Wicked gripped his bottom jaw so tight that his lips puckered up. He curved the box cutter along his jaw line causing the flesh to split, opening to the white, red-stained meat. Baldhead's eyes darted all around his head and he stomped his foot rapidly. The skin of his face leaned forth like a slice of bologna still attached to the roll. Once the blade had reached the opposite end of his victim's face, he stuck his fingers into the opening he created and got a good hold of it. While he was doing this, baldhead was still screaming hysterically. With a grunt and one strong tug, Wicked ripped the flap of skin off of his skull. It sounded like a strip of duct-tape being torn off. *Schhrrip!*

Roots didn't even flinch when he saw this. He stuck a joint between his lips and flicked a lighter until a flame licked the air. The end of the jay crackled as it met with the fire. The Jamaican's face scrunched a little as he sucked on the end of the marijuana stick, birthing clouds of smoke.

Wicked turned around, placing his victim's face onto his own. He locked eyes with the victim in the rectangular dirt smudged mirror which was broken at all of its corners. When the bald man saw all of the slick, glistening red muscles in his face, he screamed and screamed, each time louder than before causing that thing at the back of his throat to tremble. Wicked whipped around glaring at the man, looking like something out of The Chainsaw Massacre, donning the flap of skin that was his face. His eyes darkened and twinkled with madness. He clutched the box cutter in his hand tighter, causing his knuckles to turn white. He brought the lethal weapon around and swung it with all of his might, slicing open his jugular. He threw his head back and his tongue wormed around inside of his mouth.

His pupils looked like they shrunk as his eyes bulged. A searing, hot pain engulfed his neck like salt on a gash.

"Gaagggghhhhh!" His eyes stared up at his executioner as a black river oozed from the wide slit in his neck. His head bobbled after a time before it hung, his chin touching his drenched chest.

Sploch!

Wicked dropped his victim's face on the filthy floor. He approached a table in the far corner that had a little junk scattered upon it. He picked up an old tattered T-shirt and wiped his hands clean. He then wiped the box cutter free of his blood and prints before letting it drop to the floor.

"Gimme a week and I'll bring you his corpse." He said to Roots as he passed him, climbing the steps. He got about halfway up the staircase and turned around. "I forgot to ask you, what's the name of this cat whose cap you want me to peel back?"

"Donovan Cheatham, aka Don Juan."

Chapter Two

Honk! Hoonkk! Hooonkkk!
"Get the fuck outta the way!" she screamed harshly, veins bulging at her temples and neck. She was doing eight-five in a thirty-five mile an hour zone, flying in and out of lanes, narrowly missing other cars. Her heart rate was jacked, her adrenaline was amped, and she was scared as shit. Why? The love of her life was bleeding out, and bad. Her head snapped back and forth between the windshield and him, holding his bloody hand. "Hold on, baby, you hold on! You stay with me now!"

Faison was laid back in the seat, eyes blinking like mad and looking all about. His mouth was bloody and moving awkwardly. He was breathing eerily and trying not to choke on his own blood at the same time. The holes in him had saturated the lower half of his shirt red. "Ah. I'm. I'm dying, baby."

She whimpered and tears came down her face. "No! You're not gonna die, don't chu say that to me! Don't chu fucking say that shit to me!" Her head snapped back to the windshield where a Volkswagen was driving too slowly for her taste. "Get. The. Fuck. Outta. My. Waaaaayy!" She honked the horn madly.

Honk! Hoonnk! Hoooonnnk!

The driver of the Volkswagen honked his horn back and threw his middle finger up out of the window.

"Alright, bitch!" She floored it and zipped the car around, zooming real close to the Volkswagen. *Crash.* The side view mirror flew off and tumbled out in the street. She smirked and glanced out of the rearview mirror seeing the driver of the Volkswagen hop out and examine his whip. He kicked the car's front tire and turned in her direction, throwing up the middle finger.

"Hahahahaha!" She laughed aloud, staring into the mirror. "Fucking asshole!"

"Aaaaahhh." Her ex-fiancé's moans of excruciation brought her head back around. His eyes were rolled to their whites and his mouth was hanging open.

"Hold on, Faison, just hold on, we're almost there!" She slipped her hand away from his, it was stained crimson, but she didn't give a fuck. That was the least of her worries. Her main concern was getting her man to the hospital before he bled to death. She needed to focus if she was going to get him there before his life expired. She gripped the steering wheel with both hands and pressed the pedal to the metal. The vehicle accelerated, zipping down the street with her emergency flashers on and leaving debris in the air. Chevy dipped in and out of lanes, dodging other whips and nearly crashing twice.

Urrrrrrk!

A Jeep Cherokee skidded to a halt when Chevy sped by flying like a bat out of hell. *Zooooooom!* She almost clipped it, speeding toward her destination, not giving a mad ass fuck.

"Watch where you going, you stupid bitch!" the irate driver yelled.

"Home stretch, baby, home stretch!" She cracked a smile seeing the Centenela Hospital sign up ahead. She glanced at Faison as his eyes were narrowed into slits. He struggled to breathe, clenching and unclenching his fists. The smile disappeared and she adopted a scowl. "We're almost there, Fai."

She made a sharp left and the car nearly tilted over she was going so fast. She zipped right into the parking lot of the hospital, flying toward the emergency entrance.

Urrrrrk!

The vehicle came to a jerking halt and she threw open the driver side door, jumping out. She ran over to the opposite side and snatched open the door.

"Come on, baby, come on." She grabbed his hand and gritted as she struggled to pull him out. "Uhhhh!" She threw his arm over her shoulders, his head bobbled about as she walked him toward the exit. Her adrenalin was pumping so she barely noticed his weight. His legs were like cooked noodles and he was moaning in agony, but he was trying his best to stay ten toes down.

"Heeelp! Heeelp meee!" She blared like an after school bell, nearly going hoarse.

"Ahhh!" He moaned again and his legs gave out. He slowly went down and she went with him.

A moment later

Boom!

The double doors of the emergency ward went flying open. The hospital staff rushed Faison along on a gurney, tearing open his shirt and exposing the black bleeding holes in him. His eyes were hooded and his pupils moved around lazily. He was saying something, but no one could understand what he was talking about.

"What chu say, baby?" Chevy asked, running alongside the gurney, clutching his hand affectionately. Her face was soaked and she couldn't stop the tears from coming. It was like they were pouring down her cheeks in buckets.

"I love...I love you...Ch...Chevy," He croaked. "I'm sorry, baby. I'm so sorry for ever hurting you." His voice cracked and tears slid down his face as his bottom lip trembled. She'd never seen him cry, so she couldn't help sobbing aloud and wiping her eyes with the back of her hand. This was it, his last day alive. It had to be, with him carrying on talking like this. He was definitely in his final hour.

"I love you, too. I swear to God, Faison. I always loved you, babe. I never stopped and I never will."

Just as Faison was about to reply one of the doctors slipped an oxygen mask over his nose and mouth.

"Miss, I'm sorry, but you're going to have to wait outside." He told her. "We'll keep you updated."

"I'm gonna have to go, baby, but I'll be waiting for you, okay?" He slightly nodded his head. She caressed his forehead and kissed him tenderly on it.

"Miss, we've got him from here." The doctor placed a reassuring hand on her shoulder.

Chevy stopped where she was and cupped her hands to her face. She sobbed aloud and tears cascaded down her cheeks. She stood watching the hospital staff rushing her first love down the hallway toward the surgery room. She kept her eyes on them until they disappeared along the way, turning into nothing more than a few dots. Weeping, she turned around and headed back out through the double doors, her shoulders shuddering as she wept.

She never knew how much she still loved Faison until she came so close to losing him. Forever.

***

"Where. Is. He?" he asked, his tone implying, '*I'm not finna keep asking yo' mothafucking ass.*'

"Why don't chu go ask yaaahh!" He screamed at the top of his lungs with his head tilted back, the pinkness of his mouth could be seen, along with all of his cavities, and his beige teeth from years of smoking.

Thump! Another one of his fingers hit the floor.

"I can do dis all day, cock sucka! Try me!" he yelled, spit leaping from his lips.

Juvie looked up, wincing and breathing hard, chest jumping wildly. His face coated with perspiration.

"Wat chu godda say now, tough guy, huh?"

"Your breath smells like goat sex! Hahahahaha." He busted up laughing, infecting Uche, who looked over his shoulder at his brother. He was laughing, too. And just as quickly that pleasant expression was replaced. His forehead deepened with lines and his nose crinkled as his lips peeled back into a sneer, baring his teeth like a ferocious lion.

The spear whistled through the air, hacking off fingers unevenly. *Snikt! Thump! Snikt! Thump! Snikt! Thump!* The severed fingers hit the surface one after another making their own melody as they danced. By the time Uche was done playing butcher, all Juvie had was his thumbs left. He took a step back, holding his spear behind his back at an angle like he was about to attack again, his eyes never wavered from his victim. Through them it was as if he was saying '*What now, smart ass?*'

"You ready ta tell me sometin' now?" he asked, squared jaws pulsating, knuckles grasping the spear tighter, ready to decapitate his catch if he didn't talk.

Breathing hard, Juvie closed his eyes and made his lips into a tight line. He nodded and said, "Okay, okay…"

Juvie stood on the *no snitching* mantra, but with the threat of having more of his body parts hacked off, he folded like a bad hand in poker.

"Good, good bwoi." Uche patted Juvie's cheek and then examined his hand. The young hoodlum was squirting blood from where his fingers were severed. The African couldn't have him bleeding to death, so he whipped out a Zippo lighter and heated his spear until it glowed reddish orange. He brought the hot metal to his capture's severed fingers.

"Aaahhh!" Juvie's head snapped back as his eyes doubled in size. He wailed so loudly that he quaked Uche's and Uduka's eardrums. The Eme brothers winced and turned their heads, irritated by the deafening noise.

"Hold 'em steady, Duke!" Uche barked. He held tightly to the young thug's wrist and pressed the ember glowing spear head to the nubs that once were his fingers. It sounded like a cigarette being disintegrated to ash when the hot metal met the flesh, stopping the holes from spurting blood.

"Arghhh!" Spittle flew from Juvie's lips. Uduka frowned as he held him about the waist, but he still was able to squirm. The pain he felt was excruciating and he was trying to snatch away from his restraints.

"Stop ya belly achin.'" Uche balled up a rag and crammed it inside of his mouth, duct-taping it down across the lower half of his face. He wiped the beads of sweat from his forehead with the back of his hand and took off his suit's jacket. He threw it on the floor and got a better grip on his knife. "Stubborn bastard, ya stay still 'fore ya bleed ta death."

He tucked Juvie's arm under his firmly and went about the task off sealing off the blood squirting holes of his nubs. The young thug howled as loud as he could muster, feeling the sizzling hot metal pressed against his skin. Once the oldest Nigerian finished his business, he passed out cold, head hanging.

"Let 'em go, Duke." After releasing the hoodlum's arm, he turned to his brother, out of breath. He dropped down to the floor sitting Indian style and stabbed the spear into the surface. His sibling sat down right beside him. He too was panting.

"Wat do we do now, Uche?" Uduka peeled off his suit's jacket.

"We wait fa him ta come to, den we find out weah dis Don Juan character has taken solace."

"Den?"

"We make 'em regret da day he took da life of our brudda." His face contracted with hate.

***

Ta'shauna stood out on the terrace of Faison's Malibu home, dressed in a white floral knitted gown. Her pretty pedicure feet gripped the cool granite tiled floor, while her hands held on to the ledge as she peered out into the ocean. Although she couldn't see the view before her, she could imagine it. Her mind spun images of what the scenery could be hearing the water crash onto the shores of the sandy beach and smelling the faint traces of salt in the air. A smile emerged on her face as she inhaled the fresh air and then exhaled.

Suddenly, she became deathly still and her smile disap-peared, as she wondered how he'd gotten into her brother's home. Her eyes darted to their corners and fear gripped her heart knowing his botched attempt at murder had landed her in her current blind state. The only thing she could think was that he'd come to finish off the job. She couldn't see him, but he'd just entered the bedroom. She could smell him. The scent of his aftershave gave him away as soon as he darkened the doorway. She'd never forget that aftershave, he'd worn it the three years they'd been together.

"Tiaz?" She gasped and turned around.

"What?"

"Oh my God, how did you get in here?"

Recalling previous visits, she tapped into her memory for the layout of the house as she jetted off of the terrace and into the study, brushing passed him. He tried to grab her arm and ended up grasping the sleeve of her gown. She blindly swung on him, cracking his jaw. He fell to the floor taking her flower print gown along with him.

"Ooof!" He winced as he hit the floor on his side, feeling a sting in his ribs as the wind was knocked out of him. "Come here! Get back here!" He scrambled to his feet, slinging her gown to the side and holding his ribs. He staggered out of the study after her, grimacing and rubbing his side.

"Aaahh! Aaahh!" Ta'shauna screamed as loud as she could, running and spinning down the hallway in a panic, clad in just a black bra and panties. She fell on the floor and pulled herself back up on the wall. *Calm down, Ta'shauna, and stop screaming, bitch. You can't see, so you're gon' have to feel yo' way up outta here. You gotta hear 'em coming, too, so shhhh. Okay, girl, get a grip,* she coached herself inside of her head.

Being blind was very frustrating for Ta'shauna. She knew that if she lived through this that it was going to be hell trying to get adapted to her new handicap. Sight was one of the most important of the five senses. If she couldn't see then she wouldn't have an idea of where she was going or where she was being led to. It was valuable, especially giving the scenario that she was in.

Threat, Tiaz' best friend and crime partner, was sent to kill Ta'shauna once he'd found out about her playing him for her baby daddy back in prison. He'd caught the newlyweds just as they were leaving the church and didn't waste any time cutting loose on them. He domed her baby's daddy and he slumped, sending the car flying out of control before slamming into a light post. Afterwards, he hopped out of the car and strolled over to Ta'shauna, pulled her head back by her hair and put one in the top of her skull. She was thought to have been dead, but her will to survive was stronger than the grips of Death. Having fully recovered, Ta'shauna found herself out of the hospital and being ushered to the awaiting limousine by her brother Faison. That's when her ex launched a second attack that left her mother, father, uncle and Faison's hands dead. By the grace of God, she was able to escape with her life. She was brought to her brother's house out in Malibu, California where she was told that someone would come and transport her to a safe house where they would watch over her until he returned. Now here she was again fleeing for her life from yet another madman. It was like history just kept on repeating itself.

Ta'shauna pressed her back up against the wall, feeling along the wall as she traveled beside it. She made sure to keep her antennas up in case he came to finish her off. She was sure he'd come and she wanted to hear him when he decided to strike. Sensing that she'd reached the end of the corridor, she stuck her foot out and felt the first step. A smirk curled the corner of her lips and she felt a sense of relief. She was in the home stretch now. If she could just make it down the staircase and to the front door then she would be home free.

Ta'shauna was just about to make her move when a strong hand grasped her arm. Her heart dropped and her eyes bulged.

"Get offa me!" She swung wildly, catching him a couple of times in the face. He lowered his head and moved it all around to avoid her assault, still keeping a hold of her. His head shot up when she kicked him in the balls. His eyes bugged and he squared his jaws, veins bulged at his temples. *That shit hurt!* He dropped to his knees and grabbed for her. She was heading down the staircase when his hand clutched her about the ankle, tripping her up. She went tumbling down the steps, arms and legs flying every which way. She hit the end of the staircase and slid across the floor, lying in an awkward position.

He ran to the beginning of the stairs and looked down. "She's dead!"

***

Scurrrrrr!

Don Juan brought the Porsche truck to a halt. He and Lil' Stan hopped out. They jogged across the street, narrowly missing being hit by cars. Hearing screams coming from above, they looked up and were devastated at what they saw. Tiaz was standing in the window wearing a black bandana over the lower half of his face. In one hand he held a gun and in the other he held tightly to the back of a naked Kiana's neck. She grimaced and cried, tears rolling over her lips and dripping.

"Wait! Hold up!" Don Juan panicked, scared for his wife's life.

Please, God, don't let 'em hurt her!

"To hell with holding up! You fuck with the bull, you get the horns, homes!" Tiaz spat unmercifully, he was about to lynch that bitch. He wanted her nigga to feel the devastation of losing someone that he loved, like he did when he stole Threat from him.

Tiaz looped a noose around Kiana's neck and shoved her out of the window. The wind blew upwards ruffling her hair as she screamed to high heaven, eyes stretched wide open. She flailed her arms and her legs moved as if she was running on air.

"Nooooooooooo!" Don Juan bellowed, with horror etched across his face. For the first time in his life he regretted the choices he'd made, because they all had led him to this moment, which could very well be his wife's death.

"Yuuuckkkk!" An ugly noise escaped Kiana's lips as she was caught by the snag of the rope. Her face contorted and turned from red to purple, her eyeballs looking like they were about to burst out of their sockets. Veins crept up her neck, temples and forehead. She swung from left to right, trying desperately to loosen the slack from around her throat. "Gagggaggghh!" She clawed beneath her chin, breaking the skin and staining her fingers red. Her legs thrashed around wildly as she danced at the end of the rope.

"Gaaaahh!" She gagged, sounding like a choking dog. Her eyes bled her pain and fright, slicking her cheeks wet. Her vision blurred and her head began to feel light. She could feel the icy hands of death grasp her about the ankles and pull her toward the other side.

Kiana knew about the double life that her husband had led, but he'd promised to keep her out of harm's way. She believed him, but at this moment and time, she couldn't help but feel that he had failed her. She didn't have a clue of what Don Juan had done to drive a man to lynch her like an unruly slave, but whatever it was she wish he would have stayed his hand because his actions were about to lead to her demise.

"Hold on, baby, just hold on!" Don Juan screamed up at his wife.

"I'ma see if I can catch 'em, man!" Lil' Stan drew his iron and threw open the door of the complex. He hauled ass toward the elevator, punching the *up* button repeatedly. When it didn't come as fast as he wanted it, he swung open the staircase door and ascended the steps, two at a time.

Don Juan hopped into his truck and fired that big mothafucka up.

"Get outta the way goddamn it! Move!" He swept his arm around so that the bystanders would move out of his path. Cars honked their horns as he recklessly made a turn in the middle of the street, halting the traffic. "I'm here baby, I'm here! Just hold on for me!" He drove upon the curb and stopped the truck beneath Kiana. He climbed upon the roof of the car to find that she'd gone slack on the rope, slightly twitching as yellow droplets trickled from between her legs. "Awww, no, aww, baby no, don't do this to me, sweetheart. I can't live without chu." Tears streamed down his face. He wrapped both of his arms around her legs and hoisted her up, lessening the restraint of the rope.

Don Juan held her up and scanned the area. There were people standing around watching. Some wore looks of sadness, while others wore solemn expressions. "Somebody call the cops, goddamn it! Just don't stand there!"

Someone within the crowd pulled out their cell phone and dialed 9-1-1. An older white stud in a trucker cap and plaid shirt pulled a Swiss army knife from his back pocket. He triggered its blade and climbed upon the roof of the SUV.

"Hold her still, I'm gonna cut her down." He worked the knife back and forth across the rope until it came loose. Don Juan took his wife into his arms and lowered her to the roof of the truck, looking into her eyes. The stud in the trucker's cap took off his shirt and passed it to him. He thanked him and draped Kiana's nakedness in it.

"I'm sorry, Lover, I'm so, so sorry about this." He said to her as he stared into her open eyes, death lying in them. With a sweep of his hand, he closed her eyelids shut and kissed her tenderly on the lips. "I should have taken you far, far away where no one could ever touch you and DJ. DJ?" His eyes shot open when he suddenly realized that the mad man had his baby boy. He kissed his lady's forehead and jumped down into the street, just as police cruisers were pulling upon the scene. He reached inside of his truck and grabbed his gun, running inside of the complex.

Meanwhile

Boom!

The door to the staircase flew open and Lil' Stan spilled out, sweat dripping from his brows, breathing hard, and head darting all around while gripping his head bussa. He looked alive when he saw Tiaz run out of the condo with DJ held close to him. He stopped where he was and lifted his steel, sending some heat his way. Lil' Stan dove to the floor. He hit the carpet on his palms and looked up to see Tiaz' back as he broke down the corridor. The lines of his forehead deepened and he twisted his lips. He hopped upon his feet just as the elevator *dinged* and Don Juan came running out. Don Juan saw Lil' Stan raising his gun. He was about to set it off again when the Trap God bellowed.

"Stoooopp!"

Bloc!

The shot went wild and struck the ceiling, causing debris to fall when he smacked Lil' Stan's hand down. He forced him up against the wall with his arm across his chest, looking him in the eyes with a scowling face.

"Fuck is the matter witchu? I coulda got 'em!" Lil' Stan grumbled.

"He's got my son, you coulda hit 'em," he barked, spittle jumping off his lips.

"Ahh, shit." He came up off the wall.

"Come on!" Don Juan waved him on as he went after Tiaz. They fled down the hallway in hot pursuit of the buff neck thug, hoping that he didn't get away before they could get the baby back.

Coming upon the window at the end of the hall, Tiaz pointed his Beretta and let it go. *Boc! Boc! Boc!* The glass cracked into several spiders webs. He tucked the steel on his waistline and held the baby to him with both hands. He bowed his head and gritted his teeth, leaping through the window.

Craaaassh!

He went flying through the glass, carrying shards along with him as he fell toward the ground. Seeing this, Don Juan and Lil' Stan's eyes grew as big as saucers and their mouths formed Os. The Trap God raised his hand as he chased after him, like he could reach him before he made his dangerous escape. Don Juan and Lil' Stan reached the window and looked down. They found Tiaz climbing out of the trash bin with a crying little DJ. He landed on his feet and peeled the blanket the baby was wrapped in open, looking inside. Little DJ was fine. Tiaz looked up at his opposition and saluted them with the middle finger before taking off, whipping his head bussa from his waistline.

Seeing him fleeing, Don Juan tucked his banger and made to hop out when Lil' Stan gripped his shoulder.

"Wait! You finna jump?" The little nigga frowned.

"Yeah, I'm finna jump! This mothafucka got my son!" He snatched away and leaped down. *Crunch!* He landed inside of the trash bin on top of the black garbage bags and cardboard boxes. *Crunch!* Lil' Stan landed inside of the bin right beside him. Together they climbed out and landed onto the wet graveled ground of the alley. They took off down the dark path and came spilling out into the sidewalk. Their heads snapped all around, as they were trying to locate the buff neck thug. He wasn't anywhere in sight. It was like he had vanished like vapors.

"Shit! Fuck!" Don Juan vented, swinging on the air. He brought his hands down his face and blew hard. Lil' Stan placed a hand on his shoulder, trying to comfort him.

***

"Waa! Waa! Waa!" little DJ wailed.

"Shhhh! It's okay, lil' man, you gon' be alright. Uncle T is here." Tiaz steered the G-ride with one hand, looking from the windshield to the baby. He glanced over his shoulder out of the driver side window and saw Don Juan and Lil' Stan reaching the end of the alley. He saw the Trap God fuming mad and chuckled. "Bitch ass nigga. I'ma show you what time it is."

It had been Tiaz' intention to take the baby all along. He needed him for leverage.

The Game of Death had begun.

Tranay Adams

Chapter Three

Chevy sat in the waiting room with her fingers interlocked and her forehead resting against it. Her eyes were swollen and her cheeks had white streaks sprawled down them. They were dried tears. As of now she was no longer grieving. She was praying and bartering with The Lord Almighty to spare the father of her son. She knew all about Faison's dealings in the streets, as well as some of the unsavory things he'd done on his way up to Top Dawg status. Hell, her hands weren't clean of the dirt either.

The high-yellow beauty had stained her soul on her man's climb up the ladder. Not only had she helped set someone up to get knocked off on his behalf, but she used to transport guns and drugs for him in the beginning. She did this when he was a young upstart trying to get it, but he eventually hired some hands to take those risks for him. Things that she did to help the love of her life could have gotten her life behind bars without the possibility. The crazy thing about it is she wouldn't take any of it back. Not one single thing. She did it all out of love.

"Amen." Chevy finished her prayer and slowly brought her head up.

"Here, I thought you could use this."

She turned her head and found one of the nurses passing her a cup of coffee, sharing a smile of support.

Chevy took the steaming hot cup of joe and mustered a halfhearted smile. "Thank you."

"Don't mention it." She gripped her shoulder. "I'll keep your fiancé in my prayers."

"Okay. I appreciate that." Chevy watched the nurse leave the waiting room and took a sip of the coffee. She closed her eyes for a time and savored the hot liquid. It was very much needed. She cleared her throat with a fist to her mouth. Licking her lips, she was about to take another sip when a news broadcast snatched her attention.

Kantrell M. Combs was gunned down gangland style just a few blocks from the Ritz hotel. A witness reported to have seen two masked men hop out of a red pick-up truck and open fire on Kantrell's vehicle with automatic weapons. Kantrell was then pulled out of the car and shot multiple times in the chest. We were told that one of the masked men took something from out of the vehicle before hopping into the pick-up truck and leaving the scene...

The Asian reporter went on to disclose more information, but by then Chevy had already zoned out. She'd become incoherent to everything around her. Her eyes were stretched wide open and her jaw went slack, mouth ajar. She was taken off guard by the revelation. It was hard to believe that her best friend had been murdered in cold blood. With how it was done she couldn't help but think that she'd gotten mixed up with some shit Tiaz had going on. Far as she knew, Kantrell wasn't involved in the streets like that, but then again she'd put her fucking around with her man past her, too. And look what happened.

Trifling ass bitch, serves her ass right, fuck her, Chevy's forehead arched and her nose wrinkled. She found herself getting all hot just thinking about how her ex and her right-hand had played her. *Those two deserve one another, good riddance.* She shook her head and took a sip of coffee.

"Mrs. Reed." A voice came from her left and her head snapped in its direction. She saw one of the doctors that had rushed Faison into surgery on the gurney. She sat her cup of coffee down, rising to her feet prepared for the worse, but expecting the best. After swallowing hard and blinking, she stared dead into his eyes awaiting the news he'd soon deliver.

From the bewildered expression on his face she expected the worse and was about to break.

"Oh, God, no!" She shook her head and brought her hands to her face, eyes welling with tears.

"Relax, relax, Mrs. Reed." The doctor held up a hand to calm her. "He's all right, okay? He pulled through."

"Thank you, Jesus!" She looked up at the ceiling with her hands interlocked with each other. Tears broke free down her cheeks and she sniffled, wiping her face with the back of her hand.

"He's talking with some detectives now. They've been in there for a minute." He glanced at his watch. "They should be done. You wanna come back there with me to come see him?"

"Yes, please."

He waved her on and she followed him. They trekked down the hallway, with her head on a swivel. Her eyes glanced inside of each and every door that they passed. She found sickly people, some of them alone, some of them attended by family. When she looked ahead, she saw two detectives in cheap suits emerge from a room that she assumed belonged to Faison. They looked to be perturbed. More than likely pissed off that they couldn't get a word out of her man. She wasn't the least bit surprised that they came through to question him. The police were always called to ask questions once someone was shot and came to the hospital. They would even dust the wounded person's hand for gunpowder residue which was why she was glad that she'd scrubbed his hands clean before shooting him down to the emergency ward.

The detectives talked amongst themselves as they walked passed Chevy and the doctor. Once the MD reached the room the detectives left from, he turned to her and threw his hand toward it.

"Go ahead, he's waiting for you."

"Thanks, Doctor…" She searched him for a name badge.

"McCoy. And you're welcome." He flashed a smile before going on about his business, whistling and nodding at an oncoming nurse. He whipped around as they crossed paths and raised his eyebrows when he saw her bodacious ass.

Chevy entered the darkened room that Faison occupied. She found him lying in bed looking weak and exhausted with a breathing canal in his nose. Once he felt her presence he turned his head toward her and mustered up a decent smile so she'd know that he was happy to see her. She rushed to his side and pulled up a chair, sitting down.

"How do you feel, sweetie?"

"Hmmph." He smiled halfheartedly. "Besides being hit by that MAC truck earlier, I'm great."

She smiled. "I tried to call your parents to come up here, but no one answered."

When she brought this up, he closed his eyes. He opened them and they were glassy and outlined in tears, dying to be unleashed. Licking his dry lips, he snorted and cleared his throat.

"They're all dead." His voice cracked with deep emotional turmoil and suffering.

"What?" The creases of her forehead deepened. She leaned closer to him, still holding his hand. "Faison, who are you talking about? Who's dead?"

"My father…" His voice went hoarse as he went to talk. His lips trembled and his nose wrinkled.

She'd never seen him this vulnerable before. Normally, he shied away from his feelings, but now he was putting them out there on display. She gathered he must have been hurting from the inside out for him to allow her to see him grieving like this, because he'd always been the one to bottle up his feelings. He kept to himself and dealt with things on his own accord. That's just how he was, but at the moment his being sensitive was a contradiction.

"Babe, tell me who else? Who else is dead?" She squeezed his hand tighter, and wiped away the tears that fell from her own eyes. His sadness, happiness, joy, pain, suffering, all of his was hers. They felt what happened to each another like twins. It had been like this since they'd been together. They had a connection. To them this was a sign that they were made for each other and were meant to be together. No one could tell them any different, but his infidelity brought her doubt into question.

He swallowed the ball of hurt that had formed in his throat and sniffled real hard. He licked his lips before continuing, "My father, my mother…Uncle Bruce. Bird, Bone, all of 'em. He killed them all."

"Who killed them all?" The creases deepened on her forehead.

"Tiaz."

The revelation was like a punch to the kidney. It left her eyes bulged and her mouth open. She couldn't believe what he'd just told her. More importantly, she couldn't believe that she was surprised, especially with all of the shit he'd done recently. Chevy closed her eyes for a time and peeled them back open, shaking her head. Tears slid down her cheeks and she wiped them away with her fingers and thumb, sniffling.

Faison went on to tell her about Tiaz' botched attempt to have Ta'shauna murdered. And then how everybody from Don Juan, Smack, Majestic, TJ and himself were connected and decided to rid themselves of their nuisance. He told her everything along with the details. It was the hard truth. She could either take it or leave it. Nonetheless, she took it.

"When? When did he murder your family?"

As soon as he batted his eyes tears jetted from their corners and he sniffled. He went on to tell her what had happened.

"I'd like to go, but only if your father can come along." Gloria told her son. *She wanted to go to Faison's house, along with her daughter, to help her recover, but she wanted her husband right there beside her. Ms. Reed knew that her son despised his father and most likely wouldn't let him inside of his crib, but she hoped that he would have compassion due to the circumstances. All she could do was hope that he would finally come to his senses and allow his father back inside of his home and his life.*

Faison shook his head. "Ma, that man didn't want me in his house, so I for damn sure don't want him in mine."

"Junior, you and your father need to put this senseless feud behind you and..." Gloria was cut short when a bullet flew through her temple, killing her instantly and splattering blood on Faison's face. Automatic gunfire filled the air. Faison stood frozen stiff. The automatic gunfire sounded like someone punching the keys on the type writer with warp speed.

Tat! Tat! Tat! Tat! Tat! Tat! Tat!

He could still hear the cries of his family flooding his ears as they were torn apart by coal hot bullets passing in and out of them, rupturing vital arteries.

Faison closed his eyes and envisioned himself right there in the middle of that battlefield, looking all around him with his heart threatening to burst inside of his ribcage with all that he was experiencing.

Everything seemed to move in slow motion that was surrounding him. He could see the blood, brain fragments and severed body parts going up into the air like caps at a graduation. He looked over his shoulder and saw a masked up Tiaz holding a Steyr Aug, firing away as if he were on the set of a war movie. The thug whipped the German machinegun around in Ta'shauna's direction. Seeing his sister in direct danger lit a fire under Faison's ass. The coke peddler had to get to his sibling before she was taken out of his life forever.

He jetted after her running as fast as he could; silently praying he reached her before death could.

"Shaunaaaaa!" he called out, running toward her.

Just as Tiaz was squeezing the trigger, he was leaping into the air and tackling his sister's wheelchair to the ground.

Tat! Tat! Tat! Tat! Tat! Tat! Tat!

Faison jerked violently, feeling the bullet penetrate his leg again and his eyelids snapped open. There was a horrified look in his eyes and a light film of sweat on his forehead. Chevy was wincing, he looked to his hand and saw that he was squeezing her hand to the point where it had began turning red.

"Haa! Haa! Haa! Haa!" Faison breathed hard, looking all about, trying to get a grip on things. He was terrified, after reliving that episode in his life all over again. He wished he could shake the memories loose from his mental, but knew that more than likely the traumatic experience would be forever harbored inside of his mind, whether he liked it or not. He'd have to live with it like someone with herpes would have to live with that sexually transmitted disease.

"I'm sorry, I'm sorry, baby." He apologized, sympathetically.

"Why didn't you tell me before?"

"I couldn't come to you how I was all vulnerable and shit. I didn't want chu to see me like that, baby." He gave her the uncut truth, his emotions getting the best of him, but his fighting kept them back. "I just knew that if I saw you like that then I would break down. I was going to tell you, but once I got my head right and I could stand tall, you feel what I'm saying?"

"Baby, you never had to do that with me." She tried to convince him. "I'm your woman. If there's anyone you can show your all to, it's me. You should feel the most comfortable with me. I'm your soul mate." She took his hand into hers and pressed it to her chest, kissing it tenderly on the knuckles. "You are me and I am you. When you laugh, scream, cry, experience moments of joy. Those are my moments, as well."

"You're my rib, my queen." He looked into her eyes loving-ly, watching the smile etch across her lips as she closed her eyes, rubbing his palm against her cheek, purring like a kitten. "I don't know how I could have ever, ever hurt chu, Chevy. A woman like you only comes along once every lifetime and I let you slip right through my fingers."

"I haven't slipped through your fingers just yet." She said after taking his hand down and looking into his eyes.

Faison's forehead crinkled and he said, "You mean?"

"When all of this is over, I wanna start from scratch, but I swear on the graves of my parents, Faison, if you fuck up this time this next bullet is going right between your eyes." She spoke with dead ass seriousness. He believed her, too. She didn't hesitate to blast on him when she caught him with that last bitch. So, he didn't put it past her, shooting to kill him if he was to fuck around on her again.

"Alright, but this time we will do it all over again." He told her, stroking her hand with his thumb. "The courting, the getting to know you. We'll play it like two people meeting for the first time and work our way up to this forever ship. You know, you wearing my ring."

"Okay." She grinned and nodded.

"Good, gimme some lip." She leaned forward and kissed him affectionately on his lips. Afterwards she kissed him on the forehead and caressed his forehead with her thumb, staring into his eyes as if he was her everything.

Suddenly, her face morphed taking on an expression like she was thinking about something. "What's the matter?"

"Umm, where's Te'Qui?" She looked down at him.

"Where is he?" Lines ran across his forehead, he angled his head. "Didn't you come get him from my house earlier tonight?"

"What?" Her face contorted. "No, he was supposed to be with you."

"Then who?" His eyes shot to their corners as he thought to himself.

"What did he say before he left?"

"He said that you came to pick him up while I was on the phone. I dapped him up, told 'em I loved 'em and he left, that's it."

"Oh my God, Faison!" She shot to her feet. "How could you let 'em just walk away like that?" She paced the floor, running her fingers through her long blonde hair, looking like she was worried to death, which she was. This was the second time her son had escaped from her. And she didn't have the slightest inkling of an idea where he was.

"I didn't just let 'em fucking walk away, I was under the impression that he went with you." He frowned, raising his voice a couple of octaves. The sudden stress caused his heart monitor to beep aloud, drawing both of their attention. Their heads shot to the monitor and the green line was going wild.

Chevy put her hands together and pressed them to her face. She closed her eyes and took a deep breath. She was silent for a time before dropping her hands to her sides, rejuvenated.

"Okay." She blinked and exhaled. "Alright, you just relax. I'm gonna hit these streets and go looking for our son."

"Alright." He nodded and licked his lips, gathering his wits. "It's getting late, so be careful."

"I will." She leaned down and kissed him sweetly on the lips and forehead. "I love you." She pulled away, but he held fast to her hand, looking her into her eyes, like he used to. Back when he thought she was the most beautiful woman in the world and he was thanking God he'd blessed him with her.

"I love you, too." They both smiled, before she broke their embrace and went off to find their boy. Once Chevy left, Faison picked up the hospital telephone.

***

"Shit!" He hustled down the steps and kneeled down to Ta'shauna, hoping he hadn't killed her. He turned her body over and she was wearing a solemn expression. He peeled her eyelid open and took a peek, before holding a hand below her nostrils. He felt a touch of air, but to be sure he pressed his ear to her chest and listened closely. Pulling his head up from her body, a look of relief captured his face and his shoulders slumped. *Thank God she isn't dead!* He scooped her up into his arms and carried her up the staircase, her arms and legs dangling about. He stared down at her face and couldn't get over how beautiful she was. It made him wonder what she could have done to make a nigga put one in her head like they did. She had to be one wretched ass bitch for a cat to want to do her like that. That shit was cold-blooded. It was a mafia style execution hit. Luckily for her, it was botched.

He carried Ta'shauna into Faison's study, where he laid her down on the couch. Afterwards, he soaked a towel in hot water and wrung it out. Taking his time, he patted her forehead gently, admiring her beauty as she slept. Suddenly, her eyelids fluttered open like the wings of a butterfly. Recalling the situation that she was in, her eyes bulged and her mouth stretched open.

"Aaaahhhh!" she screamed, veins etching up her neck and intensity measured on her face. Sensing him in front of her, she leaped from the couch throwing them hands on that ass. He backed up bobbing, weaving and blocking her fists with his arms.

"Ooof!" He doubled over once he was kneed in the balls. *Bwap!* She slugged him across the jaw and dropped him. His head rose from off the floor, he wore a dazed and confused expression. Hearing her bare feet smacking down on the carpet as she ran toward him, he shook off the birds circling his head. He held his holster to his side with one hand and yanked his gun loose with the other. The man clutched his weapon with both hands and pointed it up at Ta'shauna, hearing the metal click in his hand froze her in her tracks. She gasped.

"Stop it! Stop it, right there or so help me, I'll shoot you!" He swore, eyebrows lowered, hoping he didn't have to make good on his threat. Seeing her chest rise and fall rapidly and her lifting her hands in the air, he went on to talk. "Now, I'm sorry, I didn't mean to scare you, but I'm not here to hurt you."

"Then who are you? Tell me who the fuck you are!"

"I'm Herby Hendrix, P.I. and bodyguard." He took one hand from the gun he had on her and went to reach inside of his suit, but stopped himself short. "Shit, I forgot you can't see."

"Who let chu in?" Her brows furrowed.

"Your brother, Faison, gave me the key. He didn't tell you that I was coming by?" He frowned. "I was hired to protect you from this Tiaz character."

"Bullshit!" she shouted. "You think I'm stupid? If that's the case then why didn't you announce yourself when you came in or respond when I called you Tiaz?"

"You're blind. I didn't wanna start speaking and startle you. I was afraid that it would lead to a situation just like this one here." He explained. "And I didn't know that you called me Tiaz. You didn't hear me when I said *what*? The way you were carrying on and reacting I couldn't get a word in edge wise."

"My nigga, you gon' have to make me a believer of this bogus ass story."

"Alright, I'll call him right now." He pulled out his cellular and it rung. His eyes darted to the screen. "Humph, well, speak of the devil. This is him right here." He pressed *answer* and brought the device to his ear. "Hey, how's it going? I got your sister here. She'd like to talk with ya. Okay. Here you go." He passed her the cell.

"Hello, Faison? Oh, thank God, it's you." She closed her eyes for a moment and sighed with relief. "Yes, I thought this man you sent here was trying to trick me."

Herby rose to his feet holstering his firearm and listening to Ta'shauna talk on his cellular.

"Okay. I love you, too." She pressed *end* and extended the cell for him to take it. He did.

"Everything hunky-dory?"

"Yeah, it's all good." She managed a smile.

"I'll tell ya, ya brotha must really love you, 'cause I sure as hell don't come cheap."

"Wow, you must be pretty good at what chu do."

"I'm the best at what I do, Toots."

"Can you help me back over to the couch, please? I'd like to sit down." She extended her hand. He took it and led her to the couch where she sat down.

"Can I bum a cancer stick off of you?"

"Sure, Doll Face."

Herby placed a cigarette in her mouth and lit the end of it for her. She took puffs and exhausted smoke, fanning away the fog. She swept the loose strands of her hair out of her face and listened closely to what he had to say.

"So, uh, I don't know if you mind me asking or not, but I have to. I mean, to be frank, it's friggin' killing me."

She blew out a cloud of smoke and said, "Shoot."

"Why is this guy after you? I mean is he some crazed stalker, you fucked around on him, you owe him money or something?"

"Uh uh." She shook her head. "He wanted me to bid, but I couldn't hack it. I'm not built to do time with nan nigga. I love dick, jewelry, clothes and the finer thangs too much."

"Is that right?" Herby cupped his hand around the cigarette and sparked it up.

"You goddamn right." She tapped her square above the ashtray, dumping ashes, after feeling around the table for it.

"Wasn't he out here holding you down?"

"Yeah, but he knew he was going to have to take some penitentiary chances if he was going to keep me." She frowned and turned her face in the direction of his voice, her expression was like *'That nigga knew what was up.'* "I have expensive taste, sweetheart. Very expensive taste. I'm too pretty to be out here working. I use what I got to get what I want." She quoted a line from The Player's Club. "Sheeiiiiit, I wish a bitch would be somebody's cleaning lady, down on my hands and knees scrubbing floors and shit. Nuh uh, that kind of shit there just ain't for me. I'ma different type of female, boo. Niggaz gotta pay if they wanna jump up and down in this pussy..."

She patted that fat coochie between her thighs. "Truth be told, I had love for Tiaz, but I didn't love 'em. Although, I did allow him to think otherwise." He scrunched his face up at her. She couldn't see it, but she could feel it. "Yeah, I know. It's fucked up. It's a dirty world, but it's an even dirtier game. I knew he was gon' get it by any means necessary, which is why I fucked with 'em. Tiaz lives by a set of old school principals. You know that providing and protecting ya woman shit. So, he was perfect. I couldn't fuck with no one 'round my way, 'cause I'd already been through them all, so they wasn't tryna see me."

A cold world breeds an even colder bitch. Herby shook his head. He hadn't been with Ta'shauna that long, but he already knew from that bit of time that he didn't like her. He wasn't going to allow his feelings to interfere with his job. Nah, he was going to remain professional and when the time came for them to part ways he was going to get as far away from her ass as possible.

Chapter Four

Chevy pulled up at a red light and a black van skidded to a halt before her. Her eyes nearly leaped out of her head and her mouth dropped open when the vehicle's sliding door was flung open. Two masked up niggaz, holding choppas, approached her car, the business end of them thangs pointed right at her. Her heart was beating so fast that she thought that it was going to jump out of her chest. Chevy released the steering wheel and lifted her trembling hands, palms showing dampness. She closed her eyes and peeled them back open having swallowed the extra spit in her throat.

Her head turned as the men rounded her vehicle counter clockwise, AK-47s poised to leave that ass as bloody as ground beef. She was visibly shaken and scared. This had never happened to her before and she didn't know exactly what these fools wanted. At first, she thought that maybe they were there on Tiaz' behalf, but that idea was dispelled. If it were him then he would have come alone. He wouldn't have sent anyone. Not to mention the only nigga she knew that he fucked with like that would have been Threat. He didn't move with a band of niggaz. Not to mention, Faison said that he was dead. At that moment, it dawned on her that these dudes had to be part of Majestic's organization. That was it. It made perfectly good sense. Mothafuckaz hopping out of vans with assault rifles on some Mexican cartel shit.

"Get out da car! Bitch, get out da car!" the tallest of them barked, startling her. "'Fore we blow yo' fucking head off!"

She went to open the door, but another bark scared the life out of her.

"Hurry up!" the shorter one barked, cocking the hammer on his weapon.

"Okay! Alright, I'm coming." Chevy's heart was beating so hard that she could feel it bumping up against her ribcage. Her legs felt like cooked noodles, but somehow she managed to use them to get out of the car. The tallest one looked up and down the block making sure no one was watching or coming. The coast was clear. It was late and the streets were naked of anyone or anything. He shoved Chevy up against her vehicle and pressed the choppa against her cheek, indenting her face, causing her to turn her head. She squeezed her eyes shut and mashed her lips together hard, waiting to hear the weapon fire and end her life.

"We know you were da one dat killed Majestic and his people." Her eyelids snapped open and her eyes darted to him. "Oh what, you think we didn't know about that? We were staked out down the block, hoe!"

"Fuck all dis talkin,' leave dis high-yellow bitch where she standin.'"

"Right." He went to pull the trigger.

"Wait!" The shorter one, was studying something in the backseat. He looked to Chevy. "What's in that bag?"

"Not. Nothing. It's just a couple of bath towels." She quivered with fear.

He gave her the side eye and twisted his lips. "Fuck outta here! What I look like, Boo Boo the Fool?" He hit the locks and recovered a Gucci duffle bag. He lifted the towels that were inside and found racks on top of racks stored. A smile spread across his big ass lips.

"What chu smilin' for? What chu come up on?" The tallest looked from Chevy to his partner, still holding that Kay to the side of her face. His man opened the bag and held it out for him to see. When he peered inside, he smiled too. "Sweet."

"How much is dis?" The short one questioned her.

"Three. Three. Three hundred grand."

They whistled, liking the sound of all of those dead white men.

"That's lovely right there."

"Sho' ya right." He closed the Gucci bag.

"Good lookin' out, lil' momma, shame we gotta kill yo' fine ass." The tallest molested her with his eyes and licked his chops. "Mmmmmm." He said like she was delicious. He went to pull the trigger, but the shorter one grabbed his wrist, snagging his attention. He frowned and looked at him like *'What's the big idea?'*

"Nah, let her slide," he told him seriously.

"Really?"

"Yeah, we done already robbed the bitch, now you wanna kill her?" He looked at him like *Damn, nigga, have some mothafucking compassion.* "One L's enough for the night. Besides..." He held up the Gucci duffle bag. "...we got plenty of loot to count up."

"Right."

"Let's go." The shorter man nudged him and sprinted to the van, climbing inside. "Come on!" He waved him over, watching him slowly back away from Chevy with his AK-47 trained on her. Abruptly, he spun around and hauled ass toward the van, gripping his assault rifle with both hands. He leaped inside and slid the door closed, locking it in place. Chevy watched the back tail light drive away until they were two bright red orbs and had eventually disappeared into the night.

With her head hung, she trekked back to her whip and climbed in, pulling the door shut. She looked at her hands and they were shaking badly. Her eyes misted and tears sprawled down her cheeks, rolling over his lips.

"Oh my God," she rasped. She was scared as hell. That was the second time Death had tackled her door, and that time he'd come close to getting inside. "Shit." She curled her fingers into fists and closed her eyes, trying to get a grip on her emotions and rattled nerves. Suddenly, she felt the bile rise up her esophagus and she hurriedly unlocked the door, throwing it open.

"Bwahhhh!" She hurled.

That night's dinner came splattering against the pavement in the form of a pinkish green goop. Just when she thought she was through, more came up. *Bwahhh!* Her head bobbed as she unleashed what was left inside of her stomach. More tears danced at the corners of her eyes and she wiped her mouth with the back of her fist. Afterwards, she retrieved a couple of napkins out of the glove-box to wipe off her tongue and chin. She balled up the napkins and threw it out of the window. Then she wiped her face with the inside of her shirt. Sniffing up the snot that threatened to drip, she licked her lips and dialed the number to her brother's contraband cell phone. As the phone rang she was overwhelmed with sadness and depressed. She felt like a complete failure having gotten the money for Savon's lawyer stolen. She didn't know what she was going to do to get that money again, so she could only pray for a miracle.

***

She bit down on her panties as he thrust in and out of her wet, creamy hole. She tried to climb the walls like she was half a spider, but he held her in place and roughly fucked her, just how she liked it. Each stroke of his love muscle caused sweat to dash on her big, luscious titties.

"Uh! Uh! Uh! Uh!" Her eyes were rolled to their whites and her arms were wrapped around his neck as he dug up in them guts. He clenched his jaws and stared into her face. It was twisted into a mask of pleasure. This let him know that he was handling his business, and damn well, that night. He pumped longer, faster, harder making her voice go up a few octaves before the sound left her.

"Uh! Uh! Uh!" He grunted, face coated in perspiration, as well as the rest of his body. Feeling her legs shaking, he looked down just in time to see her juices spraying his beaded nest of pubic hair. "Sheeiiiiit!"

"Shhhhh!" He stole a glance to see if someone was peeking in through the rectangle window, there wasn't anyone there.

"I can't help it. Damn, you got some good dick, nigga, shit." She licked her tongue at him like the freak she was, grinding up on his full potential, enticing him to keep fucking her. Old girl loved the way he felt inside of her opening and wanted to feel his one-eyed snake tickling her G-spot. She'd gotten hers off, so he went ahead and wrapped up his performance.

He rose from off of the bed and stuffed his red bandana inside of her mouth. Right after, he was pressing her up against the wall. Eyelids tightened, arms wrapped tightly around her, he grunted and ravaged her middle. She looked like a demon was trying to possess her as he galloped at her center, her white cream sliding down his swollen member. She was so wet that his hardness sliding in and out of her sounded like a nigga greasing his hands with Vaseline. He looked up at her face and cracked a smile while he worked his hips in a circular motion. The bandana fell out of her mouth as he pumped her full of raw dick. A tingling sensation greeted the head of his steel. As soon as he met it, he snatched free of her and jerked his dick on her washboard stomach, plastering it with pearly white jizz.

"Ughhhhhh!" Relief crossed his face and his tongue hung at the corner of his mouth. He went along jerking his meat until he was sure all of his children were freed from the juvenile hall that was his balls.

"Good looking out." Savon smacked the C.O. on her bare ass. He wiped off his dick and pulled up his pants. After that he kicked back on his bunk and lit up a cigarette, watching his fuck-buddy get dressed. He took casual pulls from the cancer stick as he studied her. Her face was kind of strong, but she had ass for days and titties for weeks. It helped her case tremendously that her V was some of the best he'd ever encountered. Other than her smuggling contraband into the prison for him, that was the reason he fucked with her. He hadn't been down that long, but the homies from the hood came pouring in a couple days after he'd gotten there. There were a total of twelve of them, excluding himself. Given that the Outlaws weren't the largest set there, they were one of the biggest. It was strength in numbers, so they were good on the muscle end of things.

"Well, I better get back to work." She leaned down and kissed him sensually. "See you later, handsome."

He blew out a cloud of smoke and said, "No doubt."

The correctional officer drew the sheet back on the string that stretched across the cell. As she was opening the door and leaving, Savon felt a vibration underneath his pillow. Switching hands with the cigarette, he reached under his pillow and recovered the cell phone. He smirked seeing that it was his sister. After pressing *answer* he brought the cellular to his head and his ear was assaulted with what had happened to her that night. The news prompted him to sit up on his bunk, concerned lines running across his forehead.

"You all right, sis?" He went to stand in the corner where no one could see him through the window. "Good, good, good. You make it to Steinbeck's yet? No!" A shocked expression emerged on his face. "Wait a minute, they took you for the whole shit? Oh no, oh no, this is bad, real bad." He paced the floor, running his hand down his face while in motion.

"Grrrrrr!" He growled like a lion, going berserk in his cell. "Fuck! Fuck! Fuck!" He kicked and stomped on the bunk in a rage, showing his natural black ass.

"I'm sorry, Savon, I'm so soorryyy." Her voice blared and she broke down sobbing, hearing her baby brother get crazy. "I'm so sorry."

Savon threw his cell phone against the wall, the screen cracked and it skidded across the floor. Breathing hard with teary eyes, he slid down the wall. His knees were up at his chest as he brought his hands to his face bawling. "Haa! Haa! Haa!" His head bobbed as he broke down crying, teardrops splashing when they hit the cool, filthy floor. "Ahh! Haa! Haa! Haa!" He cried long and hard, all the while hearing his sister on the opposite end of the cellular.

"Savoooonn! Forgiiive me! I'm sorryyyy! Haa! Haa! Haa!" She wailed into the cell phone. "I'm sorrryyyy!"

Savon was washed up, done for if he couldn't get his hands on some money to pay his lawyer for a good defense.

***

Chevy finally managed to pull herself together from what she thought was the final night of her life. She understood now that it was best to have her antennas up more now than ever. Them fools had caught her slipping and could have very well had her brains plastered on the inside of her Caprice. Thank God one of them felt for her. He convinced the other to let her keep her life, because had it not have been for that she'd be lying on a cold metal slab getting her body slit open during an autopsy.

Chevy pushed the thoughts into the back of her mind. Right now she had to focus on the most serious one at hand and that was finding her baby boy. She was beginning to feel like a shitty parent, having lost her son not once but twice now. All she could do was scrape her knees up to the Lord and pray that he was safe and sound. Because one thing was for certain, she wouldn't be able to live if harm came to a hair on his head. Te'Qui was her world. To her the sun rose and set on him. He was her little man.

Chevy bent the corner with an *Urrrrrrk!* Tilting the pretty black on black thang, chrome rims spinning like Wheel of Fortune contestants. As soon as the vehicle came back down on the pavement, she floored it and it accelerated. She was staring straight ahead. The window was down and the wind blew against her face, disturbing her dyed blonde hair, causing it to ruffle in the air. She blew the excess smoke from her nose and glanced down at the ashtray, mashing out what was left of the cigarette. Seeing her driveway coming up, she made a sharp right and drove upon the lawn. She threw open the door and hopped out, leaving the driver side door open as she ran around the car. Coming upon the porch, she jogged up the steps in a hurry.

"Te'Quiiiii! Te'Quiiiiii!" She called out her son's name as she went through the keys until she found the key that she was looking for. As soon as she unlocked the door and stepped inside, she took a clean scan of the living room. Her eyes were wide and her mouth formed an O. Tucking her keys into her pocket, she moved throughout the house calling her son's name and checking each and every room.

She came back inside of the living room. Stopping at the center of the room, she placed her hands on her hips and her brows bunched together. "Hmmm." She bit down on her bottom lip and that's when the thought hit her, she was hurried out of the door. Crossing the threshold and leaving the front door wide open, she made her way over to Baby Wicked's Aunt Helen's house. She jogged up the steps and knocked on the front door, glancing over her shoulders in case she saw him wandering about. It was a long shot that her baby boy would be over his best friend's aunt's house, but it was worth checking out before she went any farther.

It was taking a while for someone to answer so Chevy went to knock again. That's when the porch light came on stinging her eyes like bumble bees and causing her to wince. She heard the door locks coming undone and the knob being turned. Next, the door was being pulled open and she found a wide silhouette standing before her. From the big curly hair and the roundabout shape of the face, she could tell that it was Helen.

"Uh, hey, Ms. Helen," she started off. "Te'Qui wouldn't happen to be over here, would he?"

"N..." Helen cleared her throat with a fist to her mouth, holding a hand at her back, clutching a gun. "Excuse me, no I haven't seen him, Chevy."

Chevy dropped her head disappointedly, she hated to hear that. "Oh, uh, when was the last time you seen 'em?"

Helen blew hard thinking on when the last time she'd seen her neighbor's son. "That was a couple of days ago. He was playing basketball out there with a couple of the neighborhood kids. You seen 'em, you were out there that day, remember?"

"Yeah, I..."

"Heeelllp!"

Chevy frowned and looked up at Helen, still only able to see her silhouette. "What was that?"

"Oh, that's the TV, I'm sorry." She tucked her banger at the small of her back and stepped out on the porch, pulling the door shut behind her. The burly woman folded her arms across her ample bosom, tucking her hands underneath her armpits to keep them warm. It was kind of cold that night. "Jesus, it's chilly out here."

"Yeah, it is." She agreed wearing a saddened expression across her face. When she looked up at her, she saw her eyes rim with tears that threatened to overflow. She didn't have any kids, but her nephews were as good as her own children. The loss of the youngest one had crippled her greatly, the night before she was lying in a tub of warm murky water attempting to slit her own wrist with a Gillette shaver. She'd written a suicide note and left it on the bathroom sink. If it hadn't been for Wicked knocking on the door, interrupting her with his plan to murder the men responsible for his younger brother's death and needing her assistance she would have gone through with it. That's when she decided to fall back and kick it on earth just a little while longer to guarantee that her nephew's executioners were brought to justice.

Helen knew exactly how Chevy must have been feeling at that time and her heart went out to her. *Helen, ol' girl you need your fucking head examined,* she thought. She decided she was about to tell Te'Qui's mother that he was being held captive down in the basement by her nephew until he gave up the name of the man that had given them the drugs to sell.

"Listen," Helen began, placing a comforting hand on her shoulder. "I..." The words died in her throat when she saw Wicked driving up from down the block, headlights and music blaring. Dr. Dre's *Xxplosive was* serenading his journey.

Fuck a bitch
Don't tease bitch,
Strip tease bitch
Eat a bowl of these bitch,
Gobble the dick
Hoes forgot to eat a dick can shut the fuck up!
Gobble and swallow a nut up,
Shut up and get my cash
Backhanded, pimp slapped backwards and left stranded
Just pop ya collar, pimp convention hoes for a dollar
Six-Deuce in a plush, six-deuce Impala

Pimpin' hoes from Texas to Guatemala
Bitch niggaz paid for hoes, just to lay wit hoes
Relax one night, and paid to stay wit' hoes...

The presence of loud music stole both women's attention. When Chevy turned back around, Helen cleared her throat and focused. "Like I was saying I could get a couple of Missing Persons flyers printed up and post them up in the neighborhood if you'd like."

"Please." Chevy wiped her dripping eyes with a curled finger. "Something like that would definitely help. Thank you. I'm gonna go down to the police station and see about filing a police report. I know it's supposed to be 48 hours before you report anything, but screw that. I can't sleep at night knowing that my child is probably in his drawers and chained up inside of some psycho's basement."

Helen raised an eyebrow. She found it eerie that she'd guessed that right on the nose.

"I hear you. You do whatever you have to do to find your boy."

"Okay." She moved to head down the steps, but froze once she was called back. She turned around.

"Whatever you have to, you hear me?" She gave her a stern look, eyes glassy with seriousness. "You don't want the heartache that comes with losing a child. Believe me, I already lost one of my boys."

"Alright." She went on about her business.

Helen closed the door shut and headed back inside of the house. She wanted to tell Chevy that Te'Qui was down in the basement, but feared what Wicked would do to her if he knew that she'd ratted him out. For now, she'd play it cool until she found an opening that would allow the boy to walk without her nephew even knowing. All she had to do was get that goddamn key off of his neck. She could relieve Te'Qui of his restraints and allow him to escape. Next, she would break her own nose and make up a story. She'd tell Wicked that the kid had picked the lock of his shackle and cracked her across the bridge of her nose with a blunt object of some sort.

That's it, that's the plan. I got it, Helen thought as she headed down into the basement.

When Chevy was coming down the steps Wicked was murdering the engine of his BMW and hopping out. He locked eyes with her, but kept a neutral face.

"Hey, Wicked, sorry for your loss." She said as they crossed paths.

"I'ma be sorry for yo' loss, too, if Te'Qui don't tell me something," he said under his breath.

Chevy froze. Her brows furrowed and she turned around. "Excuse me?"

"What's up with it, Chev'?" He raised his eyebrows and threw his head back.

"Did you say something?"

"Just what's up?"

Chevy narrowed her eyes and nodded, before keeping it moving to her ride, thinking nothing of it.

***

"Uuuhhhh." Te'Qui slowly came to groaning and rubbing the lower half of his jaw. His eyelids peeled apart and he looked around with blurred vision, trying to focus. When his 20/20 finally adjusted, he saw Baby Wicked's Aunt Helen sitting in a chair before him, gripping a handgun firmly. Her face was still partially hidden by the shadows and he couldn't make out her eyes. He hadn't a clue of what she was thinking or what her facial expression was. This made him uneasy. He kept an eye on her hand as she placed a cigarette into her mouth and fired it up. She took a deep pull and polluted the air with smoke. Te'Qui gagged and coughed with a fist to his mouth, inhaling the smothering fumes. He'd always hated the smell of nicotine. It was the equivalent of a noose tightening around his throat anytime he came into contact with it.

Te'Qui's coughing ceased when he saw Helen rise from the chair. This sight set off a panic alarm inside of his head. His heart pummeled against his chest bone rapidly and he scrambled backwards on his hands and bare feet until he bumped up against the wall. His head whipped from left to right looking for somewhere to escape. Jumping to his feet, he ran to his right, moving shit out of the way and kicking it aside. His back was against the wall and he was desperate for a haven to flee to, no matter where it may be. When he didn't find anywhere to hide, he raced over to his left. He knocked boxes out of the way, pushed furniture aside, and flipped tables over, scrambling to get away.

"Haa! Haa! Haa! Haa!" His shoulders and head bobbed as he breathed hard. Looking up, he saw Helen's shadow moving up the wall as she advanced. The little nigga gasped and whipped around, zeroing in on the gun in her hand.

Thump! Thump! Thump! Thump!

His heart rate jacked up and his eyes bulged. He swallowed the extra spit that had accumulated in his throat as his eyes searched the room again for something to defend himself with. They located a dusty lamp off to the corner on top of an old tattered end table. He darted toward the end table, feeling her right on top of him. All he had to do was grab it and clock her ass. Te'Qui was in motion, moving like a track star, when— *Clingggg!*—the chain snagged him just short of reaching the lamp and he went falling to the floor, hard.

"Huuughhh!" He grimaced, feeling the wind knocked out of his lungs felt like a gut punch. Hearing Helen's footsteps at his rear, he turned over swiftly, prepared to meet his demise. His brows mushed together and his jaws squared. His nostrils flared as he looked up at his late friend's aunt, giving her a look that could cause instant death.

"Relax, I'm not gonna hurt chu, Te'Qui." She outstretched her hand.

The youngling narrowed his eyes at her hand, looking upon it like it was a venomous snake. His head shot up and he locked eyes with her. "I'm not stupid."

She took the square from her mouth and released a flutter of smoke. "Boy, if I wanted to hurt chu I would have already, trust me. Ain't nobody here to stop me. Come on." She motioned for him to take her hand.

Te'Qui weighed her words and figured he didn't have anything to lose by taking her helping hand. Smack! His palm sounded when it collided with hers, her hand grasped his and she pulled him to his feet. She snatched up a milk crate and planted it in the center of the floor, waved him over and told him to have a seat. Cautiously, he approached and sat down on the crate. She returned to her chair and sat down, tapping her Joe and dumping ashes on the floor. She took another draw and unleashed smoke that drifted in his direction like a cloud. After watching him frown and fanning the smoke away, she knew that it was getting to him.

"Sorry." She dropped the cigarette near her flat and mashed it out, her shoes spreading black ashes on the floor.

"Are you gonna let me go?"

"Are you gon' tell me who gave Brice those drugs to sell?"

"Hell n…" He caught himself and cleared his throat. "No, ma'am, I'm notta rat. I can't tell."

"I thought my nephew was your best friend."

"He is." He nodded in agreement, his face becoming somber at the mention of his deceased best friend. "We were practically the same type of person. I know he'd respect what I'm doing. In fact, he's one of the people that drilled that no snitching thing into my head. I'm only honoring his wishes and sticking to my beliefs."

She sighed and shook her head. "You boys and your codes. Not everyone sticks to those street codes, you know. Plenty of people have broken those rules."

"I'm not plenty of people, I'm Lil' Q-Ball from the set."

She looked away and massaged the bridge of her nose. "The ignorance of the youth." She licked her lips and looked up at him. "So, you're willing to throw your life away for this?"

"Yes, ma'am, I'm willing to die for what I believe in, just like any other man."

Her forehead deepened with creases. "You're a brave soul. A brave, brave soul to be so young."

"Truthfully, I'm afraid, but it's like Pac said, I'd rather die like a man than live like a coward."

"I commend you, young man."

"So, are you gonna let me outta here?"

She took a deep breath. "If it were up to me I'd unlock that shackle and let chu waltz right on outta here. But I don't even have the key. Winston took it with him. He wears it on a necklace around his neck."

"Damn." Te'Qui cursed under his breath, dropping his head. He looked back up. "You think there's any way that you could possibly get it?"

"I could try."

"Thanks." Things were silent for a time before he spoke again. "Why are you going to help me even though I won't tell you what you wanna know?"

"Believe it or not, I've always looked at you as one of my nephews." She admitted. "You being killed out there wouldn't have hurt me any less than it being Brice."

"Then why'd you go along with kidnapping me? That doesn't make any sense." He frowned.

"Winston was so goddamn adamant about finding the guy that gave you guys the drugs. Seeing the hurt in his eyes behind the loss of his brother, I couldn't turn him down." She confessed. "I was satisfied with the death of the bastard that actually pulled the trigger. His life being taken was enough for me." She clenched her fist so tightly that it slightly shook. Her eyes were glassy and glinted with madness. She blinked and opened her hand, and just like that, the hatred dissipated. Helen exhaled and ran a hand down her face. "Unfortunately, the deaths of Maniac and Time Bomb weren't going to pacify him. He won't be good until you give up that name. And I assure you that he won't hesitate to torture you for that bit of info." She spoke seriously, gazing straight into his eyes. "Winston is not all there upstairs, and I'm sure you're aware of this. He's a couple of sandwiches short of a picnic basket, you know? He's always been off, since before his parents were murdered."

"Auuntyy!" A voice called out then there was the squeaking of the steps as someone was descending them.

Helen's head snapped toward the staircase as she made Wicked's shadow on the wall of the staircase. Her eyes widened and she looked to Te'Qui.

"Oh shit!" He hopped to his feet looking spooked, taken off guard when he saw Wicked's aunt charging at him. Before he could react, she was whacking him across his dome with her gun. The blow sent him falling back, knocking the milk crate out of the way. He held the side of his head and looked up at her like she was crazy. Helen stood over the young man, looking back and forth between him and the shadow on the wall as her nephew neared.

"Shhhhh!" She hushed him, holding a finger to her lips. "I gotta make this look good, play like you're hurt." He nodded and fell back hollering like he was being beaten. She pretended to be kicking and stomping him when she felt her nephew at her back. "Lil' bitch ass nigga!" she shouted down at him and harped up a glob of spit, hawking down on his face. Breathing hard, she turned around to her nephew, wiping imaginary sweat from her forehead. "This lil' fucka's tough, Winston, I've been going in on 'em since you left and he won't come up off of jack shit."

"It's alright, he'll eventually talk." Wicked told her, looking over at a sprawled and unconscious Te'Qui. "This lil' nigga gon' have to wait though. I've got bigga fish to fry at the moment."

"What's that?" she asked curiously.

"The less you know, the betta."

"Don't go holding out on me now, you've already gotten me knee deep in this shit."

Wicked rolled his eyes and blew hard, not feeling like hearing her pissing and moaning. "I gotta cap this nigga in order for me to be square with this other nigga, the end. Okay? Ya happy now? Jesus."

"Watch how you talk to me now. I had a hand in raising you." She wagged a finger in his face with a fixed frown on her face.

"Ahhhh. You're killing me, woman." He threw his arm over her shoulders, shaking his head with a slight smile. "Come on, let's go upstairs to bed."

"I'm exhausted. I could use a couple of Z's."

"Me, too. A nigga tired as a runaway slave."

Te'Qui kept his eyes closed until he was sure that they were gone. As soon as he lifted his head from off of the floor the light inside of the basement was shut off, leaving him in darkness. He sat up where he lay with his knees at his chest, wrapping his arms around them and resting his chin on them. Closing his eyes, he hummed a song to himself that his mother used to when he was a little boy. A tear descended his cheek and he realized just how much he missed her. That night he made a promise to himself that he was going to do any and everything he had to do to get out of that hell and get back home.

Chapter Five

Bianca's forehead wrinkled when she heard knocks at the door. She looked up at the cable box and saw that it was after twelve o'clock. Creeping over to the door, she peered out through the peephole and was surprised to see him on her doorstep. She didn't know why he was there at that hour, but it had to be important for him to just pop up.

"Gimme a sec." Momentarily, she left the door and returned slipping on a housecoat. She opened the door and was taken aback when she saw him cradling a baby in his arms. His banger was tucked in the front of his jeans while his other hand clutched a black plastic bag. His head was snapping in every which direction, as if he was expecting someone to leap out from hiding and attack him. He wasn't scared, just alert. And she couldn't blame him, especially with all of the shit he and Threat had been known to be into.

"Is everything alright?" Tiaz gazed into her eyes, stiffening his jaws. He held contact for a time before looking away and blowing hard. He didn't have to say a word, she already knew what it was from the jump. Although she knew that this day was coming, she was still shocked. Her boo was active in them streets, so his death date had already been marked on the calendar. Bianca felt like the wife of a marine that had been killed in active duty. And Tiaz was the ranking officer that had been sent to deliver the bad news. *Damn!* No matter how much a person prepares for something, he still is never ready for it when it happens.

"Ahh..." She slapped a hand over her mouth, suffocating the whimper that dared to escape her lips. Her vision became slightly obscured as tears welled up in her eyes, outlining the rims of them. Her body shook a bit and tears jetted down her cheeks. She closed her eyes then peeled them back open. He heard her gasp, overwhelmed by the hurt. She took her hand from her mouth and held onto the doorway, hanging her head as she tried to pull herself back together. She took the time to try to calm down and steady her breathing. His brows furrowed and he moved to help her. She threw up a hand and said, "Stop. I'm fine. Really."

Her eyes wandered down to the baby in his arms then back up to him. She raised an eyebrow wondering what was up, because she knew for a fact that he didn't have any children. He looked from little DJ then up to her, understanding what was on her mind.

"I'll explain everything. Can I come in or are you good?" He inquired. "If so then I understand."

"No. No. Come in." She pulled the door open wider and wiped her crying eyes with the back of her manicured hand.

"Thanks." He made his way inside where he sat down on the couch. He watched Bianca close and lock the door behind him. When she turned around she locked eyes with the baby, smiling through her tears and hurt. Quickly, she wiped her face with the sleeve of her housecoat.

"Can I?" She referred to her holding the baby.

"Yeah, come take this lil' nigga." He held little DJ out. "I stopped and got 'em some diapers and some milk. You mind feeding and changing 'em?"

"Sure."

Bianca took the baby and the black bag from him. She laid the little guy on the couch and went about the task of changing his diaper. She disposed of the dirty pamper and made him a bottle of milk. After testing its warmth, she scooped little DJ into her arms and shook him so she could feed him. She grinned lovingly as she stared down into his face. Her manicured finger outlined the side of his face and tickled his chin a tad bit. Seeing the child brought her back to the night where she'd lost her own child and met the man of her dreams.

Threat was cruising in his brown El Camino, nodding his head to the infectious sounds of Westside Connection's Westward Ho. He took slow draws from a writhing blunt, allowing the fog to fill his mouth. He peeled his lips apart and smoke rolled off his tongue. He sucked it back up into his nose and blew it back out. His glassy, red-webbed eyes scanned the street and bent the corners of South Central Los Angeles' scandalous streets. The brown paper bag sitting in the passenger seat contained a bottle of Hennessy, a stack of plastic cups, Swishers, and a box of Magnums. He was en route to the motel over on 83rd and Figueroa. He had some pussy on the line that he was dying to see what it was hitting like.

He narrowed his eyes as he peered out of the driver side window. He saw some tall, light-skinned nigga with a ponytail beating on a thick ass golden brown complexioned chick. She hit the sidewalk on her hands and knees, crawling away from him with her nose trickling blood. Her big titties jiggled about as she hurriedly went down the dirty, cracked sidewalk.

"Bitch, this all the fuck you done made?" He shouted down at her and threw the balled up dollar bills at her back. "What I tell yo' ass, huh? Fuck I tell you?" He took a cautious scan of the streets as he unbuckled his belt.

Figuring that it was nothing out of the ordinary besides pimp and hoe business, Threat was about to keep it pushing. That was until he noticed that the girl was pregnant.

"Hoe ass nigga." Threat's face contorted into something heinous, he then pulled his ride over and murdered the engine. He pulled his head bussa from where it was wedged between the seat and the console, ejected the magazine, stuffed it into his back pocket, then threw open the door and jogged across the street, looking both ways. The wicked look on his face and fire

in his eyes made him resemble a slave master as he caught the flesh peddler whipping his hand left and right, his thick leather belt acting as a whip. He swung his arm from left to right with all of his might. The girl screamed and tried to crawl away, but he stayed on her, causing thick red pulsing welts to appear on her back like magic as the violent lashing tore her clothing into shreds.

"Ahh! Aahh! Aaahhh!" Her head jutted each time the leather belt assaulted her back with a vendetta. "Calvin stop, stop! Waaa!" She tried to grab the belt, but that only made him angrier and he beat her harder, faster, unmercifully.

"Bitch put cha hands down, put cha mothafuckin' hands down!" A film of sweat masked his forehead and he breathed heavily, attacking her like she'd been caught stealing. "Yo' ass gon' learn". Whap! "Oh yeah, yo' ass gon' learn." Whap!" To have..." Whap! "...all..." Whap! "...My mothafuckin' trap." Whap!

"Please, Calviiinn! Stooopp!"

"Calvin? Bitch, my name Daddy, you disrespectful ass hoe!" He walked around her and kicked her dead in the temple, causing her to fall off to the side, out cold. He then moved to her protruding belly. "Fuck you and that trick baby!" He stomped her stomach as hard as he could twice with his Stacy Adams leather shoe, blood squirted out from between her legs, staining the concrete burgundy. Old girl didn't even feel it, because she was lying unconscious.

He looked down at his handiwork proudly. A smile plastered on his face, seeing her battered and bruised as he procured his belt back on his waistline. He wiped his sweaty forehead with the back of his hand.

"Let this be a lesson to you, have not some of my trap, but all of..."

Whack!

"*Aaahh!*" *Calvin staggered forward, grabbing the back of his dome. He whipped around and took a look at his hand, it was masked red. Frowning, he looked up at his attacker and found a short, skinn,y black ass nigga who looked like he had murder on his mind. Before the pimp could launch an attack, the little nigga was on him. Whap! Whap! Whap! He held the unruly nigga by the collar of his shirt and went upside his head with that steel until his gun was stained with his own blood. He then let him fall to the ground groaning in pain.*

"*You like to hit females? You like putting yo' hands on women, mothafucka, huh? Take off yo' belt!*"

"*Fuck you!*" *Calvin winced.*

Quickly, Threat took a step back, smacked his magazine into the bottom of his weapon, and brought it up. He gripped it with both hands like One Time do and pointed it at him. The battered man looked up, peeling his eyelids open and trying to keep the blood out of them.

"*Pl—please, man.*" *He croaked painfully, head throbbing and hurting.*

"*Take off yo' belt like I said, nigga, I ain't gon' tell yo' mothafucking ass again!*"

"*Alright, alright, shit!*" *Calvin unbuckled his belt and pulled it loose from around his waistline, outstretching it. Threat snatched the belt from his grasp and tucked his banger at the small of his back, taking a cautious look around the area for police presence. Seeing that the coast was clear, he went to work beating the flesh peddler's ass with his own belt. His hand swung from left to right, up down and all around, slinging that leather belt.*

"*Ahh! Ahh! Ahhhhh!*" *He screamed louder and louder every time the belt licked at his arms and legs furiously.* "*Stop, man, stop! Waaa!*" *He tried to grab the belt, but that only succeeded in pissing Threat off further. Heated, he beat him without mercy.*

"Bitch put cha hands down, put cha mothafuckin' hands down!" Threat barked at him like he did at Bianca. "Yo' ass gon' learn." Whap! "Oh yeah, yo' ass gon' learn." Whap! "To keep..." Whap! "Yo'..." Whap! "...mothafucking hands to yo' self." Whap!

Breathing hard, with a face shiny from sweat, Threat stared down at Calvin for a second before tossing his belt beside him.

Hearing a police cruiser siren heading in his direction, he darted across the street and pulled his El Camino over alongside the curb where Bianca was lying unconscious. He took a minute, but he was finally able to get her into the front passenger seat of his ride.

One week later in the hospital

All of the lights were out, save for the one illuminating the face of the beaten girl lying in the hospital bed, looking like she was in a deep, peaceful sleep. Her head was wrapped up in a bandage and she was wearing a blue hospital gown. Threat sat beside her bed in a chair with his jacket draped over him while he slept.

"Mmmm." The girl's eyelids flickered open like the wings of a wasp. Her pupils moved around trying to process everything around her. She couldn't see clearly, so she squeezed her eyelids closed tightly and peeled them back open. She could see quite decently now. Gritting, she sat up in bed, feeling the aches of her pimp's beating. Her body was a little stiff, but she was sure she'd be alright in time. She touched the bandages wrapped around her head and looked at her arms. She donned a plastic hospital wrist band and her clothing was a hospital issued gown. An IV was in the back of her hand. Looking down

at her stomach, she frowned. Lifting her gown and saw a C-section scar, she threw her head back and shrieked. Her veins bulged at her neck and her face turned a slight red, like rose gold jewelry.

"My baby, my baby, God, why? Why? Why?" Tears rolled from the corners of her eyes and outlined her face. Her trembling hands felt her stomach missing the bump that was once there. This felt like a nightmare to her, she had to be in the Twilight Zone, this couldn't have happened to her. "What did I do? Please give her back! Please gimme back my child!" Her entire body shivered all over as she looked at her ashy palms. She started smacking and scratching herself trying to wake up from this bad dream, but nothing was happening. That was because this was her real life. She was far removed from this being a bad dream, although she wished it was.

Threat awoke and rushed over to her. Grabbing her by her shoulders, he shook her and stared down at her.

"Calm down, look at me."

She calmed down and sniffled, looking up into his eyes with cheeks wet by a tragic loss. She ran his face through her mental database and that's when she remembered he was the one running across the street to help her. It was something in his eyes that made her feel safe. Like he would do any and everything in his power to make sure no one would hurt her again. She felt like he was her guardian angel, sent down from the heavens to watch solely over her.

Bianca threw her face into Threat's chest and wrapped her arms around him. He sat on the edge of the bed, stroking her back with his hand trying to soothe her.

"It's going to be okay. You're going to be all right."

Threat held Bianca that night until she fell asleep. He eased out of the bed and grabbed his jacket off of the door. In step toward the exit, he heard her at his back calling him to her. He froze and turned around, sliding his arms inside of his jacket, straightening his collar.

"Could you...could you stay the night with me, please?" she asked with eyes so swollen from crying that she could barely see out of them.

Threat stood there for a time just studying her face, it was one of great grief and turmoil. He couldn't begin to fathom the hurt she must have felt having lost her unborn child. The horrors she must have been through or seen being a prostitute probably had substantial effects on her. How could he leave her when she needed him? There wasn't any telling how many people had turned their backs on her. He wasn't going to even try to figure it out. He just knew that he wasn't going to join that, more than likely, lengthy list of them.

"Okay." He slipped off his jacket and crawled in bed with her, hugging her into him. They shut their eyes and drifted off to sleep.

Bianca was ready for a change and Threat was the answer to her prayers. From that day forth the couple had been inseparable. Threat would enlist her every now and then to accompany him on jobs. He showed her the ropes. The ins and outs of that kick door shit, and the proper way to use a gun and evoke fear into a victim. Bianca caught on to his teaching, taking to them like a duck to water. Although down the line he made her take a step back from the game while he attacked the streets with vigor and made sure that she was well taken care of.

Coming back from her stroll down memory lane, Bianca blinked back her tears and sniffled.

"You okay?" Tiaz questioned with a creased forehead creased.

"Yeah, I'm good. Sooooo, uh, who...who does this lil' guy belong to?" She raised a curious eyebrow.

"He belongs to the man that had a hand in killing Threat." He scowled.

Bianca's face twisted and she looked down at little DJ, then back up at Tiaz.

"How do you…What makes you think that he had something to do with Threat's murder?" she questioned, tears sliding down her cheek and curling around her nose. She swiped away her tears with her fingers and wiped them on her housecoat. Tiaz told her all of what he knew about Threat's murder and those he believed were involved. The relay of the information only made her cry and hate those responsible that much more.

"But don't worry though. I took care of those dog ass niggaz off the strength of my brotha." He bumped his fist against his chest and went about the task of licking a blunt closed. He then withdrew a lighter and produced a flame, guiding it back and forth across the blunt to seal it closed.

"What about him?" She nodded to the baby. "What chu plan to do with him?" Her hand slipped inside her housecoat's pocket and settled on the Glock she had concealed. She grabbed it on her way back to the bedroom when he'd arrived. Although Tiaz was her boo's best friend, his being at her house at that hour struck her as odd. She couldn't be sure what he'd stopped by for, so it was better for her to be safe than sorry. Bianca didn't know what his intentions were with the baby, but she'd fill him with some hot shit before she allowed him to bring harm to the innocent's life.

"You can ease yo' hand off of that burner," he said, having peeped the move. "I'm not gonna do anything to that nigga'z baby." He took a draw from the ass end of the L and blew out smoke in thick clouds. "I'ma piece of shit, but I'm not the biggest piece." He assured her.

Bianca nodded and closed her eyes, silently sighing with relief. "So, what're you holding on to him for then?"

"Leverage."

"Leverage?" Her brows creased. "For what?"

"You'll see. What?" His face pulled tight at the center.

Bianca's face was scrunched up as she studied the cuts covering most of his face. She hadn't noticed them when he'd gotten there, but their bleeding had drawn her attention. Tiaz wiped his face with the back of his hand and saw a small smear of blood. "Must have happened when I went through that window."

"Window?" She looked shocked.

"Yeah." He nodded.

"Let me put him in bed and I'll grab the first aid kit to patch chu up." She carried little DJ off to bed. When she returned she patched Tiaz up and sat down on the arm of the couch. She watched him pull a burnout cell phone from out of his pocket and a piece of paper. He looked from the paper to the cellular as he punched the numbered buttons. Once the line began to ring, he placed the device to his ear and held a finger to his lips, signaling for her to be quiet. She nodded and watched as he made the call to the man that had taken away someone very special from them.

***

The front of Don Juan's complex was lit the fuck up with police and ambulance lights, their blue and red rays shining on the faces of those who were nearby. A coroner's van was also parked out front. People were standing around being nosey and talking in hushed tones amongst each other. Some of them were even snapping pictures and filming what was happening. Don Juan stood beside Lil' Stan who was chopping it up amongst a couple of the homies that had come through. They were tooled up and ready to give the business to whomever on the kingpin's orders, but he was too far gone, consumed with grief and hatred for the man known as Tiaz Petty.

The police had questioned him about what had gone down earlier that night, but he didn't tell them jack shit. Not even about his son being kidnapped. As far as he was concerned mentioning anything illegal that went on was considered snitching and he didn't want any parts of that. He was a street nigga and he was going to leave street business where it belonged, in the streets.

Don Juan's eyes were glassy and his lips were peeled back in a sneer. He stared ahead at nothing as he clenched and unclenched his fists, defining the knuckles and muscles in his hands. His jaws were so tight that the bone structure could be seen appearing and reappearing as he was seething, head tilted down, eyes staring up. His eyes rimmed with tears, but he squeezed his eyelids shut, dissipating the wetness. Hearing rolling wheels and the squeaking of un-oiled metal stole his attention. When he looked in the direction of the noise, he found his wife's body under a white sheet being rolled out on a gurney.

"Hold up," he called out to the men pushing the gurney forth. They froze where they were and he stalked over, pulling the sheet back. He found the face of who he believed was the most beautiful woman in the world hands down. She wore a solemn expression and there wasn't any indication that she'd been hung to death besides the rope burns around the neck. He placed his hand on her forehead and caressed it with his thumb, feeling the slight chill on the surface of her skin. Staring down at her face, suddenly, he leaned down and placed a tender kiss on her lips. He then whispered into her ear saying, "I'ma find this cock sucka and I'ma bury 'em for you, baby. I swear on our son, I'ma kill 'em." He then stood upright and draped the sheet back up over her face.

At that moment his cell phone rang and vibrated in his pocket, he pulled it out and took a look. He frowned when he saw the number because he didn't recognize it, but he answered anyway.

"What's up?" He spoke into the cellular dryly.

"My nigga, Don, what's cracking, homie?" Tiaz came on the line like they were old college chums. It was like he didn't just lynch his wife and kidnap his son.

"Nigga, where the fuck is my son?" Don Juan hollered into the cell phone, drawing some of the bystanders' attention, as well as his homies. Noticing, he ducked off into a recess with his crew huddling around him.

"Yo,' Don, who dat?" Lil' Stan asked.

"That's him?" One of the homies questioned.

Don Juan threw up a finger for them to be quiet. The call was disconnected right after. "Hello? Hello?" His brows furrowed and he looked down at the screen of the cell. He then placed it back against his ear. "Hello? Hello?"

"What happened?" Lil' Stan inquired concerned, looking from his boss to the cell in his hand.

"He hung up! Shit!" He called him back twice and got sent straight to voice mail. "If this nigga touch my seed, so help me God I'ma..." He was cut short by the sudden vibration and ringing of his cellular. Quickly pressing *talk*, he pressed the device to his ear. "Hello." He answered coolly, attitude having vanished.

"Let's get something straight, my nigga, you ain't calling shit here. I am!" Tiaz blared in the receiver. "And the next time you come at me talking sideways I'ma take this lil' mothafucka and chuck 'em in the river, you understand me?" He waited for a response, but didn't receive one. "Oh, you must think it's a game, huh? Well. I'ma show you how real it is this way, homeboy!"

"I understand, man! I understand!" Don Juan humbled himself, still fuming on the inside. But what could he do? That thug ass nigga had his son's life in his hands.

"Good. Now apologize."

"What?"

"You heard me, you bitch ass nigga. You hurt my feelings. I'm sensitive."

Don Juan closed his eyes, swallowing his pride and setting his ego aside. He licked his lips and said, "I'm sorry."

"Put some base in yo' voice. I can't hear you."

"I said, I'm sorry."

He chuckled and said, "That's a good bitch. Now, if you wanna see yo' son again, you'll dig up my homeboy's body wherever you buried it and bring it to me."

"You know how long that's gon' take?"

"I don't give a fuck how long it takes." He snarled in the receiver. "You dig up his body and bring it to me. He deserves a proper burial."

"Where do you want me to bring 'em?"

"Call me when you recover 'em."

He disconnected the call.

"What he say?" Lil' Stan eagerly awaited the news.

"He's sitting on junior until we bring 'em Threat's body."

"What're we gon' do?"

"Exactly what he says."

***

Tiaz disconnected the call and sat the cell down on the table as he plopped down in the chair, sitting at the kitchen table. He took a pull from the burning blunt and passed it across the table to Bianca. Her eyes were glassy pink and her cheeks were streaked wet. She stared ahead at nothing as she brought that swisher to her plump lips, taking draws. At first she couldn't believe Threat was dead, but now it was confirmed. That was clear the moment she'd heard the conversation between Tiaz and Don Juan. He had the body, so a miracle of him somehow being alive wasn't likely. In the back of her mind she knew that The Grim Reaper had come for her man, but her heart just didn't want to believe it.

"You all right?" Tiaz asked her.

"Ummhuh." She nodded, passing him back the Loud.

"You sure?"

"Positive."

"Look," he started, mashing out what was left of the swisher. "I know this is outta yo' element, so if you wanna..."

"No!" she spat sharply, slamming her fist down on the table, rattling the glass ashtray. "I'm in. We're doing this for Threat. I wanna see that mothafucka Don Juan lying belly up!"

"And I'm gon' make that happen, all I need is yo' help. You the only one I can trust right now. You all I got. This nigga'z paper'd up. He feeds our hood, so them boyz ain't fucking with me, 'cause they not tryna have they plug sever ties."

"I got cho back."

"And I got cho front." They dapped up. "Hey, you got any liquor here? I could use a drink!"

"I should have some Remy VSOP in the cabinet over the refrigerator."

"Cool." He entered the kitchen, taking down a glass from the cupboard. After he got the bottle of Remy down and grabbed an ice tray, he dropped a couple of ice cubes into a glass. They did a little dance and the dark liquor came in right behind it. He picked up his drink and swirled the cubes around in it before taking a sip. When he turned around, Bianca's fist was balled tight and her face was hard.

"What chu thinking about?" Tiaz asked curiously, seeing the look on her face.

"Threat was my man, I'ma ride for him, right or wrong."

"We both are, I'ma be right beside you, momma. We gon' get this dick sucka together."

"You fucking right we are."

Three hours later

Don Juan banged Tiaz' line as soon as he'd recovered Threat's body. He gave him the location and time to meet up. About half an hour later, he and Bianca were pulling up at an abandoned furniture warehouse. He gave her the position she was to play and posted up outside of the car waiting for Don Juan to arrive. No sooner than the Latina had taken up her post, Tiaz narrowed his eyes as the headlights of a Porsche truck pulled up. He moved his hand where his banger was stashed in case the shit was a setup. That idea was quickly put to death when the lights of the SUV were murdered. The doors of the vehicle came open, Don Juan and Lil' Stan jumped down onto the pavement. The Trap God motioned him over and he approached with caution. He pointed to the back door of his truck, but Tiaz wasn't fucking with it. He looked at him like he was stupid.

"Y'all niggaz got me fucked up if you think I'm looking in there." Tiaz scowled.

"Open the door for this nigga, man." Don Juan told Lil' Stan, throwing his head toward the door.

"Square biz, homeboy." Lil' Stan opened the door and signaled for the thug to take a gander.

Tiaz snuck a peek and found something under a sheet. He then looked to Don Juan who gave him a nod. Afterwards, he took a deep breath and expelled hot air from his nostrils. He stood there staring at the lump under the cover hoping that it wasn't his best friend beneath it, but knowing no doubt that it was. He threw the sheet from over the body and found Threat, his eyes were closed and his lips were a straight line. The short killer looked at peace, even with the dirt smudges on his face. Tiaz drew the covers back from the rest of his form and found what looked like a thousand holes in him. This made him close his eyes and lower his head, massaging the bridge of his nose.

"Fuck, Threat." He exhaled, blowing air from his nostrils and mouth. Satisfied, he draped the sheet back over his childhood friend and pulled him out. He carried him over to the pickup truck and slid him into the back, closing the door of the flat bed. Looking up, he blinked an eye and gave a couple of hand signals like he was doing sign language. When he did this Don Juan frowned and looked in the direction he'd given the signal. He peered through the darkness, but couldn't make out a soul. Afterwards, he walked over to the driver side of the truck and pulled the door open. He was momentarily stopped when Don Juan called him back, brows furrowed.

"Hold up, fam, fuck is my seed?" He was about to grab that head bussa on his waist and set it the fuck off. Tiaz ignored him as he ducked off inside of the truck. When he came back around he had little DJ in his arms. He approached his father and passed him off. The Trap God pressed his forehead against his offspring's and closed his eyes. He mouthed *'Thank you, God'* and kissed him on his cheeks, then his forehead. When he looked up, he saw Tiaz staring at him with a pair of vindictive eyes. He moved to leave, but stopped once he was called back.

"I know you wanna piece of me, homie." He began passing his son off to Lil' Stan. "And believe me, I can't wait for the day you're lying at my feet puking up blood. Oh, we gon' get active, that's on my wife's life." He spoke with glassy, red-webbed eyes, looking as serious as HIV. "But I wanna truce, at least until we've buried our loved ones. Can we agree to that?" He extended his hand. Tiaz' eyebrows arched as he studied his foe's hand like it was slick with snot. He spat off to the side and shook the man's hand. The men departed, heading towards their respective vehicles. Tiaz gave another hand signal and Bianca emerged from the darkness, slinging the strap of a sniper rifle over her shoulder. She pulled the ski-mask off of her head as she was pulling open the door, hopping inside.

"You got 'em?" Bianca questioned.

Tiaz simply nodded. He grabbed her by the wrist when she went to reach into the backseat. "You don't wanna see 'em like that, B. It's likely to give you some nasty dreams."

"I don't care." She shook her head, eyes glassy and rimming with wetness. "I gotta know that it's him for sure."

"Alright." He placed his hand back on the steering wheel.

Bianca gasped when she saw that it was Threat beneath the sheet. Tears spilled down her cheeks and smacked a hand over her mouth. Tiaz closed his eyes for a moment and shook his head. He tried to warn her, but she just wouldn't listen.

"It's him." She couldn't believe it. "He's dead. He's really dead." She wept briefly and swiped the wetness from her eyes. Sniffling and wiping her eyes with the sleeve of her jean jacket. "Fuck that, Tiaz, spin this mothafucka around." She gripped the rifle with both hands. "We gon' smoke that nigga, he's not getting away with this shit!" Her head snapped over her shoulder and she saw Don Juan's Porsche truck driving off. "He's still here. Pull up on the driver side and I'll put one through his temple. That will leave his truck immobile and the passenger at our mercy. Come on."

"No!"

"The fuck you mean *no*!" She screamed on him, spittle flying. "They killed my man and yo' best friend! That nigga gotta go and he's gotta go now!"

Tiaz pulled over and grabbed her by the collar of her jean jacket. "Listen to me, goddamn it! If we gon' do this then we're gon' do this right! By my rules! You want revenge then you follow my lead, and I'll have you bathing in blood." With that said, she settled down and wiped her face until it was damp. "Alright? Are you with me?" She nodded yes. "Good." He threw the car in drive and pulled off.

A peace treaty until the funerals are over? Shiieettt, nigga, I'm not finna let off of yo' ass, me and Bianca are right back at that ass tonight.

***

Don Juan sat in the front passenger seat cradling his young prince in his arms. Lil' Stan sat behind the wheel, maneuvering the Porsche truck through the streets.

"So, you gon' uphold that peace treaty for real or what?" He looked back and forth between the windshield and his boss.

"What peace treaty?" Don Juan asked, seriously. "I fed that nigga that bullshit for him to put his guard down. I ain't showing that dick sucka no love, young nigga. I'm about to drop a few grand on that buster ass nigga'z head, what chu thought?"

"I knew it." Lil' Stan smiled. "I knew you were playing that fool."

Chapter Six

Tiaz and Bianca hit three of Don Juan's traps that night and didn't show any signs of slowing down any time soon. The thug was trying to make the kingpin feel his pain through the loss of his loved ones and his pockets before he finally decided to shut off the lights of his pitiful existence. He got a kick out of watching the man suffer. It was something about it that gave him a serious hard-on. The night got even darker, making the glow of the moon even brighter. Sitting low in an Escalade truck not far from one of their enemy's flourishing illegal businesses were Tiaz and Bianca, staking the place out.

"Yeah, this is it, Threat took me by here before, gave me the whole layout of the place and everything." He relayed to his partner in crime. Threat had shown him one of several locations of traps, illegal gambling spots, and other operations that Don Juan had. They'd planned to strike these locations as a team, but there was a change of plans when the Lord had called his homeboy home early. *Amen!*

"How many people are in there?"

"Three, four tops," he claimed. "Which is why I brought along the equalizer." He patted the shotgun lying across his lap. "You ready?" He locked eyes with her.

"Let's do the damn thang." She held his intensity.

Tiaz pulled his ski-mask down over his face followed by Bianca's thick ass. He racked a Mossberg pump, while she checked the chamber of her Python .44 Magnum revolver. Seeing that it was fully loaded with hollow tip bullets, she snapped it closed with a flick of her wrist.

"Alright," Tiaz began, "you take the front door. I'll cover the back. Let's move."

The doors of the stolen vehicle flew open and they hopped out, closing the doors shut quietly. They stooped low and moved in on the two-story house. They were draped in all black from head to toe so they blended in with the darkness, melting into the night and going undetected by any eyes that may have been watching. Stealthily, they invaded the yard and took up their posts. Once Tiaz had made it to the second floor window, he spoke to Bianca through his Blue-tooth headset letting her know that he was good to go. On the count of three they were to burst through the entrances and seize the house.

Bianca's heart raced behind her left breast. Not because she was scared but because her adrenalin was pumping madly. She was excited and oddly aroused. In fact, she was sure if she had a dick it would have been hard right now. She loved the thrill of the impending drama, that shit gave her a high like no other.

The pistol made her feel empowered. She believed that she was a force to be reckoned with. At that moment she wished she had some iron with her that night Calvin kicked the shit out of her, because if she had, she would still have her baby. What she wouldn't give to travel back in time to that fateful night and open up on his ass.

Bianca held her revolver low, gripping it with both hands at her waist. She listened to her partner in crime do the count as she stood with her legs apart, her booted foot tapping the floor gently. She was anxious. And as soon as the countdown finished she was kicking in that mothafucking door. Once Tiaz got to the number *three* she coiled her leg and kicked the door at the lock as hard as she could.

Boom!

The door flew open sending a spray of splinters and debris everywhere. She stormed inside, waving her head bussa around and barking threats. Her trigger-finger begged for a fuck-nigga or bitch to move, so she could give their families a reason to mourn. At the center of the living room sat four men at a table littered with notepads and Boost Mobile cell phones. Their faces were plastered with terror and confusion. Tiaz emerged from the kitchen and into the living room, clutching his Mossberg. He gave her a nod, letting her know that he had her back. She returned the gesture.

"Who else is inside of the house?" Bianca asked, eyes taking in all of the faces at the table.

"N-no one. It's just us." One of the men spoke up, visibly shaken up.

"You bet not be lying or you gon' get it first and the worse." She promised through clenched teeth.

"I swear to God, it's just us." His teeth chattered like it was thirty below in the living room.

"Alright, where them bands at?" Bianca asked the man with a no nonsense attitude.

"Do you know who you're robbing? This operation is headed by…" Bianca stormed over and cracked the man in the nose and mouth with the butt of her revolver. His head snapped back. When he brought it back down, his nose and grill ran like a faucet of blood. Droplets of blood pelted the white pages of his notepad. The man yanked the handkerchief from his breast pocket and used it to try to slow his bleeding.

"You think I give a fuck about whose spot this is, my nigga?" Bianca sneered. She was still hot over the loss of Threat and had made the man the recipient of her anger. "Right now, you're the one standing between me and my come up, and if you don't move I'ma blow your face off, ya dig?"

"Please, we don't want any trouble. Just take what you want and leave us be." Another man at the table slid a tin box forth and removed a chain linked key from around his neck. He was the manager of the booking operation. Tiaz snatched the key from the man's pinched fingers and hurriedly opened up the box. Inside he found a couple of bankrolls secured by rubber bands, but nothing worth their while. He slammed the tin box shut and tucked it at the back of his jeans.

"Where the rest at?" Tiaz asked, his menacing eyes staring out of the holes of his mask.

"What're you talking about? That's it." The second man told him.

"Bullshit, this is a dummy box. Y'all set this out just in case niggaz try to rob this mothafucka." He informed him. "I did my homework, where the real money at?"

"I swear to God, that's all we have here." The man swore. "That's what we took in for the night."

"Fuck that." Tiaz pressed his shotgun against the man's forehead and licked his lips. He then settled his finger on the trigger and bore into his eyes. The coldness in his pupils made the man feel uncomfortable and he squirmed around in his chair. "Now, you gon' either come up off that or I'ma leave your thoughts on the ceiling. Fuck with me if you want to, and see if I won't call ya bluff." The man's eyes bulged and his mouth dropped open. His whole body trembled he was so afraid. His loins grew hot as he felt piss filling his bladder.

While this was going on, the third man at the table, who wore specs and a balding scalp, watched Tiaz closely as his hand crept to the .38 snub-nose that was taped beneath the table. The man in the specs got a firm grip on the handle of the snub and snatched it free, shooting to his feet. He pointed the small pistol at the thug and shouted something in his native tongue.

Blam! Blam! Blam!

The man's face grimaced when he took three to the chest, dropping his pistol. He fell back into his chair, causing it to fall back and send him spilling out onto the floor. Tiaz looked in Bianca's direction as she lowered her Glock.

"Punk ass mothafucka," She studied her handiwork as she walked over, kicking the corpse three times. She then peered into the eyes of all of the men sitting at the table. They were all shaken up.

"Now is somebody gonna tell me where that dough at?" Tiaz asked.

"If we tell you Don Juan will have us and our families executed for sure." The man holding a handkerchief to his leaking nose said.

"That cock sucker's still alive." Bianca said of the man she'd aired out. Everyone looked to the man and he was most definitely dead, but the three men at the table didn't know that for sure, because they were too scared to take a decent look. The Latina vixen straddled the dead body, careful as to not let the other men see his face. "Are you gone tell us where that money is or am I gonna have to splattered yo' shit over this hardwood floor? Fuck me? Nah, nigga, fuck you!" She shoved her Python into the dead man's grill. "Suck yo' dick, huh?"

Tiaz looked at Bianca like she'd lost her mind. He didn't know what the hell she was doing, but he wasn't about to interfere. He'd only watch on wondering what would happen next.

"I'll suck it right after you eat this..." She pulled the trigger. Blood and pieces of skull shot across the hardwood floor. The chunks of flesh and brain on the floor resembled spaghetti sauce. The men at the table shrieked and whimpered in their chairs. Bianca rose to her feet looking down at the mess she'd made as blood dripped from her ski-mask.

"Now, where's that money?" Tiaz asked again.

"In the oven," the men said in unison.

"I'm guessing it's inside of some secret compartment, so who wants to be the one to show me?"

The thug looked around at all of the men at the table.

Five minutes later, Tiaz and Bianca came strolling out of the house 140K richer. They hopped into the black Cadillac

Escalade and sped through the ghetto making it rain again, sending rushes of people out in the streets to retrieve the stolen trap.

***

After leaving Helen's house Chevy shot straight up to the police station and filed a missing person's report, telling The Boys that her son had been missing for forty-eight hours so that they could get right on it. Afterwards, she dipped through different neighborhoods looking for Te'Qui. About two hours later, she shot back up to the hospital. Defeat resonated inside of her head having not found her son, so it seemed like the walk to Faison's room was a million miles away. She thought that she'd never get there, but after a time she arrived at his door. The room was dark, save for the blue illumination of the television dancing on his face. He was wide awake watching *Problem Child*.

Feeling another person's aura near, he looked to the doorway and found a silhouette. The light from the TV was dim against her clothes, making her look like she was dressed in all blue apparel. His forehead deepened with lines when he saw that she didn't have their son beside her. He already knew what she was feeling without her saying a word. He lifted his hand and motioned her over. She darted over to his bed and climbed in beside him, balling up in a fetal position. Faison draped his arm around her and pulled her close, kissing her on top of the head. His chubby hand swept up and down her arm affectionately. He listened to her sobbing and even felt the wetness that was her tears soaking in through the fabric of his hospital gown.

Although he had his one true love in his arms again, Faison was missing his only son, his prince, his junior, his mini me. That hurt him more than the bullets he'd taken. Not knowing whether his son was dead or alive, or even worse, being abused. A wealth of emotions hit him like a punch to the gut, but he had to be Chevy's rock. Feeling himself tearing up and not wanting her to see him vulnerable again, he killed the television with the remote and nestled his head against hers.

"I don't...I don't think I'm ever going to find him." She wept, voice cracking as she clung to him.

"Shhhh, stop that now, we'll find 'em. Everything is going to be okay." He spoke with a cool and soothing voice.

"You think so?" She sniffled.

"I know so. We're gonna find Te'Qui, I'm gonna fully recover, and we're gonna have ourselves a beautiful wedding down in Jamaica."

"You promise?"

"I give you my word."

Right after, they both fell silent in the pitch black room. She drifted off to sleep and he listened to her breathing, until he met with her in Dream Land.

The next morning Chevy told Faison about her getting jacked for the money that she planned to use to pay for her brother an attorney. He told her that he would front her the loot and have her start looking for a lawyer immediately. She found what she deemed the perfect man for the job, Archie Gold. He got right on it putting together a defense for Savon. In addition to the money for Savon's defense, Faison had also given her the money to pay for his families funerals.

That night

The situation with Tiaz had gotten too out of hand, and Don Juan needed it addressed ASAP. Tiaz was nowhere to be found. He'd gone underground like Osama bin Laden, and the very moment he reared his head the Trap God wanted someone there to blow it clean off. So he sent out an invitation to all of the hungry wolves of his set. He figured they would be the most eager to get their hands on what he had to offer.

The meeting took place on a Friday night inside of Mount Carmel's gymnasium. A metal detector was set up at all the entrances of the gym. There were also armed guards at the doors and amid the audience to ward off any shit that may occur. They kept these devices on them that looked like magic wands. They swept this over the entering person to see if they were wearing any wires. Don Juan took the floor, backed by Lil' Stan. He kept his finger on the trigger of his gun as his eyes swept back and forth over the audience. Some of them he knew, while others he was vaguely familiar with.

"Ahem, may I have your attention please?" Don Juan asked in a firm, but respectable tone, careful not to offend his audience. It was as if he hadn't said a word how the men of the audience continued chatting among themselves. He looked over the faces of the men in attendance and not a soul was paying attention to him. This pissed him off, but he had to remain humble if he was going to get any help with his situation. He closed his eyes and took a deep breath before addressing his audience again. "May I have your undivided attention please?" he asked once again, but the audience ignored him.

Seeing how frustrated Don Juan had become Lil' Stan fired his ratchet into the ceiling, debris dribbled causing him to narrow his eyes. The gunshot startled the audience, but also grasped their attention.

"Alright!" Lil' Stan began. "The big homie invited y'all here, 'cause he had something very important to get off his chest. So, y'all shut the fuck up and pay attention." Once the young nigga had captured the undivided attention of the audience, the gymnasium was so quiet that a person could hear a mouse pass gas. "Thank you!" He turned to his boss. "Alright, Don, they're all yours."

"First off, I'd like to thank each and every one of you for coming here tonight. I know there are a lotta y'all that don't get along in here, and I appreciate y'all leaving your beefs at the door. Now, on to what I called y'all here for." He cleared his throat and withdrew the sheet from a poster-sized photograph of Tiaz. "By a show of hands, are any of you here familiar with this man?" Everyone in the gymnasium raised their hand. There wasn't an individual amongst them that didn't know Tiaz. He and Threat were something like legends, seeing as how long they'd been giving it up in the streets. If a person hadn't seen them get down then they'd heard about, or knew somebody that had.

"This nigga has become a real hemorrhoid, a pain in my ass! This mothafucka has murdered my wife and kidnapped my son. He's a threat to my organization, my family, the homies and me. And as long as he's breathing my loved ones aren't safe."

He snapped his fingers and Lil' Stan walked up beside him with a briefcase. He popped the locks on the briefcase and raised its lid. There was about $100,000 dollars in cash inside. The audience was in awe.

"$100,000 dollars." Don Juan began looking over the faces of the men in the audience. "$100,000 dollars for the man that brings me this cock sucka's head. Now are y'all gon' get this money or what?"

The audience erupted in talks of the bounty on Tiaz' head. Lil' Stan's eyes scanned over all of the faces in attendance and a crooked grin spread across his lips. He knew the homies were riled up now. Who didn't want a piece of that action? There was a lot a hood nigga could do with that. Satisfied with their reaction, he closed the briefcase back and locked it. Don Juan handcuffed himself to the handle of the briefcase and picked it up. Lil' Stan then escorted him out of the gymnasium as if he was his personal bodyguard.

Lil' Stan kept his banger low at his side as he opened the door for Don Juan. He held it ajar and peered about keeping a close eye on things. The Trap God was holding one hundred grand and they were in the heart of the ghetto. That was more than enough loot for a nigga to try his chance with fate.

After closing the door behind Don Juan, Lil' Stan rounded the back of the Porsche truck, giving the guards in the un-marked car a nod letting them know that everything was good. The driver returned the gesture and the young nigga hopped behind the wheel of the SUV, pulling off and glancing into the rearview mirror occasionally. He knew that the hired guns had his back, but he wanted to be extra careful. Tiaz was a dangerous man and he'd hate to be at his mercy.

"Rosa, is everything there okay?" Don Juan asked cradling the cell to his ear, as he twisted the cuff around his wrist. "Good, good. How's junior? Asleep, huh? Alright, give 'em a kiss for me. Yeah, I'll be there in a minute."

"So, what's up now?" Lil' Stan looked from windshield to Don Juan, seeing him disconnect the call.

"Nothing." He fired up the roach end of a blunt he fished out of the ashtray. "We kick our feet up and wait for one of the wolves to give this thug ass nigga his tombstone."

"Sounds like a plan."

"My greatest one yet."

***

"Mommy?"

"Duke?"

"No, mommy, dis is Uche."

"How are you two?"

96

"We're fine." He looked over his shoulder at Uduka who was sitting in the passenger seat, head lying back, mouth wide open, fast asleep. "Yeah, baybee brudda is asleep. I was just callin' to check in and let chu know dat we were okay."

Silence.

"Mommy, are you there?"

"Yes." Her voice cracked and she sniffled. She took the time to blow her nose with tissue before responding. "Yes, I am okay. You just. You just make sure you bwois get home safe."

The lines on Uche's forehead deepened and his nose wrinkled. He clutched the telephone so tightly that the plastic of it cracked.

"Grrrr!" Hearing his mother's heartache drove him over the edge. He saw a haze of red and he could feel his ears and the back of his neck growing hot.

"Uche, you hear me? Uche!"

He calmed down a little, squeezed his eyes shut for a moment and then opened them. "Yes, mommy, I heard you."

"Okay. I love you. Tell ya brudda da same and give 'em a kiss fa me, alright?"

"Sure. I love you, too."

"Bye."

"Bye." When the call was disconnected, Uche slammed the receiver into the lever that hangs the phone up rapidly. *Ding! Bing! Ling! King! Ping!* He gritted as he assaulted the lever violently, before slamming it one last time and officially hanging it up. He gripped both sides of the telephone booth and closed his eyes, pressing his forehead against the edge of it. His chest twitched with succession as he breathed hard, hot breath rushing out in spurts.

"I'ma get 'em," *Dung!* He punched the side of the booth. "I'ma keel 'em, I'ma keel 'em dead!" *Pung! Clung! Tung!* He punched it several times. "I sweah, I sweah to Gawd!" *Dung!*

He punched the booth one last time before spinning around and marching back toward the car, blinking away the wetness in his eyes before the tears could seep. He opened the driver side door, stirring his younger brother awake. He wiped the remnants of wetness left with his fingers and thumb before ducking off inside of the car.

"Everythin'okay?" Uduka's forehead crinkled.

"Yeah." He nodded and fired up the engine. He then backed out of the parking space and pulled off. "Mommy told me ta tell you she loves you."

"Right." Uduka slumped in the passenger seat and closed his eyes. "I love her, too."

Uche glanced over at his brother then brought his attention back on the windshield.

I swear on ma father's grave I'm gon' find you Don Juan and I'm gon' keel you, my word, the oldest of The Eme Brothers thought to himself.

Chapter Seven
The Next Day

The sky was sunny, yet partially cloudy while rain fell in a light mist. The wind howled and whipped wildly, disturbing the collar of his button-down and the tails of his blazer. His eyes were bloodshot and rimming with tears that threatened to spill over and down his bronze cheeks. He thought he'd be able to hold himself together, but here he was falling apart. He'd been asked a hundred times by as many people if he was okay, and he held up a convincing front. But now his tears were threatening to betray him. At that moment he was glad he'd worn his black sunglasses, they were the only thing concealing his heartache from the others.

Tiaz and Bianca stood side by side, his fingers interlocked with hers. She sobbed and tears cascaded down her face. When they rolled over her mouth, she sucked her lips inward and tasted their saltiness. It was hard for her to believe she was seeing the love of her life for the last time. She just knew that they were going to live happily ever after like some hood fairy tale, but this was real life. This wasn't some urban fiction novel. This was reality and real shit happened in it.

While Threat was alive he had made her his power of attorney which gave her the power to handle his funeral arrangements. Neither her nor Tiaz had to come out of their pockets, because he'd stashed the money for his passing in a safe place. And the only one who knew its location was Bianca.

"Damn, boo," Bianca whispered, swiping the tears from her cheeks with her thumb. "You said you'd never leave me, but you did. Far too soon."

Bianca and Tiaz watched as her lover and his best friend was lowered into the earth, into the hole in the ground that was to be Threat's final resting place. The further the coffin entered the ground, the bigger the hurt in their hearts expanded.

"I'ma get that nigga for you, Crim, I promise." He balled his hand into a fist and squared his jaws, etching out the bone structure in his face. He was hot, heated, on one and he wouldn't be satisfied until he claimed Don Juan's life.

Bianca took her hand from Tiaz' and took the time to open an umbrella. She was in a charcoal gray turtle-neck, which she wore under a Pea coat and an apple-jack the same color. Her long thick hair flowed from underneath the hat over her shoulders and down her back.

The Latina glanced at the thug, getting a profile of him, seeing a wet streak down his cheek. He was crying and that streak was the evidence. She frowned as she looked to him. Gripping his shoulder, she asked, "How are you holding up?"

"I'ma soldier, ma," he replied in a flat-tone. Standing there plain-faced with his fists clenched tight, made him look like a statue chiseled out of stone he was so rigid. He may have seemed to be remaining strong to the people in attendance at the funeral, but Bianca could feel his pain. They shared it. She could see that he was in turmoil and she wanted to do nothing more than comfort him, like a mother would her child, and tell him that she loved him and that everything would be okay. But she knew that Tiaz was the type that liked to be left alone during trying times. He didn't need anyone to hug him and tell him that everything was going to be okay. With his personality, it was best for him to be left to himself to deal with the tragedy.

Tiaz surveyed his surroundings and was impressed by how many people came out to pay their respects to Threat. All of the homies and even some of the enemies came out to show some love to the fallen street veteran. Raemar, Threat's father, stood across the way from him in a Brooks Brothers suit. His wrists, waist, and ankles were all shackled. Red-faced white men sporting caps and windbreakers with *Police* scrolled across them, stood on each side of him. Their eyes were hidden behind black sunglasses and they were clutching shotguns in their palms. The tallest of the pair chewed gum. Their heads were on swivel during the entire ceremony, watching their surroundings.

Raemar was the head of The Empire, a drug cartel that had the game on smash back in the mid-80s to early 90s. His operati on was said to have grossed him an astounding thirty million dollars. The small envelopes labeled *Frenzy* had hoods in pandemonium, hence the drug's name. Its potency had fiends falling the fuck out and brought new customers damn near every day. Raemar made enough paper to live like that nigga Sosa in the Scarface movie. With money came power and with power came influence. He had boss status and long dough. That brought women, lots of women. The kingpin had thirteen children by almost as many women. Threat was one of them. The little nigga hardly ever saw his dad. His grandmother took care of him. So, it was needless to say once a snitch brought Rae's kingdom down and he was hit with that life sentence, Threat didn't lose a wink of sleep. He didn't give a fuck. He turned his back on his old man, like his old man turned his back on him. *Karma was a bitch!* The old head couldn't blame him. His abandonment didn't stop him from sending him a letter every week trying to make amends though.

Although Tiaz' eyes were behind black sunglasses, the old head was staring directly into them. Raemar was expressionless, but his eyes were telling his son's best friend everything he was thinking. He hated himself for not being there for his baby boy like he should have been when he was growing up, because if he had it was a good chance that he wouldn't be attending his funeral right now. Oh, if he could only turn back the hands of time, but he couldn't. It was out of his hands. He had no choice but to sit back and watch things play out how the Lord had designed it. Fate.

Raemar cracked a barely visible smirk at Tiaz and gave him a slight nod. He returned the gesture. He and Threat's old man were always alright. He remembered when he and his friends use to send them to the corner store for cigarettes and beer. When they'd returned, he would always tip them twenty dollars each. He recalled how he and Threat use to take everyone's order on a little notepad when they shot dice or had card games. This brought a smile to his face, but it was quickly erased when he peeped a couple of cats he knew about to bust a move. His eyes widened and he looked alive.

What the fuck? These dishonorable ass niggaz, got the audacity to come at me at my homie's shit.

"Noooooooo!" Tiaz shrilled, outstretching his hand.

Yuckkk!

Yuckkk!

The first officer's sunglasses went at a funny angle on his face when a cat wearing a bandana over the lower half of his face, swiped a knife across his jugular.

"Gaaah!" The guard's face twisted in agony as he slumped down to the ground. His partner was right behind him grimacing, as his neck was sliced open spilling a river of blood.

"Aaarrrhhh!" The other officer was shoved aside by a second man wearing a bandana over the lower half of his face. He stared down at the guard as his life's blood drained from him, wiping his blade on the sleeve of his suit.

Tiaz drew his Beretta from the small of his back just as one of the men wrapped his arm around Threat's father's neck and pulled him backwards. He plunged his knife in and out of his kidneys, grunting with each stick that punctured his victim's lower back. Raemar's eyes went big and his mouth stayed stuck wide open, blood smearing his lips as he struggled to escape the hold. His eyes shot to his left and the other man stuck him rapidly, bloodying his button down shirt. His eyes squeezed shut and his lips trembled.

Boc! Boc!

The first bullet struck the man in his shoulder, while the other pierced his temple. He fell over onto the grass, arms and legs flopping about. Tiaz swept his head bussa around to the last man that had Raemar in his clutches. All he could see were his evil eyes which bled malice. He held the OG up using him as a human shield. The ex-kingpin was as limp as a cooked Ramen noodle in his arm. That's because his ass was dead.

"Back up! Back up, or I swear 'fore God, I'ma kill this mothafucka!"

Tiaz' eyes zeroed in on Raemar's face, he was deceased. This infuriated him. He gripped his weapon with both hands. Closed an eye and squeezed the trigger with rapid succession, causing it to jerk stubbornly in his hands.

Boc! Boc!

The first shot blew a hole clean through the man's right eye, exiting out the back of his skull with a mist of blood. The second shot made a hole the size of a nickel upon entering his forehead. He was cock-eyed when he hit the ground.

Tiaz' took in his surroundings; people were darting back and forth across his line of vision. Men, women and even children were screaming and crying trying to get the fuck out of the way, afraid of getting their lives snatched by a stray bullet.

"Get the fuck back!" Bianca's yelling snapped his head around and he found her with twin Pythons pointed at a wall of niggaz wearing menacing expressions. Some had guns, some had knives, while others only had their bare fists. Either way, they were vying for a piece of the thug's ass.

"KJ, L-Bone," Tiaz barked a couple of his homies names. "Fuck this about? What the homies tryna get at me for, crimey?"

"Hunnit racks, homeboy!" KJ responded, mad dogging him.

"Don Juan put up dat paypa, and niggaz want it!"

"Oh, so it's like that?" His face twisted as he looked around at all of the hard faces. He couldn't believe the goons. He'd looked out for most of them on more than one occasion and this was how they chose to repay him.

"Nigga threw us a bone and we gotta eat!"

"Fuck y'all, all of y'all, ya disloyal mothafuckaz!" He jabbed his banger at the air.

A deep voice roared from his right. He turned his head just in time to see a big grey blur, before he was tackled and pain exploded in his side. He and the person that rushed him fell six feet and landed hard on top of the casket that held Threat. *Thud!* Tiaz grimaced so hard his eyes turned into slits and his face crinkled. When he peeled his eyelids open he saw a big, bald-headed nigga he knew by the name of Congo. He got his moniker on the account of him looking like and being built like a gorilla.

"You killed the homie Don Juan's wife, cock sucka!" His beady red eyes bore into the thug's as saliva threatened to drip from his thick bottom lip. He squeezed Tiaz by the throat with one hand and reached for his cowboy boot with the other. A sheathed knife was there. He yanked it out. *Snikt!* Lightning flashed and thunder rumbled. The rain fell harder, pelting Congo's shiny Q-ball head and Tiaz' face. The flickering light from the lightning danced across Congo's face making him look like he'd gone mad.

"Yeeaahh, I'm gon' split chu open like a key of coke, and get dat money!" His head slightly trembled as he brought the tip of the knife toward Tiaz. He gritted his teeth and clamped his hands around the big man's wrist, struggling to keep the knife at bay as the rain hit his face and eyelashes.

"Uhhhh!"

The tip of the knife got deathly close, so close that he had to turn his head. He clenched his jaws and his eyes doubled, afraid that the blade would pierce his cheek. His eyes darted toward Threat's coffin which was beneath him and visions of himself lying inside of it flashed inside of his head like lightning.

"Diiiiiee!" Congo grunted, smacking his free hand down upon the butt of the knife and adding pressure. The sharp tip of the knife was at his cheek now.

"Fuck you!" Tiaz slammed his knee into the brute's balls, causing his eyes to bulge and excruciation to shoot through his family jewels. The pressure on the knife vanished and the thug made his move. He snatched the sharpened instrument of death from his enemy's hand and kicked him in the chest. The impact from the blow threw him up against the wall of dirt inside of the six foot plot. He went to grab for his balls and he was rushed. Tiaz tackled him and slammed the knife into the side of his neck causing blood to go spurting out. Congo gasped and his eyes rolled around in his head. He pulled the blade out of his neck and looked at it, it was stained crimson. He was pissed now. He tossed the knife aside and went to rush his attacker. He got within two feet of him before he went crashing to the dirt. *Dead!*

"Back up, y'all back the fuck up!" Tiaz heard Bianca barking orders. He looked up and she was standing with her back to the six foot hole. Both of her hands were outstretched and gripping her twin revolvers, moving them around to keep the opposition where they were. Tiaz hurriedly climbed up the dirt wall and over onto the surface. He got up on his feet, brushing his palms off on his knees and looking about. It looked like there were a hundred angry faces with their eyes on them. Them niggaz looked like they wanted to put a bullet, knife, or a fist through he and Bianca.

The roughneck snatched up the Beretta he'd dropped when he was tackled and placed his back up against Bianca's. He motioned his head bussa around making sure not a nigga jumped at him. If they did, he was going to send one through his forehead. Straight up splatter their shit.

"Man, fuck this..." One of the hard faces leaped toward Bianca and she sent one through his chest, dropping his bitch ass.

"Next one of y'all move gon' find out if there's a heaven for a gangsta!" Bianca shouted, waving her twins around ready to give any nigga stupid enough the business if he decided to test her G.

"I'ma get the car, can you hold it down?"

She kept her eyes on the crowd and said into his ear, "I got chu faded, T."

Tiaz returned in the car. He swung over by Bianca and threw open the front passenger side door, she slowly backed up, keeping her eyes and her pistols on them fuck niggaz before her. She sat one of her toys on her lap and used her free hand to close the door shut while keeping her other burner on the threat.

"Go! Go! Go!" she told Tiaz.

He floored the gas pedal and the car ripped down the grassy hill with a surge of angry ass niggaz pouring behind them. Them fools threw knifes, shoes, hats and even took shots at them. Tiaz and Bianca slumped down in the front seats and bullets that sounded like heavy raindrops pelted their vehicle. Embers tatted up the trunk, shattered the back window and even blew off the side view mirror. Tiaz made sure to keep his chin tucked to his chest as he tried his best to steer blindly. He whipped his ride out onto the paved road of the cemetery and kept the pedal to the metal, gunning it up out that bitch. Once he felt like the coast was clear he eased up in the driver seat and stole a glance through the rearview mirror, adjusting it. Those wild ass niggaz were still chasing after them, but after a while they slowed to a trot and eventually stopped.

"We good?" Bianca asked from where she was slumped low in the front passenger seat.

"Yeah, we A1." He sighed, heavily out of breath. His face then morphed with fury as he stared ahead. "I'm about to bring it to this nigga. You hear me?" He glanced at her and she nodded. "We turning the heat up on bitch-boy. If he thought he felt it before, he ain't went through shit yet."

"I'm witchu." She scowled and nodded.

That same night

Duvall was posted up on the side of the 24 hour liquor store. He could barely be seen within the confines of the shadows and he wouldn't have it any other way. He was hustling so being virtually invisible to the police was quite alright with him. The night was winding down and he wanted to snatch as many dollars as he could before he took it in. His girl had some warm pussy and a hot meal waiting for him when he got home and he couldn't wait to have his way with either of them. Duvall spat on the curb and took his 40 ounces of Olde English to the head. He brought the bottle down from his lips and wiped his mouth with the back of his hand.

A crackhead wearing a jean jacket two sizes too small and tattered Reebok Classics approached him with a handful of wrinkled dollar bills. Duvall quickly served the crackhead and sent him on his way. He went to stuff the wrinkled bills into his pocket and made someone at his left. Duvall frowned and clenched his jaws, thinking it was a junkie that owed him some paper. His facial expression and body language projected the hostility he felt for the advancing man and he didn't bother to conceal it. He had it in his mind to pull out his joint and leave his noodles on the curb for the shit he'd pulled the last time he'd seen him. About two weeks ago, the approaching man had copped a couple of twenties off of him with counterfeit money.

"I know that ain't Ravone," Duvall said in a way that *said Nigga, you know better than to be showing your face around here.* "If it is, my nigga, you better have some money or some bullets for me, 'cause yo' black ass ain't leaving off this block in one piece unless I got some paper in my hand or some slugs in my dome." He looked him up and down with disgust.

"Relax, homeboy, I came to drop that on you and shop with chu." He produced a healthy knot from his pocket and peeled off a few bills, making sure to keep his head out of the light.

Duvall snatched the bills from him and tried to get a good look at his face. It was too dark to ID him, so he said fuck it and shrugged his shoulders.

"This shit better be authentic, nigga." He held the bills up into the dim street light and examined them. Seeing that the money was official caused a smile to stretch across his face. He licked his big chapped lips, and when he brought the money down, he gasped. His eyes were wide open and so was his mouth. He was staring face to face with a Beretta. Before he could utter a response the trigger was being pulled.

Boc!

His head bobbled about and the light left his eyes. Smoke rose from his forehead where the bullet was embedded as he slithered down to the ground. The few people that were standing around on opposite corners took off scrambling and running, like marbles from a punctured bag. Tiaz tucked the warm gun on his waistline and relieved his kill of his money, drugs, and cell phone. He took a couple of pictures of his dead body and sent them to Don Juan. He then tossed the cellular device aside.

Urrrrrrk!

The G-ride came to a halt alongside the curb. Bianca leaned over the front passenger seat and threw the door open. Tiaz ran and hopped inside, closing the door shut behind him. He pulled the money and drugs out of his pocket, dropping it all on his lap.

"Bend this corner right here." He motioned with his finger, pointing the street out through the windshield. When she bent the corner, the creatures of the night were shuffling about looking to secure their next fix, looking like the zombies in The Walking Dead. Tiaz pulled himself out of the window and sat on the sill. As the G-ride blew past the unsuspecting crack heads, he threw out all of the money and crack he'd stolen. They sent the streets into pandemonium. Fiends were running about screaming, hollering, and fighting one another trying to get their hands on the dollars and crack.

Duvall wasn't the last to fall at the twosomes' hands. That night a few more followed. Tiaz kicked in the door at the last trap and slaughtered the men there with a machete, while Bianca held them at gunpoint. He left them all dismembered and used their blood to leave his nemesis a message: *I'ma raise hell 'til I see a grave or a cell. This ain't over, you bitch ass nigga. I'm just getting started.*

Chapter Eight
The Next Day

Guru sat inside of Wing Stop hunched over a box of chicken wings and fries. He sunk his teeth into the wing of the fried bird and pulled back, tearing the meat from its bone like a lion. Guru sucked the crumbs off of his fingers before taking another bite and wiping his hands on a napkin. Once he'd wiped his hands off, he snatched up a couple more fresh napkins and wiped off the greasy lower half of his face. When he was done he balled up the napkin and set it aside before picking up his fountain drink and taking a sip of Coca-Cola.

Although any other day he would have been caught rocking a tailor-made suit and some leather Mauri shoes, that day he opted to wear something a little more comfortable. On top of his dome and cocked to the side was a navy blue Red Sox snapback with a pair of red socks on the front. His skinny form filled out a matching long sleeve, navy blue T-shirt. He didn't have on any jewelry, save for the gold and diamond ring on his pinky finger. It twinkled under the lights of the establishment and was worthy of the boss of an organized crime family.

"Y'all niggaz don't won't nothing to eat, man?" Guru asked Shank and Tink, after stretching and yawning. They shook their heads no. The young wolves went wherever the OG went and were his own personal security. Though they didn't speak much, violence was their strong point. They had enough bodies between them to open up their own cemetery. "Suit yourself, you missing out though, this chicken good than a mothafucka." He was about to tend back to his box of wings when he saw Tiaz pull into the parking lot and hop out of his whip.

As soon as Tiaz crossed the threshold into the establishment, Shank and Tink moved in on him. It wasn't until Guru gave the okay that they parted and allowed him to enter their boss' personal space. He motioned to the empty chair across from him at his table. Taking his cue, Tiaz pulled out the chair and planted himself in the seat.

"You want a chicken dinner?" Guru looked up from his chicken box.

"I'm not hungry. I do need to holla at chu though."

"What's on yo' mind?"

"I got into some shit and I'm gon' need some heat."

"Speak on it."

Tiaz looked to Shank and Tink.

Guru picked up on him not wanting to speak in their presence. "Yo, Shank, Tink, y'all take the employees and chill out front for a minute. Me and my homeboy need to chop up some game." The bodyguards retrieved the employees from out of the kitchen and made their way outside. The employees went their separate ways while the muscle posted up just outside the doors of the establishment.

Guru wiped his mouth and hands with a napkin. He balled up the napkin and tossed it aside, then folded his large arms across his chest. "What's on your mind?"

Although there was no one inside of the establishment besides Tiaz and Guru, he still took the time to look around and make sure no one was listening to what he was about to say. Seeing that the coast was clear, he leaned closer to Guru. "You know my man, Threat, took a bad one, right?"

Guru frowned and leaned forward. "Threat's locked up again? Shit, I know they threw the book at his lil' wild ass, that boy there just like a pit bull."

"Nah." Tiaz shook his head. "They took my man out."

The OG made his hand into the shape of a gun and he nodded his confirmation. This let him know that their mutual friend had been murdered. Shocked, he looked away and closed his eyes, shaking his head. "Well, I'll be goddamned. We're losing more and more homies every year." He locked eyes with the roughneck. "Who laid the homie down?"

"Nuh uh, he's mine."

"I feel you, youngsta. I know how close you two were."

"Right." He nodded. "That was my mothafucking brotha. So I'ma represent and get down for him, but I'ma need some heavy artillery if I'm gon' get some get back, you feel me?"

Tiaz wasn't a dummy. He knew that if he told his big homie that Don Juan was the nigga that he planned on bringing it to, that he wouldn't put him into contact with the cat he needed to see for the firepower, so he made sure that he was discrete. Niggaz in the hood loved Don like they loved hood rat pussy. He was a ghetto celebrity in his own right.

On more than one occasion he brought the neighborhood kids school clothes and shoes, paid mothafuckaz gas and electric bills, and blessed niggaz with work on consignment. He played the game like a politician making sure he was in favor of the people, so even the homies that fucked with Tiaz tough, would more than likely turn their backs on him if they knew he had an issue with him. He couldn't blame them though. How could they bite the hand that fed them? When it came to making a decision on whose side they were on, it was going to be a no brainer on who they'd pick. Tiaz understood this and he couldn't do anything but respect the game.

"Alright, well, if you tryna get cho hands on some Commando, Rambo type of shit I could plug you with my man Remo. He's got some shit, some really nice shit."

"Cool." Tiaz rubbed his hands together. He couldn't wait to feast his eyes of the toys Guru's people would have.

"Let me hit 'em up." He stuck a toothpick into his mouth and took the cellular from off his hip. He found the number he was searching for and pressed *dial*. "Yoooooo, Darlene, how are you doing, sweets? Good, good, good. Listen, is Remo in?

What?" His face tightened at the center and he looked up at Tiaz who frowned. "Okay. You be sure to tell 'em to let me know if he needs anything. Alright now, take care."

"What's up, G?" Tiaz questioned, concerned.

Guru blew hard, saying, "My man got picked up by the feds last night."

"Sheeiiiitt." He slammed his fist down on the table, startling Guru's chicken box.

The OG lowered his head and stared down at the table as he massaged his gray stubbled chin, thinking. Suddenly, his head shot up and he snapped his fingers like *eureka*. "I know where you can get chu some tools from. Mothafucka right in our backyard, I can't believe I didn't think of him before."

"Who?" Tiaz asked anxiously, sitting up in his seat.

"Gatz."

"Gatz? Last time I remember he was slinging them piece of shit 9s."

"Nah, he's got his weight up since you been gon.' From what I hear he's hooked up with some Arabian mothafuckaz. He gets shipments on some pretty nice stuff too, or so I've been told." He picked up his fountain drink and took a sip. "I could hit 'em up, but you and Gatz are good money, right? Y'all square?"

"Aw, hell yeah, me and the homie always been straight."

Tiaz rose from the table at the same time that Guru did. He stepped around the table and embraced him with a gangsta hug, patting him on the back.

"Good looking out, G."

"Don't mention it," he said, arm over his shoulders. "Look here, you don't hesitate to shout me a holla if you need some back up for this cock sucka's program you 'bout to get with."

"Fa sho.'"

"Alright then." He patted him on his back and watched him take his leave. He then motioned Shank and Tink back inside before getting back to the business of devouring his chicken dinner.

***

If Wicked was going to track down Don Juan then he was going to need some information on him. The only person he knew that could help him was this BBW he used to knock down back in high school by the name of Diana. Diana was a fairly attractive, brown-skinned chick with eyes the color of almonds and a short haircut. She'd been in love with Wicked's crazy ass since middle school. He was her first love and she was his first nut. She fell in love while he fell in lust. But how couldn't he? She had a sex game like a porn star and an ass he could hitch a trailer on.

Wicked circled the block of the Hope Street Department of Motor vehicles four times looking for a parking space. Figuring he'd have better luck laying low inside of the parking lot and waiting for someone to leave, he drove back and did just that. It was taking a while so he sparked up the pinch of blunt he had left in the ashtray. As he sucked on the end of it, smoke manifested, filling the interior of the car with a foul stench. He cracked a window to let a little cool air inside. He leaned forward and narrowed his eyes seeing an old Chevy pickup backing out of its parking stall. A crooked grin formed on his lips and he flicked the piece of the blunt out of the window, sending embers flying. He cranked up the engine and was about to swoop into the stall once the pickup was gone. He got about five feet away when an Infinity truck with blaring speakers slid right inside and murdered its engine.

"No the fuck this nigga didn't." Wicked couldn't believe he'd gotten jacked for his stall. He squared his jaws as lines formed across his forehead, hopped out of his ride and approached the driver just as he was getting out of the SUV. He was a tall light-skinned nigga rocking an LA snapback and light jewels.

"Say, homeboy, you didn't see me waiting to get this spot?" Wicked dripped with attitude, just waiting for old boy to pop off at the mouth.

"Yeah and?" He looked him up and down like '*Nigga what the fuck you gone do?'*

Wicked took a deep breath and thumbed his nose, thinking clearly, *this dude doesn't know who I am*. He lifted his shirt and revealed that thang-thang on his waistline. The sight of that steel made the bitch bleed up out of homeboy, his eyes got big and his mouth trembled. He kept his eyes on the weapon as he raised his hands, swallowing the nervousness in his throat, knowing a parking spot wasn't worth his life. There was something about the look in Wicked's eyes that let him know he'd have no problem taking it there.

"Say, say, say, bro, I…"

"Get cho punk ass in the car and get up outta here!"

Smack!

His ashy palm went upside his head. He ducked back inside of his truck and backed out. Wicked watched the backlights of his SUV as it pulled out of the parking lot, smiling victoriously.

That encountered reminded him that he was truly one of the hardest niggaz walking the earth. See, he needed that. He felt like a bitch ever since he'd taken an order from Roots.

"Humph." He returned to his ride and pulled into the stall. Snatching his key out of the ignition, he stuffed them into his pocket and headed for the entrance of the DMV. When he crossed the threshold he couldn't help but notice that the place was packed out. This wasn't anything new. The Department of Motor Vehicles was notorious for being overly crowded. He wasn't studying it though, because he didn't have to wait on the line to thin.

Wicked glanced at the woman he'd come to see, giving her a nod. He saw her whisper something to one of her co-worker's and grab her purse. He nodded to the women's restroom and ducked off inside. She was right on his heels. She looked both ways to make sure no one had seen them enter together before closing the door shut, locking it. When she turned around he was leaned up against the sink with his arms folded across his chest.

"'Sup, sexy?" He cracked a smile, still looking like his namesake.

"Hey, baby." She smiled as she approached, flipping her hair out of her face. He collided with her, tonguing her down so hard the sounds of saliva could be heard sloshing around inside of their mouths. "Ooh." She cooed and smiled, feeling his strong hands cuff, then squeeze, her big old ass. When he pulled away they wiped the extra spit at the corners of their mouths, grinning as they did so.

"You got that for me, boo?"

"Yeah." She nodded, reached inside of her blazer and pulled out a manila envelope. He took the envelope and opened it, pulling out several documents, all of them loaded with Don Juan's personal information. He looked through a couple of them, coming across one of them that was a copy of his driver's license. After studying some of the info, he stacked the papers neatly at the edge of the sink and slid them inside of the manila envelope. He then tucked the envelope at the back of his Levi's 501 jeans, pulling his shirt over them.

"Thanks, baby." He tilted her chin up with a curled finger and kissed her again, this time passionately. *Muah!* He kissed her lips once more before headed for the door. He stopped short once she called him back. "'Sup, boo?"

"Umm." She twisted her manicured nail at the corner of her teeth, seductively, dying to get a taste of that thick dick of his. "Do ya think I could getta quickie before ya leave?"

Wicked didn't even have to think about that one. He hadn't had any ass since he'd been home. Her request immediately caused him to rock up.

"Yeah, I can break you off." He smiled devilishly, unbuckling his belt and watched her slide off her purple panties. She kicked them off of her high heel and turned her back to him. Facing the mirror, she hiked that enormous ass of hers up. Diana became wet watching her man through the restroom mirror, approaching her from behind and stroking his hardened meat from its base to its head. He licked his lips in anticipation of feeling her wet, warm passage hug his dick. Stepping to her rear, he smacked her violently on her wide dimpled rump.

"Uhh! Uhh!" He frowned, the smacks growing louder and louder. She closed her eyes and threw her head back, gasping and sucking her lips inward. They were louder than a mothafucka inside of that restroom, but neither of them gave a damn about getting caught because the sex was just that good.

"Mmmm." She murmured, liking that kinky shit. Rough sex was the best to her. She threw that ass back, bumping against his endowment. His shit was so hard that it jumped occasionally like it had a nervous twitch. He bit down on his bottom lip, stroking his dick and then spanking her on her behind with it. He beat each of her cheeks, going back and forth as if he were playing a drum set. She looked over her shoulder at him, sliding her tongue along the outline of her full lips. She bounced up and down, making her ass applaud, trying to entice him. He rubbed her buttocks and slid his hand up and down his steel slowly. He then drew back and slid gently into her gaping pink hole. Her shaved lips swallowed his member and she contracted her walls around it.

Smack!

He whacked her butt with his ashy palm telling her, "Throw that ass back, momma, I wanna see that pussy eat this dick up." She sucked on her bottom lip and looked over her shoulder as she threw that thang back into him. Her coochie making his wang disappear and reappear, getting wetter with each glide. "Sssss, ahhhh." He tilted his head back and rolled his eyes, mouth hanging open. "Yeah, yeah, that's it. Faster." He smacked her booty, causing her to wince and moan, but she did as he commanded though. She loved when he gave her that thug love. Looking down, he admired his stroke being gobbled up and spat back out. He flipped the end of her blazer up so he could get a good view of her cakes. Wicked frowned in ecstasy, feeling his rod swelling with jizz, he gripped each of her butt cheeks, causing the meat to bulge between his calloused fingers. "Hold still, baby, I got this." Her movements ceased, he spread her ass apart and pushed them up. He thrust himself in and out of her roughly, watching her pussy's vanilla pudding glaze his diamond hard dick.

"Ooohhh, shhhhhieeett, that's it, work it, baby, work this mothafuckin' pussy!" Her eyes shone white and she bared her teeth. He got a good grip of her short hair and pulled her head back, he looked at her watching him fuck her in the reflection of the glass. His face was twisted hostilely, he was beating that bitch back up and she was loving every bit of it. The blissful smile on her face and her fluttering eyes made this apparent.

"Arrrhhh!" She growled.

Still, staring at her through the mirror, he smacked her on her buttocks and talked that shit. "You like that rough shit, don't chu! Don't chu, you freaky mothafucka you!"

"Yes, yeess, yeeesss, I fucking love it!"

He harped up saliva and turned her face to the side, spitting on it twice. The hot goo splattered against her face as he worked her bottom, the nappy hairs of his V slapping against her cakes. Diana tried to lick some of the spit off as it rolled down her cheeks with her nasty ass.

"Arrrrh!" Wicked gritted, feeling his nut build up in his pipe. He kept at it until the last possible minute. "Here I come, here it go!" He snatched his glistening beef out of her and jerked it. The head of his meat swelled and shrunk as his dick was pumped until finally, *Ahhhhh!* His cream oozed and pelted her brown booty. He smacked her on the butt again and rubbed his flaccid penis in the glaze he'd stained her with.

"You did that, boy." She smiled at him through the reflection in the mirror.

"You ain't gotta tell me, I was there." He smiled with a forehead beaded in sweat.

He grabbed some paper towels for them both and they cleaned themselves up. After getting dressed and straightening themselves out, they exited the restroom minutes apart from one another.

Diana was going back to work, while Wicked was off to put another notch under his belt. Don Juan's life was his to claim.

***

Don Juan stood in front of the dresser's mirror tying his tie and adjusting it. Smoothing the slight wrinkles out of it, his eyes came across the wedding portrait of him and Kiana sitting on the nightstand. He made it through the reflection in the mirror's glass. In that instant the weight of his guilt hit his shoulders like a three hundred pound barbell. His shoulders slumped and he hung his head, blowing hard. He ran a hand down his face and stopped at his nose massaging it. Taking his hand away, he looked up at his reflection. His eyes were pink and rimming with tears.

"I'm sorry, Ki." The tears shot down his chocolate cheeks. "I swear on my soul, baby, I am so sorry. If I could trade places with you, my right hand to God I would." He pressed his forehead against the mirror and closed his eyes. His shoulders shook as he sobbed quietly, tears splashing on the dresser. He sniffled and lifted his head up. Staring at the broken image of himself in the mirror, made him realize that he was broken just like it. He had tried so hard over the years to keep his life from her to keep her safe, but in the end it had not been enough. His dealings in the streets had come right to their door, claiming her life and putting their son in the hands of a ruthless thug.

Hearing a knock at the door took Don Juan back to the here and now. He wiped his eyes with the sleeve of his suit's jacket and cleared his throat.

"Who is it?" He called out.

"Lil' Stan. Are you ready? The homies waiting for you."

"Yeah, gimme a sec." He straightened himself out and gave his reflection one last look. Opening the dresser drawer, he picked up his gun, opened his suit's jacket and holstered his weapon. With that done, he opened the door and found his second-in-command holding his son. He took him into his arms and kissed him on his chubby cheek. The little dude was wearing a suit identical to his father's. They were matching from head to toe. Ever since Tiaz had launched that attack on his home, Don Juan was even more protective of his son, even to the point of being obsessed with his safety. He considered leaving the child at the house with a nanny and one of his men to watch over them, but felt that his baby boy would be safer with him.

"Come on, DJ, let's go send yo' mommy off."

***

Bianca pulled up across the street from Gatz' house and executed the engine. Tiaz looked from the head bussa in his palm to his front door as he check the magazine of his weapon, making sure that mothafucka had a fully loaded clip. *Click! Clack!* He chambered a silver hollow tip bullet into the black gun and tucked it inside of his jacket. He looked over to his accomplice.

"Keep this bitch running," he told Bianca after surveying his surroundings. Although Don Juan said he was good until the funeral, he wasn't going to throw caution to the wind on his word. He was a gangsta like he was, which meant he was willing to do whatever he had to do to come out on top. *Fuck his word!* He rationalized, grabbing two extra magazines from out of the console and smacking it shut. He leaned aside and stuffed them into his jacket's pocket, eyes still focused on the front door of Gatz' place. He could be walking into a setup and if it was so, he wanted to have plenty of ammo to get himself out of a tight squeeze. "If shots start flying, you gimme three minutes and then you pull yo' ass up outta here."

"No."

"What?" He leveled his eyebrows and narrowed his eyelids.

"I'm not leaving you behind, we're a team." She informed him. "First sign of trouble and me and this bitch coming up in there laying down bodies." She stroked the Magnum revolver in her lap like it was a Persian feline.

"Gangsta to the core, my brotha knew how to pick 'em." Tiaz cracked a slight smile, holding out his fist.

Bianca smirked and dapped him up. "I'll be back." He hopped out of the car and jogged across the street, looking over both shoulders.

Tiaz knocked on the door and called out Gatz' name for about five minutes. When didn't answer he pressed his face against the window and cupped his hands around his face, peering inside hoping to see him. He could barely make out anything through the slight opening of the curtains, so he made his way around the side of the house, looking to try the backdoor. He was just about to head up the steps of the back porch when a foul stench assaulted his nasal passages. He whipped his head around and found the garage. He darted right over and knocked on the door, calling his name.

"Gatz! Gatz!" He called out. "Yo,' it's Tiaz, homie!" He waited for a reply, but didn't get one. Noticing the light shining out through the lining of the aluminum door, he grabbed the handle and lifted it up. When he saw Gatz strapped to the iron table with bug eyes and a wide mouth, he was taken aback. He glanced over his shoulder and hurried inside, closing the door back. He approached the table and looked upon him. Flies were swarming all around him. There were some on his eyelids, nose and mouth, all drawn to the repugnant odor. Nearly every inch of him was covered with gashes and his clothes were soaked with so much blood that he looked like he was wearing the color from head to toe. Tiaz smacked a hand over his mouth and narrowed his eyes, walking backwards. The stench nearly made the roughneck gag. The gun merchant was dead and stinking worse than a sack full of sweaty assholes.

Bump!

Tiaz stepped into the side of the refrigerator, he whipped around to it and recognition flashed inside of his head. He remembered when he'd last bought some guns from Gatz. He specifically recalled him showing him his merchandise which was stored inside. He pulled open the freezer and the refrigerator, rummaging through the weapons and the boxes of bullets. He withdrew two M-16 assault rifles and few boxes of bullets for them. After lying out a sheet on the floor, he laid the weapons and ammos down upon. He rolled the items up and tucked them under his arm. Opening the garage door, he turned around to Gatz crossing his heart in the sign of the crucifix.

"Rest in paradise, homie." He smacked his hood over his head before ducking off outside and making his way down the path.

After securing the weapons, Tiaz hopped back into the rental and into Los Angeles traffic. He scoured the streets looking for a ride identical to the rental. A smile stretched across his face when he found one, a '97 Nissan Pathfinder with a crash bar. He parked six cars down from the whip that was identical to his own. He hopped out of the rental and jogged over to the Nissan Pathfinder. He kneeled down and unscrewed the license plate with a screwdriver. Returning to the rental, he swapped its plates with the stolen one and hopped back inside of the SUV. Bianca pulled off. They were on their way to execute their mission.

Chapter Nine

Don Juan rode in the back of a limousine with Lil' Stan and his baby boy. He picked up a glass and dropped several cubes of ice into it. After picking up a bottle of Louie XIII and filling the glass, he sat the bottle aside and tilted the glass to his lips.

"You still haven't heard from that nigga Juvie?" Don Juan asked Lil' Stan.

"Hell naw, I've been blowing that fool up. He still hasn't hit me back." He frowned as a thought crossed his mind. "You think that nigga Tiaz caught up with 'em?"

Urrrrrrrk! Craaashh! The impact of the crash caused the Trap God to spill the liquor into his lap, making him glad to be wearing black.

"What the fuck?" He looked down at the water mark on the crotch of his slacks. He sat up where he was perched and Lil' Stan did, too.

"Hell was that?" Lil' Stan frowned.

"I don't know, I'ma see." He descended the black tinted window and stuck his head out. He gasped when he saw a masked man who he knew in his heart was Tiaz jumping out of a truck with an M-16. He didn't even turn his head as rounded the hearse holding his weapon with both hands, hugging the trigger. His assault rifle bucked wildly chewing up the windshield, cracking up all of its glass. There wasn't any doubt in his mind that the driver of the hearse was dead.

What Don Juan saw next surprised him. Tiaz opened fire on the side of the windshield where the chauffer of the limousine was, but luckily for him the vehicle was bulletproof, because all of the shots deflected off of it. The rush of gunfire startled everyone, but what came next came as a surprise.

Boof! Boof!

The front of the limousine tilted forward as the front tires were burst from beneath it.

"It's him, it's Tiaz!" Don Juan blurted, pulling his head back inside of the limo.

"Oh shit!" Lil' Stan watched him grab a gun out of a hidden compartment inside of the limousine. He checked its magazine and slapped it into the chamber of that bitch.

"Tell the wolves to tool up!"

"Right." Lil' Stan pulled a burnout cellular from his suit's jacket and speed dialed someone. "Y'all niggaz banger up, it's on!" Was all he said before flipping the cell phone shut.

"Watch my son, you guard my seed with cho life." He stared into his little homie's eyes, all glassy and serious. "You hear me, lil' nigga?" The Trap God inquired, hating himself for being so in his grief that he let his guard down. He wasn't so much afraid for his own safety, but for the safety of his child.

"I got chu, Don. Ain't shit gon' happen to lil' man that don't happen to me first."

Don Juan gave a nod and threw open the door of the limo, leaping head first into the action.

***

Tiaz glanced at Bianca. She was wearing the same look of determination and vengeance as he was. He cracked a slight grin. He respected her G. She was as down as any nigga he'd rubbed shoulders with.

"What's up?" Bianca asked off of his look.

"Nothing." Tiaz regained his focus.

"Okay."

"That's them right there." He pointed to the windshield at a vehicle and cocked a live round into the M-16. He sat up in his seat, drumming his fingers on the stock of the weapon and tapping his boot on the floor. He was ready to get it on and popping out that mothafucka.

"Alright. Here we go!" Bianca bit down on her inner jaw and pressed the pedal to the metal. The SUV accelerated, flying down the lane and whisking passed cars, nearly side swiping them.

Urrrrrrk! Craashh!

The Pathfinder slammed into the side of the hearse, stopping all of the trailing cars behind it. The buff neck thug pulled his ski-mask down over his face and threw open the front passenger side door, jumping down into the street. He ran around the front of the truck, hastily approaching the vehicle that contained one of the most precious people of Don Juan's life: his wife. Tiaz let loose on the windshield of the ride where the driver was sitting, tattering the glass. The bullets came in a rush making the captain of the car dance where he was perched. The driver slumped with his chin touching his chest, the front of his shirt stained crimson.

Tiaz looked up and spotted the limousine that he believed Don Juan was in. He figured this because this was the only limo in the lineup of vehicles and the limos in funerals normally carried the family of the deceased. When the chauffer of the limousine shook off his daze and saw the thug, his eyes nearly leaped out of his head. He went to start up the car, but the engine wouldn't turn over. Right after he was greeted by rapid fire from his M-16. Sparks flew left and right from the windshield, the limo was bulletproof.

"Fuck!" Tiaz cursed. He then aimed his weapon at the front tires and blew them bitches out, insuring that the vehicle wasn't going anywhere. Next, he focused his attention on the rear of the hearse, hoisting up his assault rifle.

Crack! Craackk! Craaackkk! Craaashhh!

He slammed the butt of the rifle into the glass window of the vehicle until it gave. He then reached his gloved hand inside and unlocked the door, yanking it open. Hoisting the deadly weapon over his shoulder, he pulled the coffin out of the rear of the vehicle. It made a loud thud as it was dropped onto the ground. He opened the box's lid and revealed Kiana with her hands folded at her waist. She was dead, but looked like she was in a peaceful sleep. Tiaz took the time to observe her appearance as he angled his head. *Snikt!* He drew his machete and the sun's shining caused it to gleam, sweeping up the entire length of the blade.

Pedestrians halted where they were looking on in shock, while some of the approaching cars stopped and gazed on at the gruesome act that was about to be committed. All they could do is watch in horror as the roughneck pulled Kiana's rigid, lifeless body out of the coffin, dragging it out into the middle of the street. He held her head steady by her hair and cocked the machete back, swinging it with brute force. It whistled as it cut through the air.

Whack! Crackk! Thwhack! Chack!

The audience cringed. Some of them even squeezed their eyelids closed and turned their heads, unable to stand the sight.

"Noooooo!" Don Juan bellowed, hopping out of his chauffer driven limousine, gun at the ready. His henchmen spilled out, brandishing guns of their own, poised to address the drama with some hot shot.

Haackk! Shaackk! Whaackk!

The blade bit into the side of Kiana's neck as it hung half way attached to her neck. Her eyes were shut and her lips were a straight line. Her body slightly jerked with each and every encounter with the machete until it happened. The head came loose and the severed carcass fell out in the street.

Thud!

"Mothafuckaaaa!" Don Juan slowed to a trot along with his men. He clutched his gun with both hands and lifted it to take a shot, his crew was right behind him.

Blurrrat! Tat! Tat! Tat! Tat! Tat!

Bianca let loose out of the driver side window with that M-16. Cutting down all of the Trap God's men and tatting up some of the cars. Broken glass and blood flew everywhere.

Ping! Ting! Zing! King!

Don Juan dove to the street and hastily crawled behind a nearby car, leaning his back up against the vehicle's bumper. Holding his gun up at his shoulders, with his heart throbbing inside of his chest, he occasionally peeked around the corner of the car to see if the gunman was headed his way.

Bianca hopped out from behind the wheel of the Pathfinder with her assault rifle trained on the street. She kept the door open and her neck on a swivel, her eyes taking in the streets through the holes of her ski-mask.

Tiaz climbed upon the roof of the hearse and turned to his audience. He fished around inside of his pocket until his hand found a Zippo lighter. His thumb swept down the jagged dull edges of the metal ball. *Shhickk!* A flame shot into the air and he guided it to the thick hair of Kiana's severed head. The fire started off small, but quickly began to consume the head, the smell of flesh cooking filling the air. Tiaz watched the head be devoured by the flames for a time before throwing it out into the street. It rolled up the block looking like a small burning ball of hay. Seeing a fireball tumbling near him through the shiny bumper of the Nissan Dotson before him, Don Juan's forehead deepened with crevasses and he narrowed his eyes. When he went to go look, the fireball stopped along beside him, burning. Staring into the face of the crackling flames, it became clear to him that it was his late wife's severed head. *Oh my God,* he mouthed, sitting down his gun and quickly peeling off his suit's jacket. He tossed his jacket over the burning head and patted it, snuffing out the fire. When he drew the jacket from off of the head, it was nothing more than a ball of charcoal.

"You're next!" Tiaz pointed at the car Don Juan was hiding behind.

"My baby," he uttered sorrowfully, a tear descending down his cheek. Everything seemed so surreal to him. His entire world had been turned upside down because some fucking parasite wanted to take what was his and he retaliated. He didn't understand. What the hell did Tiaz think he was going to do when he violated him? Lie down and take it? Who the fuck did he think he was dealing with? That would be the day that he got fucked up the ass and asked for more. He would fight like he always had, with everything in him.

Don Juan's nostrils flared and his top lip twitched, thinking about how the thug had gotten at him. That shit had him on one. He'd be damned if he folded. Fuck that! It was time to give this buff ass nigga a taste of his own medicine.

He snatched his weapon up from off of the ground and came up, both hands gripping his banger. "I'm next? You're next! Fuck you! Fuck you! Fuck you!" He pulled the trigger rapidly, the gun recoiled each time it spat heat.

Ping! Ting! Zing!

Holes punctured the double backdoors of the getaway ride as it drove off with Tiaz and Bianca. Police car sirens filled the air as several cars were en route to the location. Don Juan continued to open fire on the SUV until his banger was empty. He dropped the hand holding the gun to his side and watched the truck for a time as it sped off. He then turned around, wiping his eyes with the back of his hand. He looked over all of the dead bodies sprawled out in the middle of the street. Niggaz was laid the fuck out, black holes littering their forms and running with streams of blood. It looked like a mothafucking Iraqi warzone out there.

Spotting his wife's severed head, he kneeled down and picked it up. His eyes pooled with tears as he stared down at her chipping charcoaled face. Big teardrops fell from his eyes and splashed onto the face of the severed head. "I'm sorry, baby, I'm so sorry." He kissed it on the lips and hugged it to his body. His head snapped up and he peered up into the sky. "I'ma get chu nigga! You hear me, homeboy? I got something for that ass! Haa! Haa! Haa!" He pressed his head against the forehead of his wife's head and squeezed his eyelids closed tightly. Tears burst from the corners of his eyes and transcended down his face as his shoulders trembled. "Haa! Haa! Haa!"

There alone in the middle of the street with his niggaz watching, the Trap God cried his heart out. It was then that he promised himself that he wasn't going to stop until Tiaz was being lowered six feet into the ground.

Later that night

"Yo' this the spot right here." Ralo tapped Chance as he leaned forward staring at the house they'd just pulled up on.

"Hold up, lemme see." Chance slid on his glasses and looked over the slip of paper with the address they'd obtained.

After smacking the magazine back into the bottom of his head bussa and cocking that bitch back, Ralo stole a glance in his homeboy's direction. He snickered and shook his head. "Blind mothafucka," he said under his breath, amused.

"Fuck you say?" Chance looked away from the slip of paper.

"What? You deaf, too? I said you *blind mothafucka.*"

Chance held up a middle finger and allowed it to linger.

"Sorry, but you aren't my type." He smirked and opened the glove-box, pulling out two ski-masks. He kept one and passed the other to his partner in crime. "That's the right address?"

"Yeah, it's the right one." He removed his glasses and folded up the slip of paper.

The men pulled the ski-masks over their faces and adjusted them so that they could see out of the eye holes.

"Come on." Ralo made to hop out of the truck.

"Hold on. Let me hit this nigga Don up and let 'em know we got this fool in our sights." Chance withdrew his cellular and sent a text to the man that had put the contract out on the Super Thug. He deposited the device back inside of his pocket. "You got upstairs and I got the back doe, alright?" Ralo nodded. "Alright then, let's get this money."

The two hit men hopped out of the Navigator and hunched over, hurrying into the yard. The night was as black as their hearts and their trigger fingers were itching. They planned on leaving the house with a body and one hundred thousand dollars richer.

***

Once she'd taken off her clothes, Bianca wrapped up her hair, threw on a wife beater and some blue boy shorts. She grabbed a gun box from out of the top of the closet and sat down on the end of the bed. She popped the locks of the box and removed a chrome long-nose .44 Magnum revolver Python. She popped open its chamber and dumped out the silver bullets that inhabited it. She removed the items she'd need to clean the weapon from out of the box and went about the task of cleaning the weapon. This was something she'd done once a week to make sure that the weapon was fully functional when she decided to use it. Bianca loved her gun almost as much as she loved Threat. He had given the pistol to her as a gift for her last birthday. She hadn't done any dirt with it, but she'd taken it out to the gun range a couple of times. The Python was huge and lethal. Its bark was as loud as its bite. Not to mention, that just one shot from the big bastard was enough to kill a man. The Python was bigger than Bianca and kicked back like an aggravated mule. Although it was powerful she had gotten the handle of the thing and could fire it expertly.

Bianca was busy cleaning the Magnum when Tiaz emerged from out of the bathroom having just stepped out of the shower. He was clad in pajama pants and slipping a black tank top over his head. He stepped before the dresser mirror and gave himself the once over before turning around to his accomplice.

"Yo' I'm 'bout to…" The words died in his throat when he saw a lone tear slide down Bianca's cheek, as she was cleaning out the huge revolver. The skin on his forehead bunched together showing his concern. He sat down on the edge of the bed and tapped her ankle. "Aye, you okay, momma?"

She wiped her face with the back of her hand and her fingers, sniffling. "I…I…I just miss him so, so much." Her voice crackled and she licked her lips. Closing her eyes and trying to pull herself together. "He was my soul mate. I know that I'll never find another love like him."

"I feel your pain, sis." Tiaz shared her grievance. "Me and Threat been down for each other since free lunch. That was my brother. Blood couldn't make us any closer. That was my mothafucking family, you know?" His eyes became glassy and he felt stinging in them, tears rimmed his lids. He tilted his head back to stop them from falling. Threat's death had crippled him emotionally. He was hurting. A lone wolf howling up at a full moon. Soon the streets would feel his pain, all of it. Tiaz batted his eyelids and dissipated the accumulated water in his eyes.

"I'll tell you one thing though. This nigga here…" He smacked his hand up against his chest hard, facial features displaying the animosity that he held captive in his heart. "Ain't gon' stop until that punk bitch out there…" He referred to Don Juan, pointing a thick finger outside. "…is lying face up and gurgling on his own blood with me standing over him, you feel me?"

Bianca sniffled and wiped her eyes with her fist. "I'm gonna be right there with you." She claimed, looking through the holes inside of the chamber of the revolver.

"I know you will, momma, and I know my nigga, Threat, wouldn't have it any other way."

Bianca finished, closed the pistol and placed it back inside of the gun box before snapping the locks closed. She carried it over to the closet and slid it all of the way back on the top shelf. She then turned around to Tiaz, eyes still bleeding her hurt. To her surprise his eyes were, too. She knew he must have been feeling their loss as much as she was, because men were known to keep their emotions hidden. She'd heard how he was in the trenches. And from what she had gathered, he wasn't anything to fuck with. That was for damn sure, so for him to be standing right there in front of her with his feelings on display, he had to really be feeling it.

"I think we both need a hug." She swiped the tears from her running eyes and opened her arms.

"This shit right here is steel…" He slammed his fist against chest, but the hurt in his glassy, pink eyes betrayed his words. He needed it like she needed it.

"I know. Well, can I have one for myself, Mr. Gangsta? I could really use it." He nodded and they embraced. They melted in each another's arms. Their souls hungered to be comforted, and this was much needed. It was healing. Not just for their minds and their hearts, but their souls. Eyes closed, deep breaths taken, they allowed the pain to be reduced in that moment. Then they pulled back. The display of emotions was awkward and they didn't know what to do afterwards.

"Thanks, I really needed that." Bianca told him.

"No problem." He cleared his throat. "Listen, I'ma go kick-back downstairs, probably watch some TV."

"Okay. I think I'm gonna go shower."

"Alright. Goodnight." He threw up a hand as he made his departure.

"Goodnight." She waved before opening her dresser drawer to retrieve some underwear.

***

Tiaz came down the stairs and headed to the closet beneath the staircase. He went to retrieve something, but stopped short once he heard a noise. His brows furrowed and he stopped where he was, holding the door open as he listened for the sound again. When he didn't hear anything, he closed the closet shut and plopped down on the couch. He picked up the remote control and turned on the flat-screen. He flipped through the cable channels until he landed on *Justified*. Tiaz got so engrossed in the show that he didn't even hear the soft footsteps of the masked man that had entered the house through the backdoor. The gunman smiled fiendishly, sliding his wet tongue across his top row of teeth like a hungry dog. He got about half way across the living room when Tiaz jumped to his feet. He whipped around, holding a shotgun at his hip. His eyebrows arched and his lips peeled back in a sneer.

"Surprise, mothafucka!"

He pulled the trigger and the deadly weapon jerked at his side as it roared furiously.

"Oh, shhhh…" The hit man was cut short as his eyelids stretched open. The blast lifted his monkey ass off of his feet, carrying him into the kitchen. He skidded across the floor and slid up against the kitchen cabinet, slumped. He struggled to lift his head up, hooded eyes looking ahead, seeing the two blurred images of his assailant as he approached him clutching his pump.

When he heard feet hurrying down the staircase he whipped around just in time to see the second hit man. He stopped where he was and raised his head bussa about to open up Tiaz' face.

Bloom!

The blast slammed the hit man up against the wall. He slid down to the steps wearing a grimace and clutching his gun. Behind him was a red splatter running down the wall.

Seeing that he'd dispatched the gunner successfully, Tiaz advanced toward the kitchen, both hands gripping his powerful weapon.

"Wheeze! Haa! Wheeze! Haa! Wheeze! Haa!" The first hit man's vision came into place as his glassy eyes looked ahead, his cheeks swelling and releasing as his lips dribbled his blood.

"Who sent chu? Let me guess, that faggot ass nigga, Don Juan, right?" The gunman nodded yes. "Why am I not surprised?" Tiaz asked as he descended upon him, barrel smoking. "The vindictive prick." He shook his head shamefully. The hit man's eyes shot to their corners seeing his .9mm within arm's reach. His gloved hand almost grasped it when it was kicked aside, sending it spinning in circles. It clanked up against the refrigerator. The thug pulled the ski-mask off of the gunman's head and tossed it to the side. He then racked the shotgun again and pressed it against his dome piece. He fished around inside of his pocket and pulled his cellular free. Flipping it open, he scrolled through the list of contacts until he found the name

Don. He pressed *dial* and passed it to the hit man. His trembling gloved hand brought the cell phone to his ear, still wheezing. "What's cracking?" Don Juan answered.

The trigger man's eyes shifted up to Tiaz who was wearing a stone face. "Tell 'em 'we fucked with the wrong one.'"

He trembled all over realizing that he was on the brink of death. Closing his eyes briefly as tears ran down his face. He swallowed hard and said, "We fucked with the wrong one."

Tiaz pulled the trigger and thunder rumbled. *Bloom!* The gunman's head disintegrated, sending blood and chunks of brain splattering all over the kitchen cabinets. His head hung and his chin touched his chest. His hand fell, but he was still holding tight to the cell phone. The screen of it was speckled with blood.

Tiaz picked up the cell, sat the shotgun down on the table, and snatched a butcher knife from out of the knife block. *Snikt!* Cool, calm, and steady, he returned to the living room whistling where he dispatched the second hit man slumped on the staircase. His victim stared up at him with blood gurgling and bubbling inside of his grill, spilling over, dripping from off of his chin. When the roughneck stepped foot on the first step, he grabbed at his leg. He tried to plead with him, but the crimson fluid pooling his mouth stopped him.

"Get cho fucking hand off of me, nigga!" Tiaz kicked his gloved hand from off his leg. He then kneeled down to him and pressed his head up against the wall. With a growl, he slammed the butcher's knife into his chest bone repeatedly. Yanking it out and slamming it again, until it finally got stuck. He clenched his teeth, and twisted it around until half of it broke off inside of him. When that was done, he drove the broken half of the blade into his neck and dragged it around to the opposite end, spilling a river of black blood. The knife clanged when it hit the step. He wiped his red stained hands off on the deceased hit man, whose eyes were staring off into their corners. He picked up the cellular and said, "You missed mothafucka," before disconnecting the call.

Hurried footsteps snapped Tiaz' head to the top step. He found Bianca with a towel wrapped around her ample bosom and holding a gun up at her shoulder.

"You alright?" she asked, concerned, seeing the dead man at his feet at the bottom of the step.

"Yeah, I'm breezy." He nodded as if it wasn't a big deal. "There's one slumped inside of the kitchen, too. We're gon' have to get rid of these fools and get up from outta here. If they found this place then there's no telling who else knows where we're laying our heads."

"Okay. I'm gonna get dressed."

"Cool." He hoisted the body up and carried it off to the kitchen. He laid it beside the cat whose head he'd blown off. He then went about the task of cleaning up. Afterwards, he and Bianca would dispose of the bodies.

***

"We fucked with the wrong one." The hit man said from the opposite end of the cellular.

Bloom!

Don Juan's eyes shot open and he nearly choked on his champagne. He listened attentively as he heard Tiaz' whistling and then him saying, "Get cho fucking hand off of me, nigga!"

Then there was the growling and stabbing. Afterwards, the thug came on the phone. "You missed mothafucka." The call was disconnected.

"Fuck!" Don Juan threw his bottle of Belaire into the wall and it exploded, sending black shards flying everywhere. He'd just heard the roar of Tiaz' shotgun when he murdered Chance.

He didn't know how the young niggaz had found the man that had been the pain in his ass, but he was happier than a jailhouse sissy. He was counting on them to shut his lights off, but boy was he in for a surprise.

"What happened?" Lil' Stan's forehead creased with concern.

He wiped his mouth with the back of his hand and turned around to his second in command. "He whacked out Chance and Ralo."

"Hell they miss this nigga? They were right on 'em just a minute ago." He said all riled up. He couldn't believe the young wolves were so close to having Tiaz' people draped in all black and ended up on the wrong side of his gun.

"I don't know." Don Juan looked defeated as he massaged the bridge of his nose and shook his head. He then looked up at the ceiling. It was like he was talking to God when he said, "Fucking amateurs."

"Don't even trip. We bound to get 'em, one of the homies will murk this fool." Lil' Stan stated confidently. "A hunnit racks. Who couldn't use that kinda loot?"

"You right, you right." Don Juan gripped his shoulder and patted him on the back. He was grateful for having such a stalwart soldier in Lil' Stan. The young nigga was loyal, fierce, and followed orders to the T.

Lil' Stan's eyes followed his boss as he headed up the spiral stairs of the mansion he'd rented. His head was bowed and he was dragging his feet. This thing with Tiaz was really weighing heavily on his shoulders. He knew he couldn't get a decent night of rest until the South Central terror's name and face was scrolled across an obituary. The thug had killed several homies, murdered his wife, violated her corpse, kidnapped his son, and attacked his traps. Lil' Stan knew exactly what Tiaz was doing.

He was causing Don Juan great emotional pain and stress before he ultimately delivered the Death Blow.

Tiaz is one of the most ruthless niggaz I done came across in a minute. A nigga don't like 'em, but I can't help but to salute his gangsta, he thought before standing to his feet.

"Yo' Don!" His voice echoed throughout the mansion causing the Trap God to stop and turn around, throwing his head back like *'What's up with it?'* "We gon' get this nigga, we just gotta stay focused." He quieted and waited the Top Dawg's response. He licked his lips and nodded before carrying his tall frame up the stairs.

Don Juan retreated to the baby's room where he approached his son's crib. A slight smile creased his lips as he stared down at his baby boy lying peacefully asleep. His booty hiked up and his tiny fists balled. He looked so beautiful and serene in his current state. He reached his hands into the crib and picked his offspring up, laying him against his chest and kissed the top of his curly head. The baby nestled closer to the warmth of his dad, sleep undisturbed. Don smiled as he carried the little dude out of his room and headed into his study where he laid him inside of the extra crib in there. Afterwards, he decided to make himself a drink.

He placed a glass on the desk, dropped a couple of ice cubes into it and poured up the Louie XXIII. He took the bottle of the expensive dark liquor to the head before sitting it back down on the desk. Picking up the glass, he swirled the alcohol around inside of it and carried it over to a book shelf. He pulled on one of the books and the wall beside it shot up into the ceiling. This was the panic room. A panic room is like a safe haven in the event of a break-in, home invasion, tornado or terrorist attack. Don Juan had the place made up like a Man Cave so he'd feel comfortable in case anything popped off. The space was encased in concrete so there wasn't any way in hell anyone was getting in, but whoever was on the inside could get out.

When the wall shot up into the ceiling, the blue illumination from several TV screens shined out from the dark room. Don Juan entered the room and turned to his right. He lifted the small square glass case up and pressed the big red button. There was the sound of air compressing and then the wall slid back down. Don Juan took a sip of his drink and sat down at the sectional desk before a row of small televisions. These televisions were to the surveillance cameras that monitored the inside and outside of his estate. Don Juan pulled open the desk drawer and dipped his hand inside. When it came back out, he was gripping an automatic handgun with a silencer attached and an infrared laser sighting. He didn't even bother to check it, because he already knew that thang was cocked, locked and ready to get off, if need be. He sat the black tool down on the desk top and grabbed two extended fully loaded magazines, which he sat beside it.

The Trap God focused his dark brown eyes on the rows of televisions as he took sips from the glass. He'd already lost his wife, so there wasn't any way in hell he was going to lose his son behind this war with Tiaz. See, he was more than willing to lay down his life and anyone else's to protect his prince. There wasn't any doubt in his mind that gunfire was going to be exchanged until either he or his enemy was lying in a puddle of their own blood. The only thing he could do was hope that after the smoke cleared he was the last man standing.

Chapter Ten
The Next Day

"This should be quick," Tiaz said, buttoning up the shirt of a janitor's uniform. He was in the back of the stolen van getting dressed. "But if I'm not back in twenty minutes, you get the fuck from up outta here, you hear me?"

"No." She told him, sitting behind the wheel.

"What?" His face scrunched up.

"I'm not leaving you here. We're a team. When you're done I'll be right out here waiting on you."

"Alright then." Tiaz cracked a grin, happy to have a down ass bitch riding shotgun with him. He smacked a cap on his head and adjusted it at the brim and the back. He pulled out his gun and checked its magazine for a fully loaded clip. Satisfied, he smacked that ho back in and racked it. Brand new strap, for a brand new murder. He tucked his head bussa in the front of his pants and threw his shirt over it. Afterwards, he reached into his duffle bag and pulled out a detonator. He looked into the side view mirror where he could see the entrance of the hospital. There were visitors walking through the door and being checked at a metal detector. A couple of security guards stood off to the side taking inventory of everyone that crossed the threshold.

Yesterday, he'd snuck into the hospital and placed bombs in the restrooms of the thirteenth floor. The explosives weren't enough to take out the floor, but it could cause some damage if someone was in close quarters. He'd placed them there to create a distraction. This would give him a sufficient window of time to slip inside undetected and with a ratchet. *The perfect plan!*

Tiaz looked back and forth between the detonator and the side view mirror, watching the hospital entrance. He pressed the red button and *Boom! Boom! Boom! Boom! Boom!* The bombs went off in a domino effect on the thirteenth floor. From the outside, a mesh of screams and cries could be heard. Not even a minute later a rush of staff and visitors came flooding down the corridor in pandemonium. Tiaz hopped out of the van and made his way toward the entrance of the hospital. He navigated his way through a herd of people running for their lives, bumping into a couple of them along the way. Stopping, he looked up at the twelfth floor window and locked eyes with Chevy. She looked to be shocked to have seen him there. He smiled evilly and darted inside of the establishment, shoving people out of his way in a hurry.

***

"He's still out there and he's not gonna stop until he knows I'm dead." Faison told Chevy.

"I know and I'm not gonna let that happen." She squeezed his hand gently and patted it with her hand. "I already called those people of yours. They said they'd be here in an hour. We're gonna be safe. Even if he does know where we are and he just so happens to get past security, your wild ass cousins are gonna be right up here waiting for him."

Faison closed his eyes and took a deep breath. "You're right. I'm tripping. JT and my cousin, Lil' Chris, don't play no games, especially when it comes to family."

"Oh, believe me I know." She raised her eyebrows and gave him a knowing expression.

Boom! Boom! Boom! Boom! Boom!

Thunder erupted five times in a row startling both Chevy and Faison. The entire building quaked. Faison was nearly thrown from the bed and Chevy almost fell to the floor. Right after, they heard screams and hollers along with stampeding feet. Someone came over the loud speaker announcing to the hospital staff and guest what to do, but they couldn't hear it over all of the noise. Chevy got to her feet and rushed over to the window. When she looked down, she saw people pouring out into the parking lot. A janitor was walking against them heading in the opposite direction of the crowd. Feeling a pair of eyes on him, he stopped and looked up at her, locking with her gaze. A creepy smile etched across his lips and she instantly realized who he was.

"Tiaz." She gasped. Eyes wide, mouth open. Her hand pressed against her chest.

She kept her eyes on him until he went darting towards the building, knocking scared people out of the way, trying to clear a path to the entrance. Chevy whipped around. Worry emerged on Faison's face when he saw the shocked expression she was sporting.

"What's the matter? What's going on?" He panicked, heart monitor going crazy.

"He's here!"

"Who?"

"Tiaz. We've gotta get chu outta here." She ran out of the door and ran straight into a surge of people, all fleeing for their lives. No one was paying attention to the hospital staff that was trying to restore order. Men and women were shoving people out of the way and trampling over them, not giving a fuck if they were hurting them.

Chevy tried getting help from someone out of the staff, but they weren't paying her any attention, because they were too focused on trying to get people to leave the hospital in an orderly fashion. She stopped where she was and her eyes scanned the crowd flooding in her direction, searching desperately for someone that could help her get Faison out of the room before Tiaz arrived.

"Fuck it!" She ran back into the room, pulling the patches free from Faison's chest.

"Aye, what chu doing?" He winced, feeling pinches as the patches were yanked from off him.

"I've gotta get chu outta here before he comes up." She took cautious looks over her shoulder as she removed the IV from out of his hand. The entire time her heart was beating wildly inside of her chest.

Chevy knew that Tiaz was a tyrant willing to do any and everything in his power to crush the people he felt that had wronged him in some way. She understood better than anyone that he wouldn't have any problem killing her or Faison and he'd probably be vicious because of what he'd been through with them. With this knowledge in mind, she was going to do whatever she had to do to protect herself and Faison, even if it meant going toe to toe with the vindictive killer. There wasn't any way in hell that she was going to lose him again. She'd just recovered him from the hands of Death.

All she was worried about now was getting a weakened Faison out of bed and finding somewhere for them to hide, until she figured out how she was going to get out of the hospital undetected.

***

Tiaz came through the staircase door, bumping into droves of people going into the direction from which he came. He pulled his silenced gun from the front of his pants and made his way toward the corridor. Going down the hall, he met a surge of hospital staff and patients, getting clipped at the shoulder and dropping his weapon. *Fuck,* he thought. His head moved all around as he searched the floor for his gun. Not being able to spot his piece beneath the stampeding feet, he looked up and down the corridor. When he spotted a metal push cart with surgical tools which someone had abandoned, he started in its direction.

As he walked past it, he swept up a scalpel and stuck the blade inside of the sleeve of his shirt's cuff. Tiaz' head moved from left to right looking for Faizon's room number. When he spotted it, a grin curled the corner of his lips and he rubbed his hands together mischievously. Taking a cautious look over both shoulders, he snatched the scalpel from his sleeve. The lights in the hallway deflected off of it and it twinkled.

His massive hand pressed against the door and he made his way inside, eyes peering around the dimly lit room. Figuring that his target was hidden behind the curtains, he drew the curtains back and found an empty bed. His forehead wrinkled and he whipped around. He sniffed the air and inhaled the scent of perfume. The scent was familiar, very familiar. He'd smelled it before on Chevy. It was her fragrance. Chanel #5.

Tiaz followed the aroma out of the room and into the corridor where he made a right. He hurriedly jogged down the hallway. A herd of people came stampeding across his line of vision at the opposite end. He made a left just in time to see the restroom door closing. *Ah ha,* he thought inside of his head, a devilish smile came across his face. He did tricks with the sharp instrument between his fingers, real fancy like, maneuvering it like a mini baton. He jogged down to the women's restroom door and kicked the door open. It bounced off of the wall. His head snapped from left to right, looking for his prey. Suddenly, he jumped down to the tiled floor and looked under the stalls. He was smiling until he didn't see any feet underneath. Quickly, he jumped back up to his booted feet and made his way down the line of stall doors, kicking them in one by one.

"Come out, come out, wherever you are." He snickered with a balled up face and a wicked smile.

Boom! Went the first door. *Boom!* Went the second. *Boom!* Sounded the third and fourth.

"Ah, the fifth and final door, I wonder if you're behind it. We shall see." He said with his hands planted firmly against the door. The side of his face pressed against it as he listened closely. He licked his lips and found his dick nudging his zipper. He was so excited his member grew hard.

Chevy sat propped upon the commode with a weakened Faison in her arms, their feet up on the wall. She took a good hold of his chain, the one that was passed down to him from his great grandfather. She looked from the chain to the stall's door. Making up her mind on what she had to do, she kissed her man on the side of the head.

"Lil' pig, lil' pig, let me in." He stepped back, placing one hand firmly against the wall and coiling his leg about to kick in the stall's door.

Boom!

The end stall flew open and Chevy slid out twirling Faison's chain around in circles, the end of it was a blur. It whistled loudly and spun like a helicopter propeller. Her head was tilted and she was staring up at Tiaz wickedly, jaws so tight that they pulsated. Her teeth were clenched and her chin was wrinkled, she was ready to get it in. Tiaz took a step back, but kept his blade extended. If that chain was to hit his head, it would crack his skull open, maybe even kill his ass. He had to be careful, quick and calculated if he wanted to body her and get to Faison.

"You wanna play with me, bitch? Come on then, I'm game." He maneuvered the scalpel between his fingers like it was a coin.

"Let's get it on then, bitch-boy." She countered, moving counterclockwise with her rival. They were locked into a very intense stare. Neither one of them blinking or flinching. The wrong move could put either one of them in a bad way.

Whook! Whook!

Tiaz swung the scalpel back and forth causing Chevy to jump back, but she kept the chain spinning. When he pulled back she swung it at his head, he bobbed, weaved and leaned all of the way back. His spine bent like he was playing Limbo. His eyes bulged and his mouth dropped open seeing the chain miss the tip of his nose by a half an inch. When the chain drew back he came up and staggered back, quickly regaining his equilibrium. He touched his nose and looked at it, thinking he'd see blood, but he didn't. He flipped the surgical blade over in his palm and gripped it firmly.

"Yeeaahh, come on." His forehead deepened with lines and his nose wrinkled, while his tongue pierced his lips and he slid it across his top row of teeth. Adrenaline pumping, like it always did when he was in the face of danger, his blood was rushing furiously, his pulse was thumping rapidly, and fat veins were on his temples and forehead.

They circled each another counterclockwise, weapons brandished and ready to go. They were locked into the other's gaze, intensity at its all-time high. The combatants were ready to lock ass and draw blood. Chevy swung the chain fast and sharply, he moved swiftly barely managing to dodge the lethal weapon. "Arghhh!" His face tightened with pain, feeling the sting of the chain strike his elbow. It hurt like hell.

"Uh huh." Chevy smiled triumphantly and licked her lips, feeling herself having injured her enemy. From there she went at him swinging the chain wildly trying to tear his fucking head off of his shoulders.

Chevy was enraged from all of the shit Tiaz had put her through. The lies, the cheating, the deceit, the broken promises, he'd hurt her to the core of her being. His selfishness pierced her heart and soul like a harpoon. She wanted to hurt, maim, and kill him, right here and right now.

Whook! Whook! Whook! Whook!

Tiaz wore a face of concentration as he dodged the chain, with it barely missing him. When she brought the chain back, he made his move, jabbing at her chest and torso. Her face tightened feeling the scalpel poking up her middle, small red spots quickly expanded. She staggered back and almost fell. Righting herself, she found the thug about to swipe her jugular with the blade. Refocusing, she swung the chain and knocked the weapon from his hand, sending it flying across the restroom.

Tiaz looked to his naked palm then back at his enemy. She was about to attack him again, but before she could bring the chain around, he kicked her in the chest. The impact sent her slamming up against the tiled wall, wincing when she bumped her head. Chevy dropped the chain to the floor and slid down the wall, leaving a red streak. She moaned, barely conscious, and felt the stinging at the back of her skull. The blonde bombshell lay slumped up against the wall with her legs separated in a V.

Tiaz' head whipped all around the restroom looking for the scalpel. Seeing a twinkle at the far corner, he smiled and stalked over. He picked up the surgical tool then turned around to a discombobulated Chevy, gripping the blade so tight that his hands turned white at the knuckles. Reaching her, he outstretched his hand to grab her by the hair and slice her fucking throat open. He'd just pulled her head back to open her up when a shrill came from his left. Faison tackled him and he slammed up against the restroom mirror. His head bumped into the glass, cracking it into a spider's web. The roughneck's face balled up and he dropped his weapon in the neighboring sink.

"Bitch ass nigga, put cho hands on mine!"

Wap! Wop! Wamp! Bwhack! Crack!

Tiaz' head whipped from left to right while he staggered back. That nigga Faison was throwing haymakers on his big, buff ass. He was weakened from his wounds, but seeing his lady in trouble ignited a fire inside of him.

The husky man went to throw another right and it was blocked by Tiaz' arm. Faison came back with a right cross and followed up, with several bone rattling blows to the thug's face backing him up. Once he kicked his adversary in the chest and he stumbled backwards, he tackled him hard. They slammed up against the tiled wall, denting it and cracking it into what appeared to be a million pieces. Faison squeezed his eyes shut and squared his jaws from the excruciation in his back and head. He quickly shook off his lingering pain and tackled Tiaz to the floor.

They rolled over on the linoleum, hands wrapped around each other's necks, trying to choke the life out of each other. Faison ended up on top squeezing his foe's neck as hard as he could with a face masked by hatred.

Cock sucka, put me in the hospital! Stole my woman, had my son slinging crack, murdered my family, and blinded my sister for life! I'mma kill you, you mothafucka!

Veins rolled up Faison's forehead as well as his opponents. These big ass niggaz struggled for power and Faison seemed to be holding his own even with his injuries. That was until Tiaz snatched his hands from his neck and stabbed his fingers into his bandaged wounds.

"Aaarrr!" The coke peddler threw his head back and his eyelids snapped open. His mouth stretched wide enough to see his uvula when he screamed. Tiaz' fingers sunk into the holes of his gunshots, expanding the blood in the bandages wrapped around his torso.

"Shit hurt, don't it?" He gritted with arched eyebrows. "Uhhunh." He then grabbed the collar of his gown and pulled him down while throwing his forehead upward. *Bwhrack!* Faison's eyes rolled to their whites and a reddened line encircled his nose, as it was broken, running red streams. He released the grip on his foe's neck and fell off to the side, moaning in pain as his eyes flickered whiteness.

Tiaz scrambled to his feet breathing hard and looking at a defeated Faison. Turning around to the row of sinks, his eyes searched them until he found his scalpel. He recovered it and straddled the husky man. He wrapped both of his hands around the surgical tool and raised it above his head, staring down at his opponent with madness in his pupils. His head shook slightly as he clenched his jaws, the bone structure in them shown.

Chevy's head bobbled and her eyes fluttered open. Her vision came into place and she saw Tiaz about to murder her man. She was stiff at that moment, but seemed to come alive seeing her son's father in danger.

"Noooo!" She outstretched her hand, making to get up, but it was too late.

"Lights out, big man!" The scalpel gleamed at its razor sharp tip under the restroom's light. Tiaz moved swiftly to stab it into Faison's heart.

Boom!

Tiaz' head snapped up as the restroom door swung open and two police officers poured inside, dispatcher rattling off on the radio transceivers on their shoulders. They had their guns drawn on him, fingers settled on their triggers ready to leave him holier than a weak alibi.

"Drop the weapon and put your hands behind your head!" One of the Caucasian cops yelled, veins visible on his temples as he turned red in the face from yelling. Hands still held above his head clutching the scalpel, Tiaz looked down at Faison to the cops trying to make up his mind on whether to force their hands or not.

"You're one lucky son of a bitch, you know that?" he told Faison and dropped the blade, placing his hands behind his head.

I guess the fat woman has sung, huh? A nigga got snatched up by One Time right before I could finish these bastards. Damn. He shook his head regretfully, hating having been caught. *I had three more niggaz to take out before Threat could finally rest in peace. Fuck it though. It's alright, my name still good in the streets. I can call in a couple of favors and have these bitches whacked out from behind the wall.*

One of the cops kept his gun trained on Tiaz, while the other ordered him in a position so that he could handcuff him. Chevy scrambled over to Faison lifting his head off of the floor and peeling back his eyelids to see if he was still alive. His moans of pain were confirmation enough for her. She kissed his cheek and pressed the side of her face up against his, mashing them together.

"Thank God you're alive, baby." She sighed with relief and looked up at the ceiling. "Thank you, Lord, for having mercy." She kissed him again and held her face up against his lovingly. Tears pooled in her eyes and came pouring down her cheeks in buckets. The moment before was so intense that she didn't know what would have happened if the police hadn't shown up. For the first time in her life she was actually happy to see The Boys in Blue.

Tiaz stared down at the couple with murderous thoughts running through his mental as he was pulled to his feet and read his Miranda rights. Chevy's eyes darkened and she stood up holding his angered gaze. Intensity passed between them for a time before she hauled off and cracked him in the mouth, whipping his head around.

I can't believe I ever loved his ass!

When Tiaz turned back around to her, he had a mouth pooled with blood and his lips were partially red. He cracked a smile and swallowed, licking his lips. "Taste almost as sweet as your pussy." He laughed as he was ushered away by one of the officers. The other stayed behind to attend to Faison and ask Chevy questions.

Finally the mad man's reign of terror was over.

***

Ta'shauna stood completely still as Herby slipped a white bulletproof Kevlar vest over her head.

"Hold your arms up for me, Doll Face." She did like he ordered and he strapped the vest down under her arms. He kneeled down and strapped it down around her waist. "There we go." He stood erect, adjusting the vest making sure that it would hold up against her frame. "Yep, nice and snug like a bug in a rug." He passed her a gray hoodie and she slipped it on over her head.

"Alright, ya ready to go?" Herby asked, sticking his gun into the holster underneath his arm.

"Yeah, I'm ready." She took his hand and he snapped a handcuff on her wrist, her brows wrinkled, turning her head in his direction, her expression reading 'What the fuck are you doing?'

"Relax." He threw up a hand to put her at ease. "This is just in case someone tries to snatch you up. I'll be coming right along with you, and giving them hell all the way." He patted his holstered firearm. "Now, come on, I've gotta get you to the safe house." He smacked a hat on his head and grabbed his overcoat, heading for the door.

Herby hopped on the freeway taking the 105 going East. Once he adjusted his rearview mirror, he glanced up at it to make sure that there was no one following them. Next, he turned off the radio. His eyes were open and he wanted his ears to be, as well. He needed to be well aware if some shit was going to pop off.

"Sooooo." He looked from the windshield to Ta'shauna. "Who's this cat you left Tiaz for?"

"My son's father, Orlando. What about him?"

"Hmmm." He wondered. "How'd that happen? Weren't you two broken up?"

"Nah, we weren't broken up, but I let Tiaz think that," she shamelessly admitted. "Honestly, my baby daddy put me up on the dude. He was a lick. He used to see 'em at gambling spots and strip clubs. My nigga had grips. I mean he rocked heavy jewels, drove the latest foreign whips, dressed in the flyest of clothes, the whole nine. My nigga was holding a big bag and all these hoes out here were tryna dip their hands into it. But the nigga had on his choosing shoes and chose me. Not that I'm surprised, 'cause you know." She shrugged, turned her head his way and smiled. "A bitch is all of that, a bag of chips and a free soda."

"How long were y'all together?"

"Three years."

"You got away with playing him for three fucking years?" He raised his eyebrows, surprised with what she'd relayed. "Impossible. You're lying, you've got to be." He shook his head, believing wholeheartedly that she wasn't telling the truth. "No way."

She smiled bigger, then said, "What reason do I have to lie?"

He froze the image of her smile inside of his mind. She looked so pretty and angelic at that moment in the passenger seat beside him. He'd heard before that looks were deceiving and it had been proven in that instant. The woman sitting beside him was as scandalous as they came.

How can you smile? Tell me how in Jesus' name you can sit there and smile like that after what you did to that poor bastard? Trifling whore, you deserved that bullet in the top of your fucking head. My piece of shit wife did the same thing to me, sucked me dry, the fucking vampire. Took everything I had worth having. I swear if I wasn't hired to protect this broad I'd let her foul ass out right here and right now on the fucking freeway, so help me God.

"None whatsoever." He managed a halfhearted smile. "I'm not mad at you, get yours."

"Not to worry, 'cause I did, every nickel of it and then some."

"How'd you managed to keep both relationships going though? I mean, three years, he had to catch on to something. Excuse me, I'm not one to be nosey, but I'm curious." Not being in the know was eating him alive.

"Please, Tiaz was a street dude. He wasn't home most of the time, no way." She let him know how it was back then. "I got my chances to sneak away with Orlando often. The only real problem I had was getting Jaden to keep his mouth shut. That water head boy of mine almost got me caught up twice. Luckily, a bitch is quick up on her feet. I played that shit off cold, if I do say so myself." She laughed, but stopped once she realized he wasn't laughing along with her. "I bet chu think I'm some kind of monster, don't chu?"

Ta'shauna didn't feel any kind of way about how she'd played Tiaz. The only thing she regretted was getting shot and having to be blind for the rest of her days. Still, that wasn't going to stop her from hustling her pussy. Just as soon as this thing blew over she was going to be right back out there courting herself another baller for sponsorship.

"Naahh." He shook his head. "Just a young lady doing whatever she can to survive in this cold, cruel world."

"I'm glad you see it for what it is."

"I'm glad you tell it like it is, Sweets." He narrowed his eyes and peered closely out of the windshield. "Alright, this is it."

Herby pulled into the driveway of an old, white modest house with a neatly trimmed lawn and bushes. He parked his car in the garage and closed it shut. He was discreet as he led her to the backdoor of the house, keeping his gun in his free hand while the other unlocked the door. Once he opened the door, he ushered her inside and quickly closed it shut. He took a gander through the back porch window then hastily moved from it with Ta'shauna by his side. He maneuvered through the dark, carefully, until he discovered the picture window. He peeked out through the curtain. There wasn't a soul in sight.

"Alright, safe and sound." He removed the handcuff. "Now, let me put a text in to your brother to let him know that we're alright."

Herby shot the text to his employer, removed his overcoat, and made himself a drink. He watched Ta'shauna attentively, mesmerized by how much of a low life that she really was. He really hated being in the same space as her. The bitch made his skin crawl. He would be relieved once this job was over so he could get paid and move on.

Tranay Adams

Chapter Eleven

Juvie had been sending The Eme brothers on a wild goose chase for the past couple of days. He took them to several traps of competing drug dealers, promising that Don Juan would show, but he never did. He was trying to stall the brothers for as long as he could, so he could find a way to escape their clutches, but so far he hadn't come up with a plan that would spring him free of them. He and Uduka played the station wagon, while Uche kicked in the trap in search of their younger sibling's executioner. Not even five minutes later, Timon and Uma's first born came strolling out tucking his banger at the front of his pants, looking over his surroundings, an angered expression fixed on his face. He'd kicked in the door of the trap, shooting niggaz in their legs and shouting threats if they didn't tell him where Don Juan was, but no one knew who the hell he was.

As soon as his brother hopped into the backseat and slammed the door shut, Uduka pulled off in a hurry.

"Dese is fuckin' bullshit," Uche fumed, slamming his fist on the backdoor panel, frustrated. His head snapped in Juvie's direction and he was looking scared as shit. "Dese cock sucka is sending us on a wild goose chase."

"I'm telling you where the fuck he is, man! Ain't ma fault the nigga ain't here!"

"Ya play games, huh? Do ya?" he asked with madness in his eyes. He looked insane and like he was up for the challenge of making him talk. "You think we not serious? I'ma show yo' punk ass." He whipped out his .45 and pressed it into his kneecap. Before he moved his leg, he was pulling the trigger. The gun was so close it sounded like a cap gun was being fired.

Juvie's head snapped back and his eyes pooled with tears. He went to scream, but the oldest of The Eme brother's slapped his hand over his mouth to muffle the sound. His head snapped in all directions to see if anyone had seen or heard him do what he'd done, but there wasn't a pair of prying eyes in sight. Uduka was staring up at the rearview mirror, having seen all of this happen. He watched as his brother focused his attention back on Juvie, observing the agony written across his face as his muffled screams continued.

"I'm gonna take ma hand off of ya mouf and I sweah on ma brudda's grave, if ya make so much as a peep I'm gon' shoot cha dead in ya face, ya heah?" The young hoodlum nodded as tears wet his cheeks. "Good." He removed his hand and he doubled over in pain, squeezing his eyes shut and silently sniffling. "Now, I want an address where this deek sucka is more than likely at. If we get there and he's not dere, guess whose deek I'm choppin' off."

"Alright, okay, there's only one of two places he'd probably be." Juvie winced. "They're like a safe haven for him. Only me and my nigga, Lil' Stan, know where they are."

"Okay. Now we're gettin' some weah."

Uche picked up a roll of duct tape from off of the floor, and extended a lengthy strip before tearing it with his teeth. Afterwards, he smacked it over his mouth and rubbed it down so it would stick.

"Alright, pull off." He ordered Uduka.

Sometime later

Uduka pulled up a few feet away from the liquor store that Don Juan had just entered. Their eyes were glued to the entrance, watching him attentively, as he made his way inside.

"Alright, keep her running and keep an eye on that piece of shit back there." Uche threw his head to the backseat where Juvie was gagged with his wrists duct-taped behind his back. He then checked his magazine, smacked it back into the bottom of his .45 and chambered a round into it. The blood of Boxy's killer would be his.

"Hold on." Uduka grasped his wrist as he was about to hop out. His head snapped in Don's direction. He had a furrowed forehead. "Some guy in a red hoodie just went in behind him. Let's wait 'til he's alone."

"Okay." He nodded his approval and the waiting began.

***

Wicked pulled up across the street and a few cars down from where Don Juan had parked. He killed his engine and watched him emerge from his Porsche truck and slam the door shut. His head was on a swivel as his eyes followed him inside of the gas station. Once the Trap God was out of sight, he popped open the glove-box and grabbed a pair of latex gloves. He slipped them on one at a time and flexed his fingers inside of them to make sure they were good and snug on him. Next, he reached inside of the glove-box and withdrew a handgun. Once he screwed the silencer on the end of his weapon, he made sure there was one in the head and threw open the driver side door. He took one last look at the picture of him, Baby Wicked and his Aunt Helen when they'd come to visit him while he was in youth authority.

I miss you, bruh bruh, I'll be up there one day. But for now I'ma 'bout to send this nigga up there to kick it with chu.

With that, he hopped out of the car and slammed the door shut behind him. The nigga pulled his hood over his head and jogged toward the gas station with his hands in the pockets of his hoodie, keeping an eye out for witnesses.

***

161

"Alright, there our mon is." Uche made Don Juan emerging from out of the restroom, with a father and his son retreating from him. He was so absorbed by his finally getting to murder him that it never even crossed his mind why the man and kid were hurrying away from him. The taller of the African's hopped out of the car as his prey was approaching the sidewalk, ignorant of his presence.

Seeing one of his abductors with his gun low about to creep up on his man and serve him a clip full of some hot shit, Juvie scooted over to the cracked open window of the backdoor and leaned his head up against the door panel. Using his tongue, he jabbed at the duct tape, causing it to nudge up from his face until it came up from his mouth, hanging loose from one end. It flapped over his lips and he blew it hard to keep it from sealing his grill closed. He swallowed and screamed as loud as he could, veins throbbing at his temples and neck.

"Don Juan, watch out!" His breath fogged up the glass and spittle hit it.

"Shut da fuck up!" Uduka's head snapped to the backseat and he whipped out his thang-thang. He reached into the backseat, cracking his punk ass over the dome repeatedly.

"Ah! Ahh! Arghhh!" The hoodlum winced with each strike of the steel against his melon. The assault left him dazed and confused. He moaned in regret and pain. The younger of the African's settled back down in his seat, laying his gun on his lap and focusing his attention through the windshield.

***

Don Juan had spent the greater part of his day getting shit-faced at The Barfly which was a dive on the lower eastside of Los Angeles. It was a place that an abundance of unsavory characters frequented. Nonetheless, he fit right in. The place was like the ghetto version of Cheers and he was just as known as any employee there. The recent widower took about six glasses of Hennessy and Coke to the head and would have taken more had the bartender not refused him service. Seeing that he'd overstayed his welcome, he dropped a couple of bills on the bar top and made his departure.

Don Juan knew that it was against his better judgment to have gone out and gotten drunk that night. But with all of the drama going on in his life and the shadow of death following close behind him, he needed to escape his harsh reality, even if it was only for a couple of hours.

On his way home, his bladder constantly nagged at him, so he figured he'd pull over at this gas station that he knew wouldn't deny him access to their restroom, being as how he supplied its owner with the drugs he sold. Not even thirty minutes later, Don Juan was hopping out of his truck and hurrying inside like he was being followed. He staggered into the men's restroom, struggling to keep his balance. He shuffled over to the urinal like a dead man and unzipped his jeans, pulling his meat free from its denim prison.

"Aaahhh!" A look of relief crossed his face and he threw his head back, bladder emptying as he whizzed. Once he finished, he shook his member twice and put it away, zipping his jeans back up. He moved over to the sink and turned on the faucet, pumping pink liquid, foamy soap into his palm. He rubbed his palms together and lathered them up, as he rinsed his hands beneath the cool flowing water. His drunk ass was whistling when a man in a red Champion hoodie over his head entered the restroom. He clocked him walking toward the stalls, but paid him no mind, feeling as though he was just minding his business.

Don Juan looked down at his hands and rinsed the soap from them. Once he looked up, Champion hoodie was pointing a handgun with a silencer on it at him. His eyes stretched wide open and his mouth damn near hit the floor. The sight of the lethal weapon sobered his ass up quick.

"Haa!" the kingpin gasped.

Tiaz, the name of the nigga who sent the hit man resonated inside of his head. Right after, he saw the gunman's finger bending around the trigger. Swiftly, he dove out of the way just as the first shot was fired. *Choot!* The bullet crashed into the mirror and cracked the glass into a cobweb.

"Ooof!" He hit the linoleum with a grimace and his head snapped up. Seeing the gunman swinging his head bussa around and pulling the trigger, he rolled on the floor like he was on fire, narrowly missing the embers meant to take his life.

Pewk! Pewk! Pewk! Pewk!

The floor shattered as it was shot the fuck up. The Trap God rolled up against the wall. He looked up, breathing hard and hoping not to be shot. His worried eyes found him about to bust on him again and his voice caught in his throat.

Click!

He flinched expecting a hot one in his dome. When he saw the gunner trying to un-jam the round that clogged up the slot of the weapon, he knew then that it was the perfect time to react. Don Juan's face twisted with madness and he sprung to his feet, charging at the shooter. The gunman had just un-jammed his weapon and moved to point it. He'd half expected his head to be blown off, but to his surprise he didn't get his shit splattered.

"Uhhh!" The shooter was tackled by Don Juan and lifted off of his feet, being slammed on his back. The impact sent his gun up into the air then dropping to the floor, sliding up against the wall beneath the row of sinks.

"Tryna kill me, huh, nigga?" Don Juan fumed with darkened eyes and his lips sucked inwards. He balled his fists tight and threw solid blows at the man's face.

Thwap! Wop! Wamp! Bamp!

The gunman's face winced and he saw flashes of white when each blow landed.

"Yuuckk!"

The Trap God's eyes went as wide as golf balls and he wrapped his hands around his neck. His foe jabbed him dead in his jugular with two strong fingers. Using both of his palms, he then clapped his ears at the same time.

Clapppp!

"Aaarhh!"

The assault set off an eerie siren in his ears and left them stinging.

"Uh huh!" The gunner snarled, making his fingers into the peace sign, he jabbed his enemy in the eyes.

"Ahhhh!" His mouth stretched open and he smacked his hands over his eyes.

Bwap!

The shooter punched him in the jaw, knocking him off his person. He scrambled to his feet, looking for his gun. Spotting it underneath the sink, he went for it, but was tripped up once Don Juan grabbed his ankle. He fell forward and his chin went slamming against the edge of the sink, knocking him out cold. The Trap God got to his feet and quickly snatched up the head bussa. He pulled the hoodie from over the gunman's head and pressed it into his face, indenting his cheek. He squeezed his eyelids shut and turned his head, so the blood wouldn't get into his eyes. His finger curled around the trigger, he went to pull that bitch back and a knock resonated at the door.

"Lucky ass," he said, standing erect, looking down at the dispatched gunner. "I ain't gon' kill you in here and risk a charge, nigga." He tucked that thang on his waistline and threw his shirt over it. Afterwards, he unlocked the restroom door and pulled it open. He found a patron and his son there. His eyes shot from him to the nigga he'd left sprawled out on the restroom's floor. Scared, he clutched his son's hand tighter and hurried away.

Don Juan left the restroom, blinking and massaging his eyes. They were sore and he still felt stinging in them. He winced and wiped his tearing eyes with the back of his hand, frowning. He marched toward his car in a hasty fashion, paying no attention to his surroundings. He was oblivious to The Grim Reaper on his heels. The shadow on the cracked, black-spotted sidewalk was damn near on top of him. An object the shape of a gun was extended at its side as it moved in on him, ready to deliver that fatal shot.

"Don Juan, watch out!" A voice came from his right and he snapped his head in that direction. He found a tall African there dressed in a cheap suit trying to creep up on his mothafucking ass. Fear ripped through his heart. He dove to the sidewalk, tucking and rolling. He stopped in a kneeling position with that banger extended. Both hands clutching it, he hugged the trigger. The head bussa jumped as it spat that heat.

Splocka! Splocka! Splocka! Splocka!

The tall man dove behind a car with bullets narrowly missing him. They *Ping! Zing! Ting! Clinggged!* Off of the vehicle's bumper and side view mirror. Don Juan whipped out his own piece and cautiously crept on the fool that had come for him.

"You come knocking on Death's door, and The Reaper may just answer!" he bellowed, guns held up at his shoulders, moving out into the street to see if he could catch him slipping from the opposite end. "Who sent chu, nigga? Tiaz? The Mexicans? The Jamaicans?" Just then, the gunner from the restroom came sprinting out. He stooped low and pulled the .38 revolver from his ankle holster. Don Juan had just crept upon the tall man without his acknowledgement. He smiled wickedly and licked his lips as he pointed the deadly ends of his toys at him.

Goodnight, he thought as his fingers curled around the triggers of his burners.

Bop!

Crash!

The back window of the Ford Mustang he was standing beside shattered, garnering his attention as well as the nigga he'd snuck up on. When he whipped around, he saw the homeboy he'd left staring up at the ceiling in the restroom. He turned his gun on him and banged back, empty copper shell casings leaping over his hand. He retreated toward his truck letting both of his guns go ham, backing the gunner down. A noise to his left stole his attention and he spotted the tall man again, rising to his feet, heat in hand. Don Juan whipped his second gun around in his direction, letting him get in on the action as well. Once the second banger was spent, he tucked it into the front of his jeans and got busy with the first, nearing his car. His hand jerked violently as he banged it out, narrowing his eyes into slits as he backed up.

"He's mine!" the tall man barked, seeing the other cat busting on his prey. He turned the fury of his weapon on him.

Poc! Poc! Poc!

The gunner's banger clicked empty and Uduka came beside Uche, letting his tool act a goddamn fool. *Poc! Poc! Poc! Poc!* He gave it to that nigga all in his mothafucking chest bone, causing him to stagger backwards and fall on his ass. When he and his brother whipped around to Don Juan, he was in his Porsche truck flooring it away from the battlefield.

"Shit!" Uche slammed his fist down on the trunk of a car and kicked its bumper several times. "I was this fucking close." He showed his brother with his thumb and forefinger, which were a half of an inch apart.

When The Eme brother looked to the gunman that was made victim by their guns, he was long gone on some Michael

Myers shit. They exchanged glances with surprised expressions across their faces. Hearing approaching police sirens, Uche nudged his brother and they retreated back to their car.

Uduka pulled away with his brother cracking Juvie upside the head with that steel, talking plenty of shit.

"Punk ass beesh." Uche mad dogged Juvie as he laid moaning and bleeding from the side of his egg. He turned to his sibling. "Jump on the 105 and punch it up ta a hunnid miles an hour." Uduka locked eyes with his brother through the rearview mirror and nodded. He followed his orders, hopping on the freeway and gunning it. It was dark and all that could be seen in addition to the lights over the signs were the red and white backlights of speeding cars. The windows of the G-ride they were in were cracked open, so the cool air rushed inside, ruffling their clothes.

Holding his .45 on Juvie, Uche reached over him and unlocked the door. After he shoved it open, he set his sights on the young thug, maliciousness dancing in his eyes.

"Dis is as fah as ya go, neega!" he yelled over the sound of the blowing winds, rushing against him and causing the collar of his shirt to slap up against his chin, repeatedly.

Juvie slowly came to moaning, feeling the wind blowing onto his face. His eyes fluttered open and he looked about. Spotting the backdoor open and seeing the asphalt speed past him in a blur, scared the shit out of him. His eyes nearly flew out of his head and his jaw ached from screaming.

"Nooooooo! Noooo! Please, God!" He threw himself toward Uche and busted the older African's lip. He grimaced and shoved him off, touching his lips with his fingers and coming away with blood. When he grabbed him by the front of his shirt to throw him out, he started biting on his hand and arm.

"Argh! Son of a…" He squeezed his eyelids shut and tightened his jaws, showcasing his teeth. Growling, his eyes snapped open and his hand was like a blur. *Crack!* He knocked Juvie upside the head with that thang again, but he couldn't even feel the pain with his adrenaline being jacked up as high as it was. Uche leaned all of the way back in the seat and kicked on the youngster. His dress shoes struck him in his chest, neck, and chin, before landing a blow flush in the mouth. That was enough to send that ass flying out of the car screaming.

"Ahhhhhh! Ooof!" He hit the ground and went flying back hastily. The darkness seemed to swallow him. Uche looked down the road at the tumbling body. He didn't even blink as it was run over by several oncoming vehicles speeding toward him. The boy came apart like a Mr. Potato Head and his spleen and bladder were quickly squashed by the cars down the road.

Uche closed the backdoor and settled back down in his seat. His nostrils flared as he breathed hard, chest rising and falling rapidly.

"You okay?" Uduka looked up through the rearview mirror at him.

"Yeah." He threw his head back and closed his eyes, swallowing his spit. They'd been leaving quite the trail of blood behind them on their road to revenge and with each life they took their souls darkened just that much more. It didn't matter to them though. They'd forfeit their souls if it meant that they were going to finally get their hands on their loved one's killer. The oldest of the Nigerian's peeled his eyelids open and sat up, clearing his throat with a fist to his mouth. "Go back to the house where we followed him from, Duke. He's sure to return their since his son is there."

"Alright." Uduka responded, following his brother's orders.

Today they'd get their man or die trying.

Chapter Twelve

Once order was restored back at the hospital, Faison was placed in another room on a different floor. His cousins stood outside the door tooled up in case some more shit was to pop off.

While they held it down, Chevy was getting the back of her head stitched up and her bodily wounds attended to. She stared off into space thinking about her son and where he could possibly be at that time. It had been a couple of days and the police didn't have any leads on his whereabouts. She posted missing persons pictures of him all over her neighborhood, in hopes that someone would contact her, but she hadn't had any such luck yet. Just thinking about never seeing her baby boy again turned her eyes glassy. She'd been a ball of emotions since he'd gone missing and knew that she'd never be the same without him. Chevy blinked her eyes and mashed the wetness out of them. Exhaling, she ran her hand down her face and cleared her throat.

"I'm almost done, sweetie." The nurse told her as her gloved hands patched up the holes in her.

"Okay." She looked to her and nodded.

Chevy's thoughts drifted off to Helen the night she'd gone to see her about Te'Qui. She didn't know what it was, but it was something that was definitely off putting about her behavior. Although she didn't notice it then, she'd been analyzing the situation since she'd left her house. It was like she was hiding something from her. She didn't know exactly what it was, but she had a feeling that she may have had something to do with the disappearance of her son. Chevy didn't want to think that she had anything to do with her boy being kidnapped, but she was starting to feel that it was more than likely. She remembered hearing someone yelling for help when she came to the door that night. And although Helen claimed that it was the TV, what she heard didn't sound like it came from the television to her. The voice was kind of muffled like it was far away or deep down somewhere. *Maybe the basement,* she thought to herself, forehead creasing with curiosity.

Chevy massaged her chin as she gave it some thought. Her mind switched from Helen to her oldest nephew, Wicked. She'd heard some of the God awful things he'd done and she wouldn't put anything past him, not even kidnapping. The only question she had was why would he want to kidnap Te'Qui? What reason would he have to snatch up her little man? Hmm, she pondered on it harder this time, going to her encounter with the mad man. He'd said something that was suspect to her, real suspect. The crazy thing about it was that she couldn't quite recall what it was, so she rewound the interaction inside of her head, going over it many times.

Chevy closed her eyes and visualized her encounter that night with Wicked, rewinding that moment back multiple times trying to figure out exactly what he was saying.

"I'ma be sorry for yo' loss, too, if Te'Qui..."

"I'ma be sorry for yo' loss, too, if Te'Qui don't..."

"I'ma be sorry for yo' loss, too, if Te'Qui don't tell me something."

"Helen's basement." Chevy's eyes shot open and she sprung to her feet, shoving the nurse aside and darting out of the room. The sound of the nurse's voice could be heard echoing down the hall as she asked Chevy if everything was alright. She sprinted down the hall where she saw Faison's cousins, JT and Lil' Chris shooting the shit outside of his door.

"Nigga, you ain't fuck Pam witcho lyin' ass." Lil' Chris laughed heartily, with his hand on his stomach.

"That's on momma." JT declared, lying his ass off.

"Lil' Chris, I need your strap." Chevy slowed to a stop, panting out of breath.

Lil' Chris frowned and chuckled like '*This bitch can't be serious.*'

When JT looked to Chevy and saw the seriousness in her eyes, the smile immediately fell from his face. He didn't know what drama she had on her hands, but he wanted to help her. But unfortunately, all he could offer her was a banger being that his place was there protecting Faison.

"Hell you need my strap for?" Lil' Chris inquired, needing to know what shit she'd gotten into that she needed a burner.

"I don't have any time to explain, just let me get that."

"Man, I'm not finna..."

JT nudged his younger relative and said, "Gon' and give it to her, fam."

"You can't be serious?" He looked at him with furrowed brows.

"Nah, give her that."

Lil' Chris blew hard, hating to have to part with his gun. Giving the area a cautious look, he whipped out his Glock and cocked one into its chamber, passing it off to Chevy on the low. After concealing the weapon on her waistline, she gave him a grateful nod.

"Thank you." She made a mad dash down the corridor, heading towards the elevator. Seeing her disappear down the hallway, JT and Lil' Chris exchange somber expressions.

"Yo,' what chu think she needed that banger for?" Lil' Chris asked.

"I don't know, but it must be serious." JT theorized.

30 minutes later

Chevy pulled up a couple houses down from Helen's house, killed the engine, and hopped out of her Caprice. She slammed the door shut and jogged toward the house. Nearing it, she hunched down and made her way through the yard. She crept along the side of the house and got down on her knees where the basement window was. The glass was filthy as hell, so she narrowed her eyes trying to peer through it. She thought she saw someone lying down on the floor in the far corner, but couldn't be for sure. Harping up a glob, she spat it on the window and rubbed out a circle with the sleeve of her shirt. Her eyes widened with hurt when she saw her baby boy down in the basement dirty and crazed looking like a delusional homeless war veteran. Seeing him in such a state made her feel as though she had failed him as a parent given his current situation. She was distraught and heartbroken, but she knew that she had to do all within her power to rescue him.

"Don't worry, baby, I'ma get chu outta there, okay?" Chevy spoke to no one in particular. She pulled the gun from around her back that Lil' Chris had given her and chambered a round into that bitch. Her mind was on some *Taken* movie shit. The plan was to kick in the door and go in there squeezing off on any threat to her and her son. She made to do just this, but her better judgment prevailed. Looking from the gun in her hand to the basement window, she decided that her idea was stupid. If she pulled a stunt like that she could be killed before she was ever able to rescue her son. For all she knew she could be running into some kind of child prostitution ring with a few gunners in there guarding it. What good was her gun against several others? She wouldn't make it out alive and she was sure of it. Chevy tucked her steel at the small of her back and paced the ground beside the house, thinking hard. She snapped her fingers and pulled out her cell phone, jogging back to her car she dialed up a number.

***

"What chu watching?" Wicked came through the door, finding his Aunt Helen on the couch watching television. He'd just come through the door as Chevy was pulling up outside.

"Dr. Oz," she responded, seeing the burn holes in his hoodie where'd he'd been shot. "I'm not even gonna ask."

"Good."

He headed inside of the kitchen and cracked open the refrigerator. He grabbed a bottle of Hennessy and removed the top, tossing it into the trash can. Standing where he was, he turned the bottle up, guzzling it.

"Ahhh." He hissed with closed eyes, shaking his head. The dark liquor was acquired to lessen the stinging of his wounds. Next, he unstrapped the bulletproof vest and tossed it onto the kitchen table. On his way back into the living room, he stopped at the oval shaped mirror with the unique golden frame. The crazy son of a bitch took swigs as he looked over the red swellings were he'd been shot. Oddly enough, he was thankful for them. It was better these bruises than real live bullet holes in his ass.

"Fucking Don Juan." Wicked said to no one in particular, just then his cellular rung. He pulled the device out of his pocket and saw that it was Roots. Once he pressed *answer,* he brought the cell to his ear. "'Sup with it?" He took a swallow of the liquid fire.

"Ya took care of dat?"

"Nah, I missed, some otha niggaz were there." He spoke like it wasn't a big deal.

"Da blood clot? Ya godda make sure ya sleep dese nigga. Beena long time comin' now. Ya understand me?"

"Man, fuck dat, I'm through with this shit. You want this nigga then you get 'em ya damn self." Wicked raged, spit flying from off of his lips. He was sick and tired of being Roots' slave. He knew that popping shit off at the mouth like that was likely a death wish but he'd had enough. If the Jamaican decided to send his people at him then he was going to take a couple of them with him before he met up with Satan in the afterlife.

"Watch ya mouf bwoi, me got da mind ta take ya off ya feet."

"Oh, yeah?"

"Yeah?"

"Suck my mothafucking dick, old pussy ass nigga!" He disconnected the call, feeling cocky and sure of himself. "Fuck them spaghetti heads. What they think? They the only gangstas out here? They got guns and I got guns. We can do this shit in broad day light, in the middle of the street."

"Is everything all right?"

"Yep." He plopped down on the couch and kicked off his red All-Star Chuck Taylor Converses. His banger was digging into his hip, so he whipped it out and rested it on his thigh, keeping his finger around the trigger. "That wasn't 'bout nothing." She stole a glance at him and noticed his bloodshot eyes and the bags below them. That and the nasty bruises on his body made him look like he'd been through hell. He was exhausted, having run around the city trying to track down Don Juan and peel his mothafucking thinking-cap back.

"Those bruises look kind of bad." She made her observation, a line deepened across her forehead. "You want me to get chu some ointment?"

"I'm good, Aunty, don't wet it."

"Well, alright." Her eyes studied the key around his neck. It twinkled every time the illumination from the television danced on it. It was as if it was daring her to take it from its owner. She took it as a challenge. One she'd rise to meet. Helen focused her attention back on the TV, occasionally glancing over at her nephew and then at the clock above the refrigerator.

Before she knew it, he was slumped and snoring, Hennessy bottle leaning toward his lap, threatening to spill every time he took a breath. Helen slipped off of the couch. Slicking her lips wet with her tongue, she crept towards him with the stealth of a feline. Making her way around the couch, she took pinches of his necklace with both hands. As soon as she made to lift it, he snorted an octave louder and smacked his lips, adjusting his head. She paused, but kept the necklace pinched between her index fingers and thumbs.

Her eyes shot to the gun in his hand and her heart jumped angrily at her left breast. She closed her eyes and swallowed the lump of nervousness in her throat. After waiting until she felt that he was back in his slumber, she gently lifted the length of jewelry from around his neck and looped it over his head. Helen moved to head for the basement and caught another look at the steel in her nephew's hand. Tempted to try for it, she gave it some thought and decided against it. If she were to get caught, that would be it. It wasn't any doubt in her mind that her nephew would dome her with one of the hollow tips that the weapon held. With her mind made up, Helen departed to the kitchen and grabbed a steak knife before dipping off to the basement to release Te'Qui from his shackle and into the free world.

***

Helen crept down the steps as quietly as she could until she met the floor. She pulled the drawstring and brought the basement to life. Te'Qui's head shot up from the surface and his eyes narrowed from the bright illumination of the bulb. He wiped the crust that had formed from the corners of his eyes and watched his late homeboy's aunt approach him.

"I got the key." She whispered, holding up the key to the shackle. This caused a smile to stretch across his face.

Helen leaned down and passed him off the steak knife. She then unlocked the shackle and pulled it free from his ankle.

"What's going on here?" A frowning Wicked looked from Helen to Te'Qui. She nearly leaped out of her skin, hearing her nephew's voice boom at her back. She and Te'Qui were so engrossed in what they were doing that they didn't hear the maniac creep up on them.

Helen whipped around wearing a guilty expression, looking like a child that had gotten caught with her hand inside of a cookie jar. Te'Qui's heart was beating so fast that it feels like it was about to explode inside of his chest. All he could do was stare into the mad man's eyes and wonder what was going on inside of his twisted mind.

"Nothing, I was just checking on him." Helen delivered the thought as soon as it was birthed in her mental.

Wicked's eyes narrowed into slits. He had a feeling something was up.

"I need to talk to you in private for a second, come upstairs with me."

"Okay." She tucked the gun into the small of her back and walked past him, climbing the steps. Wicked stood at the bottom of the staircase watching her, he pulled the steel from off of his waistline and pointed it at her. She'd just turned her head to the side to look over her shoulder when he pulled the trigger.

"Nooooo!" Te'Qui screamed from where he lay, reaching out.

Pop!

"Aaahhh!" A hot one entered her back causing her to throw her head back and scream aloud, face showcasing all of her excruciation. She fell awkwardly, tumbling down the stairs hard and fast, sliding across the floor. Helen lay on her back staring up at the ceiling. Her eyes twinkled with tears at the corners of them and she murmured. An approaching shadow brought her shade and her eyes darted to their right. She saw her nephew standing over her. She tried to move, but her limbs wouldn't cooperate. Her mouth went to say something, but before the words could be formed death greeted her.

Pop! Pop!

He put all of that heat in her scalp and kicked her corpse. "Fucking Judas."

Wicked turned around to Te'Qui and advanced in his direction, taking his time like he was on a stroll through his neighborhood. The little nigga looked from Helen's strewn dead body to the face of her crazy ass nephew. Te'Qui's chest was jumping crazy and his eyes were frighteningly wide. He swallowed the lump of nervousness in his throat and closed his eyes for a moment, pulling himself together. There wasn't any way in hell he was going to die scared and on his knees, he'd meet his demise head on, middle fingers up high. Te'Qui pushed off of the filthy floor and stood up. The young man stared his would be executioner directly in his maddening eyes, showing the maniac that he wasn't afraid of a mothafucking thang. He harped up some phlegm and spat it aside on the ground, setting his eyes back on the evil soul approaching him.

"You've got balls, lil' homie, big, gigantic balls." He showed the size of the balls with one hand while the other held tight to his gun. He cocked his arm back and made to crack the youngster upside the head. A sudden movement that was too fast to clock caught him by surprise. "Arghhhhh!" He grabbed his eye grimacing, dropping his head bussa, having been jabbed in the pupil with a knife.

The next jabs came quick and without warning, poking up his chest and forearms. Then there was that one attack that made him scream the loudest, he got that in the side of his throat. "Gagghhhh!" His good eye bulged and he smacked a hand over the spurting hole in his neck. He staggered backwards, giving Te'Qui enough time to react. He finished unlocking the shackle with the key Helen had left in it. After letting the key fall, he tossed the shackle aside and it clanged on the surface.

He then jetted toward Wicked, bumping his shoulder as he ran past him. Suddenly, the mad man's hand shot out and he grasped his neck causing him to howl in pain. The pain was so intense that it caused him to drop the steak knife, his aggressor kick it away. It slid across the floor, spinning in circles until it was lost beneath an old deep freezer. Te'Qui grabbed a hold of Wicked's wrist and winced, feeling his neck being jerked back violently.

"Lil' fucka!" He slammed his forehead into the railing of the staircase and released him. The boy hit the floor on his back, eyes closed, mouth shut, snoring like he was asleep. He was knocked out cold. With his one good eye, the crazy bastard stared down at him, gritting teeth and clenching his fist. "Grrrrrr!" He growled like an old junkyard dog, before going blindly mad with rage. Hand pressed down on the hole in his neck, he stomped and kicked the little nigga until he was bloody and bruised. He was furious. First his aunt had tested his gangsta. Now this little pipsqueak had the nerve to try him.

"Haa! Haa! Haa!" He breathed like he'd just finished running a marathon, studying the injuries he'd given to the youngster. His head snapped up and he met an old antique mirror at the back of the basement wall. Its frame was gold and filthy, while its glass had amassed dirt. He hurried over to the back of the room, carefully looking over his reflection as he held his neck.

Wincing, he slowly peeled open the eyelid of his wounded eye to take a look. He was completely blind. The pupil had been gouged out and some colorful gunk was oozing out of it. His head snapped away from the mirror, his eye anxiously searched the room until it fell on something. Wicked rushed over to the table and snatched up a roll of duct-tape. He pressed two fingers down on the wound as he stretched the tape out and began wrapping his neck up with it. Once he was done with it, he then tore the length of tape with his teeth and tossed the roll of it aside. Keeping his eye on the reflection, he pulled the black sunglasses out of the breast pocket and slid them on. He turned his head from side to side making sure he got a good look at himself.

Through the mirror he saw Te'Qui lying out in the floor unconscious. This made him mad all over again. His eyebrows arched and his nostrils flared.

"I got something...I got something for that ass." He stormed over to his worn brown leather bag and unzipped it. He dipped his hand inside, rummaging through the torture tool collection he had amassed. Once he found the one he was looking for, he withdrew it. It was long with jagged edges. He smiled evilly as he stared at the shiny, bladed weapon. A gleam swept up its entire length and illuminated his face. He chuckled wickedly before licking his chops and marching over to Te'Qui's strewn form, ready to perform his fatal operation.

"Yeeaahh, it's about that time." He grabbed his bony wrist and made to drag him when he heard a loud noise coming from upstairs. His brows mush together and bewilderment enveloped his face. He listened closely as the noise continued. His head swung around to the small basement window where he saw several booted feet headed in the direction of the house. It was the S.W.A.T Team. Soon after, he heard a helicopter flying toward the area. He really looked alive when he heard a succession of thunderous booms as the police were ramming the door. While all of this was going on, he went about the business of duct-taping up Te'Qui's mouth, wrists, and ankles. When he grabbed the kid under his arm, he heard a *Boom!* and the front door banging off of the wall. Right after came a stampede of boots trampling throughout the house.

Wicked dragged his capture across the floor until he met with a rug which he threw back, revealing a secret trap door. He grabbed the door's handle and flung it open.

"Clear!"

"Clear!"

"All is clear up here, too."

"Check the basement!"

He heard the collage of voices coming from above him. Then he heard the basement's door being assaulted by the battering ram. He tossed Te'Qui through the secret door and he landed on the dirt floor beneath the house. He then pulled the door closed as he headed down the short steps. As soon as the door clicked shut, he heard the basement door come crashing down. Wicked grabbed the youngster under his arm, dragging him through the dirt as he climbed toward the gated passage beyond him. It was gated and light was illuminating through it. At the corner of the gated passage, its wiring was bent up and he saw a couple of rats ooze through. He paid them no mind as he navigated toward his freedom, taking the time to smack a baby spider he felt crawling up the side of his face. The further he crawled, the more light shined on his face until he was dead smack in front of the passage.

Thud! Thud!

He looked over his shoulder and two of the S.W.A.T Team members were crawling after him, one African American, the other Caucasian.

"Stop, you fuck!" the Caucasian one blared.

"Fuck y'all niggaz, Blood!" Wicked shouted back, yanking open the passage with two strong tugs.

The white cat aimed his automatic weapon at him about to blaze his back up until the black one grabbed him by the wrist.

"Wait, he's got the kid with him!" the African American warned him.

"Shit!" the Caucasian pounded the dirt floor with his fist.

Wicked crawled his way out from underneath the house. When the street lights hit him, he was dressed in dirt from head to toe. He reached back inside of the passage and grabbed Te'Qui under his arms, dragging his little ass out. His head snapped up, hearing the locks of the back door being undone. Swiftly, he hoisted the youngster over his shoulder and sprinted off toward his BMW. He popped the trunk with his remote control, opened it, and deposited him inside. *Thunk!* He slammed the trunk closed and ran over to the driver side door. Bringing the vehicle back to life, he stole a glance out of the window. The S.W.A.T Team was coming from underneath the house and through the back door. Wicked threw his whip in *reverse* and floored it, sending the rear of his ride crashing through the gate and tearing it down. He then switched the gears into *drive* and mashed out down the alley, leaving a cloud of dust in his wake.

Vrooooom!

Wicked flew out of the alley and into the street, turning left passing Chevy. She cranked up her Caprice and mashed the pedal, but it died on her.

"Ahhh, fuck, come on, come on." She turned the key in the ignition several times and mashed the gas pedal repeatedly, but the son of a bitch wouldn't start up. "Damn!" She smacked the dashboard heatedly. Clenching her fists, she went to assault the steering wheel, but stopped herself while in motion. She put her hands together in prayer and closed her eyes. "Lord, let this car start, so I can go after this bastard and rescue my son, please, please, please." She begged, then took a couple of deep breaths. With her eyes shut, Chevy said a silent prayer and turned the key in the ignition. The Caprice cranked right up.

"Thank you, Father, thank you." She looked up at the ceiling. Right after, she pulled away from where she was parked and went after Wicked.

***

Once Wicked figured he'd put a good distance between himself and his Aunt Helen's house, he took a couple of glances over his shoulder to see if the police were on him. They weren't. He took his flask out of the glove-box and screwed off the cap, taking a long drink. He hissed, feeling the dark liquor course down his throat. The alcohol wasn't because he wanted a drink. He needed it because his wounds were kicking his ass and it was just the remedy.

Wicked screwed the cap back on the flask and tossed it into the front passenger seat. He adjusted the rearview mirror and took a good examination of his injuries. Seeing the work Te'Qui had done on him angered him further and he clenched his jaws. *Lil' mothafucka,* he looked over his shoulder and punched the ceiling rapidly. He pulled over alongside the curb and popped the trunk, grabbing his torture tool from underneath the seat. Slamming the door shut, the nutcase made his way around the back of the car.

Fuck it. I got baby bro's killa, he can rest in peace now. I'll let the streets catch up with homie that hit Brice off with that work. But this lil' nigga here gotta go. Wicked stepped to the trunk and lifted it.

"Ooof!" His eyes bulged and he doubled over, dropping his Instrument of Death. The weapon clanged when it hit the street and a scowling Te'Qui swung the tire iron across his head. Pling! The mad man flew off to the side and hit the ground, moaning in pain. The little nigga had used the pointed end of the tire iron to cut himself free of his restraints. He jumped down into the street, dropped the tire iron and took off yelling and hollering for help.

***

Tiaz rode in the backseat of the police cruiser, hands cuffed behind his back and neck on a swivel. Although he was taking in the scenery as he was driven down to the precinct. The thug looked more like he was trying to find an address or the name of a street the way he was going about it. Hearing a voice at his back the police officer riding in the front passenger seat looked over his shoulder through the gate at the suspect.

"Hey, buddy, do me a favor and shut the fuck up back there, will ya?" He settled back down in his seat.

"What's going on?" his partner inquired.

"Fucking whack job is talking to himself."

"Yeah?" His forehead wrinkled.

"You mean you don't fucking hear 'em back there?" He looked at him like '*How didn't you hear him?*'

"Yeah, you're close, real close." Tiaz spoke just above a whisper.

"Aye, I'm not gonna tell you again!" the officer roared at Tiaz. "You open your big mouth once more and you're gonna get real acquainted with this here night stick!" He held up the black metal rod. The roughneck stared at the officer with a solemn face, but then his lips went on to form a smirk. "Hell are you smiling about?"

He turned his head slightly to the left and the law enforcer saw the ear bud. His eyes grew big and he went to say something.

Craashh!

A car slammed into the police cruiser and it fishtailed out of control, bumping up against a light post. When the cruiser had stopped, the police had bloody gashes in their foreheads and were moaning in pain. Tiaz peeled his head back from the ruined back door window. It had cracked into a spider web when his head went whamming against it in the crash. He grimaced, feeling the throbbing in his head. Tiaz popped his thumb bone out of place and slipped his hand out of the handcuffs. Afterwards, he snapped his thumb back in place and looked his hand over. He then went about the task of getting out.

He was about to start kicking at the back window glass to break it. But that's when she arrived. Bianca, assault rifle in hand, slamming it into the driver side window, cracking it until it gave. She reached inside and popped the locks to the back door before pulling it open. Right after, she was handing Tiaz the handcuff key. He unlocked the cuff and threw it aside, following her to the van. He jumped into the awaiting vehicle and she was right behind him pulling off.

"You okay?" she questioned, driving off.

"Just a lil' banged up." He winced bending his neck and back. "You get that from 'em yet?"

"Yeah." She opened the glove-box and passed him an envelope. He hastily opened it and pulled its contents loose. He smiled deviously. "Don Juan's current address, now we know exactly where to find this lil' pissant." He looked at a smaller sheet of paper inside. It was the size of a sticky note. He held it open with his thick thumbs. "Uh huh, everything has fallen into place." He passed Bianca the sticky note. "Get me here."

He then climbed into the back of the van and opened up a duffle bag, pulling loose a sweat suit, among other things.

"What about ya boy, Faison?" she asked, looking from the windshield then over her shoulder.

Click Clack!

He chambered a hollow tip round into the brand spanking new Beretta before replying. "We'll double back, but right now I wanna get this one bad, real bad. This heartless mothafucka has it coming."

"Right." She laid the sheet of paper down on the front passenger seat. They were off to their next destination to tie up another loose end.

***

"Well. You don't have to worry about it, Toots." Herby patted Ta'shauna's thigh. He'd just finished telling her how he'd been hired to guard her with his life and he'd give it up without a second thought if it meant her salvation. Although she popped a lot of shit off at the mouth, she was truly scared to death of Tiaz coming after her.

"Thank you." She grasped his hand firmly. "I really mean it."

"Don't mention it, Sweets."

A knock at the door put a pause to Herby and Ta'shauna's conversation. Seeing the worry etched across her face, he placed a reassuring hand on hers and slightly squeezed it. "It's okay, relax, it's probably your brother." He rose from the couch and approached the door, gun at his side. He leaned forward and took a gander through the peephole. Confirming who it was, he tucked the burner into its holster and turned to Ta'shauna. "It's Faison." When he relayed his discovery, she sighed with relief and relaxed a bit. "See, all of that worry for nothing." He unchained and unlocked the door, pulling it open.

"Where's Ta'shauna?" Faison stepped through the door.

"Faison?" His sister rose to her feet excitedly, hearing his voice.

"Hey, baby sis." He hastily approached and she opened her arms. She'd never been happier around him. They embraced. She closed her eyes and rested her chin in the nape of his neck. He swept his hand back and forth up her back as he relished in the tender moment of affection.

"Arghhh!" Her eyes snapped open and her jaw dropped, she staggered back looking at him in turmoil. She touched her torso and her trembling hand came away wet with blood. She looked up at her brother accusingly. "Wh-why, Faison?"

"Not Faison," Tiaz spoke into the voice changer device then threw it aside. "Tiaz." He glared up at her and smiled menacingly, snickering. He was wearing a hairnet, gloves and hospital moccasins over his shoes so he wouldn't leave any forensic evidence for the murder he was about to commit.

She gasped and screamed. "Ahhhhhhh!" Turning around, she ran for her life, but she didn't get very far. *Bump!* She ran dead smack into the wall and fell out. She lay on her back with a knot forming on her forehead as she moaned, moving her head from left to right. Breathing sporadically, heart racing, she blindly scrambled upon her feet. She could feel Tiaz' presence, but she didn't know exactly where he was. Unbeknownst to her, the thug stood behind her, watching as she moved in circles feeling for something that wasn't there. Evil was in his eyes and a gun was in his hand. He lifted his silenced weapon and put one in her spine and two into her cabbage.

"And that's that," Herby said from over his shoulder.

Tiaz looked to find him slipping his suit's jacket back on. He then opened up the thick ass envelope he'd given him upon entering and quickly thumbed through the dead presidents inside. Figuring that it was the amount due to him, he closed the envelope and secured it inside of his suit.

"Well, it was nice doing business witcha. I'ma get going."

"Nah, you stay here with her."

"Wha…" His head snapped back as a hot one pierced his forehead. He fell to his knees and leaned all of the way back, sitting up awkwardly. Tiaz reached inside of his suit and removed the envelope, stuffing it into his back pocket. Pulling out a bandana, he wiped the murder weapon clean and tossed it beside Herby. He used the bandana to open the door and turned around, his eyes giving a quick sweep of the room before descending out of the house.

Tiaz hopped into the front passenger seat and slammed the door shut. He pulled a cigarette loose from a pack of Newport 100s and stuck it between his lips. After ripping out a match from a book, he raped it across the black strip and a flame awakened with a hiss. He fired up the square and took a couple of puffs, fanning the flame of the match out. A victorious smile curled his lips having finally gotten his hands on Ta'shauna. It had been a while coming, but thanks to Herby he was able to get his revenge. He'd hired the man as soon as he found out Ta'shauna had survived the fatal wounds. He believed that if anyone could find her, a private investigator could. And he was right.

"Where are we off to now?"

Tiaz took the Joe from out of his mouth, blowing smoke from his nose. "Don Juan's."

With Ta'shauna finally out of the way, Tiaz could now move on to the rest of the niggaz that had wronged him. The people on his *Shit List* were growing fewer and fewer. His victims would feel his pain and forget that mercy ever existed.

Tranay Adams

Chapter Thirteen

"Alright, I'm finna come out now." Lil' Stan disconnected the call and stashed it into his jeans pocket. He mashed out his blunt in the glass ashtray and stuck it behind his ear. He snatched up the duffle bag and headed for the door. The bag's content was all of the money from his boss's traps and illegal businesses. Earlier that day, he was sent to gather up all of his scratch and sit on it until he came to retrieve it. The thought of running off with all of that money came to mind several times for the young hood. He could do a lot with what he was toting, but the theft wouldn't be worth all of the heat that would come behind him from stealing from Don Juan. Having made up his mind to play it fair, he picked up all of the money and sat on it until it was time for the pick-up.

The front door of the house came open and Lil' Stan slammed it shut, hustling down the steps. He kept a firm hold on his .40 cal as he crossed the threshold out of the yard en route to Don Juan's Porsche truck. He wore a solemn look on his face, seeing him talking to someone on his cellular. From the exchange he could tell that conversation was getting heated. His eyes bugged and his mouth opened to shout a warning, seeing someone hastily approaching the SUV with a gun pointed. Before the words could leave his lips the shots were already on their way.

***

After the shootout back at the gas station, Don Juan hit up Lil' Stan and told him to get all of the money he'd made from his traps that week. Next, he called Rosa and had her pack luggage for him and his little man. Cali had gotten too hot for him, so he decided to blow town and lay low for a while. He needed to get his head together and figure out how he was going to handle this situation with Tiaz.

At first, he thought he was going to be able to squash the thug like a cockroach and be done with him, but he proved to be more of a nuisance than he imagined. He never thought that one man would give him so much trouble, but when he bumped heads with Tiaz, he got a headache that he really didn't need. Regardless, he was going to take care of him in time. He just needed time to kick back and gather his wits. He was driving out to South Carolina to stay with his Uncle Benny and Aunt Cookie to chill for a time. They were good, country folks and he was sure they'd welcome him and his son with open arms. It would be a nice little getaway. One that he sorely needed after all of the shit that had went down those past couple of weeks. All of the business he had to take care of in the next couple of weeks would be turned over to Lil' Stan. He was going to hold things down while he was away.

"You alright back there, lil' man?" Don Juan cracked a smile, looking at his son through the rearview mirror. His baby boy smiled and kicked his little legs, excitedly. This made the Trap God's smile broader. Hearing his cell phone going off, he pulled it out of his pocket and looked at the screen. Seeing that it was one of his biggest customers, he pressed *answer* and brought the device to his ear.

"DJ, wat's up?" the caller asked.

Don Juan took the time to take a pull from his blunt and blew out smoke. "What's up witchu, Roots?"

"How long have we been doing business?"

Don Juan whistled thinking of how long they'd been dealing with one another. "Man, I'd say we been at it for quite some time now. What's this, a social call? 'Cause I gotta…"

"Dis is notta social call. Dis is me coming ta ya ta ask ya ta give me ma money back."

The Trap God slumped his shoulders and blew hard, releasing some of his frustration. "Like I told you before, I didn't have anything to do with yo' people getting hit, fam."

"Listen, me gon' ask you 'bout ma money and if ya still say ya dunt know wat happened ta it, den…"

"Mothafucka, you threatening me?" He frowned and snatched the blunt out of his mouth.

"Brudda, ya can take it howeva ya want."

"Nigga, fuck you! Take that however you want!" His head bobbed from side to side as he spat harshly into the receiver. "You send any niggaz this way and I'ma send 'em back to you in body bags. Best believe that, homeboy!"

"Is dat a fact?"

"You goddamn right. Make ya next move ya best move, playa."

Pewk! Pewk! Pewk!

Shots whizzed through the driver side window, peppering Don Juan with glass and causing him to drop his cellular on the floor. The sudden eruption of gunfire startled the baby and sent him into a crying fit.

"Waa! Waa! Waa! Waa!"

Don Juan hunched down to avoid the gunshots. He stole a peek through the shattered window and saw a tall, dark-skinned nigga with high cheekbones approaching, sending fire at his ass. The Trap God threw his truck in *reverse* and slammed into the Plymouth behind him. He threw it back in *drive* and slammed into the Neon parked in front of him. After reversing again, he pulled the steering wheel to the left and mashed the gas down, tires screeching as he peeled off.

Don Juan pulled his .9mm from underneath the seat and sat it in his lap. He stole a peek through the side view mirror and saw the cat that was getting at him hop into the front passenger seat of a station wagon. The vehicle was driving off right behind him in pursuit. He glanced into the backseat at his baby boy and he was wailing as loud as ever, tears slicking down his chubby cheeks.

"Waa! Waa! Waa! Waa!" the baby continued to cry.

"You alright, lil' man, huh?" He glanced back at his son, checking him for wounds. He was straight. "You good, DJ, hold tight. Yo' daddy gon' have to get with a couple of fuck-boys program right quick." He turned back around gripping his thang-thang, and stealing a look through the side view mirror. The station wagon was speeding upon him.

***

Lil' Stan's eyes bugged and his mouth opened to shout a warning, seeing someone hastily approaching Don Juan's SUV with a gun pointed. Before the words could leave his lips the shots were already on their way.

Poc! Poc! Poc!

The gunman opened up fire on the driver side window of the truck. Lil' Stan watched as the Porsche slammed back and forth between two parked cars before peeling off. As soon as the SUV took off, the station wagon toting the gunman was pulling off right behind it. Lil' Stan was about to run out into the street and get off behind it, but seeing the silhouette of someone creeping upon him slowed his roll. His head whipped around and he made Tiaz with that Beretta held low, creeping on his dog ass. The young nigga slung the duffle bag to his side and brought his head bussa around, sending some heat at him. Tiaz ducked low to avoid the heat wave before he came back up with a deadly response.

Boc! Boc! Boc!

Sparks flew from off the side of the parked Neon and shattered its side view mirror. Lil' Stan broke up the block, gun in one hand and duffle bag in the other. It was like his sneakers were on fire as fast as he was running, heels kicking him in his ass, he was moving so swift.

"Nuh uh, both of these niggaz ain't getting away from me." Tiaz went after him, gun held at his side as his sneakers pounded the sidewalk, covering ground.

Where the fuck did that other nigga come from? I almost had Don Juan's bitch ass. Damn! It don't matter. As long as somebody get that ass. I know one thang though, I'ma get this lil' mothafucka right here, on my momma, Tiaz thought as he got after Lil' Stan, moving like a pistol was fired in the air to start a race.

Bianca was just a few feet away tailing him. As soon as the thug turned that young ass nigga'z life off he was to hop back into the car and get the fuck out of dodge. Lil' Stan rounded the corner coming off of the residential block out onto a main street. His forehead was beaded with sweat and he was huffing and puffing, had him wishing he wasn't a nicotine fiend and visited the gym regularly. When he glanced back, Death was right upon him in the form of a very determined Tiaz. Beretta held up at his shoulder as he ran, he was behind that nigga like he was his shadow. He stopped for a second and pointed his banger, letting her rip.

Boc! Boc! Boc!

Gunshots rang out causing the few pedestrians occupying the sidewalks to scatter and scream in panic. Lil' Stan ran like he had a lynch mob behind him, breathing heavily and occasionally glancing over his shoulder. His forehead shined from the sweat. His adrenaline was pumping madly and fueling his stamina to run. He was so jacked up off of fear that he could probably make it to Montana on foot.

Clenching his .40 cal tighter, Lil' Stan spun around and let two fly. Smoke and sparks rushed from the cal's barrel behind the twin bullets. The first shot narrowly missed its mark as he hunched over and darted behind a parked cab. The second shot went through the cab's back window, shattering it into pieces. Lil' Stan turned around and continued on his way. Tiaz peeked over the trunk of the cab and saw the young nigga moving like a track star. Seeing his kill getting away, he jumped back to his feet in hot pursuit.

Tiaz knew he had no business chasing down Lil' Stan on a busy street with his face exposed. He had plenty of witnesses to point him out in court if he was to ever get pinched for the murder, but at the moment he'd seen his bitch ass he threw logical thinking to the wind. He had a vendetta against Don Juan and his lieutenant. They had stolen his best friend from him and he was determined to take their lives. He knew he wouldn't be able to sleep a wink at night if both of them weren't dead. The roughneck had a score to settle and he was going to settle it that night.

Lil' Stan turned around and dumped on Tiaz, twice more. The first shot missed his head by an inch. The second one hit the building at the end of the alley he'd ducked into, causing a spray of debris to mist the air. Leaning against the brick building, Tiaz checked the magazine of his head bussa and smacked it back in. He had more than enough rounds to get the job done, but knew he'd better hurry because the police were sure to be on the way with a firefight going on in the middle of the city. Tiaz went to take a quick peek around the corner of the building and caught debris in his eye as a chunk of brick was blown off by one of Lil' Stan's bullets.

"Arghhh!" He yelped and grabbed his eye, doubling over.

Thinking that he'd critically wounded Tiaz, Lil' Stan cautiously advanced on the alley with his gun arm erect. While his right-hand clutched his .40 cal, the left one held the butt of it. He knew that he'd injured the foe, but he didn't know if he was so bad off that he couldn't bust his gun. Just as that thought entered the youngster's head, the thug threw himself out of the alley on his side, squeezing off shots.

Boc! Boc!

A hole opened in the little nigga'z abdomen and his shoulder. A hole exploded in his hand and he grimaced and dropped his gun. He went to pick it up and it was shot out of his reach.

Police sirens wailed in the distance, heading to the rivals location, no doubt. Tiaz ignored the blaring noise. He had to end this feud tonight for good and at any cost. Lil' Stan looked up from where he was about to pick up his gun and saw Tiaz with his burner aimed at his forehead. He closed his eyes and waited for the bullet that would send him to Heaven or Hell.

Click!

Lil' Stan's eyes popped open and he saw Tiaz examining his weapon, it had jammed. Using the distraction to his advantage, he fled. The buff neck thug stood to his feet. After fooling around with his gun for a moment, he finally managed to un-jam it. He looked up and saw Lil' Stan ducking off into a music store.

Tiaz followed him into the music store, gun hanging at his side. When the patrons and cashier saw his weapon they were too petrified to move. They cowered where they stood, eyes bugged and mouths open. Lil' Stan looked for some place to run, but there were none. The only other door was at the back of the store chained and locked. He found himself cornered, but realizing that he was in a store full of people put him a little at ease. He knew that the nigga that was on him was a killer, but even he wasn't crazy enough to pop him in an establishment full of witnesses. Or so he thought.

Police cars pulled up to the store while a scowling Tiaz was en route to Lil' Stan. The youngster didn't show any fear though. He was G with his. His scowl matched the thug's own.

"You got balls, my nigga, but I don't think you're crazy enough to pop me with a room full of witnesses and The Boys at the door." He cracked a smile, displaying a perfect top row of white teeth and bunched bottom teeth.

Tiaz spat on the floor and pressed the barrel of his gun between the little nigga'z eyes. The whole time he kept his game face. His heart quickened, but he refused to leave this world anything less than a gangsta.

"Freeze, motherfucker!" A cop bellowed from the doorway. He had his gun drawn on Tiaz. "Drop the gun now!"

Neither Tiaz nor Lil' Stan heard the police officer. They had completely blocked him out and were now in their own world. They stared each another down. Neither one flinching, neither one blinking, one not afraid to die, the other not afraid to kill.

"I'm not gonna tell you again, asshole!" the cop barked.

For a moment there was silence. Tiaz and Lil' Stan stared each another down. The thug's eyebrows arched and his lips twisted. They stayed like that for a time before transforming into a toothy smile. And then it happened. *Boc!*

The music store erupted into cries and screams.

The bullet whizzed through Lil' Stan's forehead and exited out the back of his skull. Red goo and brain matter splattered everywhere, speckling nearby CDs on racks. The youngster's eyes were as wide as saucers and his mouth was hanging open. He fell to the floor in what seemed like slow motion. Tiaz wore a wicked smile on his face, but not for long. A bullet struck him in the back and he grimaced. He whipped around, bringing his head bussa along. He went to pull the trigger and a second bullet hit him low in his abs. He looked down wearing a frown, seeing the crimson stain expanding. He looked up ready to kill the cop and a third bullet slammed into his shoulder, causing him to stagger backwards. He bumped into a rack of CDs and fell over with it. There was a loud crash and he rolled over onto his side. Spotting his gun, he went to pick it back up and another bullet struck his hand.

"Gahhh!" He cradled his hand, bawling. When he looked up the cop was right up on him, pointing his pistol down at his face and kicking the head bussa out of his reach.

"Move, and that's your ass!" the cop shouted down in his face.

Tiaz' let his head drop to the floor and sighed. His lifestyle had caught up to him. It was finally over. After murdering Lil' Stan in front of a cop, with all of his priors, he was sure he was going to be locked away for a long time. The funny thing is that he didn't mind. All of his killing and shady dealing had gotten the best of him and he couldn't wait to get a piece of mind.

***

Te'Qui ran as hard as he could, constantly looking over his shoulders, his bare feet smacking against the pavement. His chest swelling and deflating. He was breathing hard, real hard, and his lungs felt like they were warming. The fear he was experiencing was like an adrenaline shot. His legs seemed like they were moving with hyper speed. Every time he'd start to slow down from fatigue, he'd look back and see Wicked. He was hauling ass after him and holding a hand over his injured neck. His other hand was gripping the same Instrument of Death he had down in the basement that he'd planned to use on him. From his facial expression, he knew if he caught up with him he was going to chop his little ass up into tuna.

Te'Qui's head was snapping around in all directions. There were plenty of bystanders out and about and none of them were trying to help him. It seemed that those seeing a little kid about to be slaughtered like cattle, would do something to stop the mad man that was after him.

"I'm gonna kill you, you lil' shit! You're dead! You're dead!" Wicked swore, glassy-eyed and veins bulging on his forehead and temples.

"Ooof!" Wicked was tackled to the ground by what looked like a blur. He hit the sidewalk, tussling with a man who decided to intervene on the youngster's behalf. *Big mistake!*

Crack! Whack! Bwap!

Wicked knocked him to the ground and snatched up his deadly weapon. "That's yo' ass, nigga!" He grabbed him by his throat and lifted the torture tool over his head. The man's eyes bulged and he gasped, then it happened, the sharp instrument bit into his face, repeatedly. Blood specs clung to Wicked's face and clothes. He looked like a fucking lunatic.

His head snapped up and he saw that Te'Qui had stopped to watch the tussle he was having with the bystander. When the youngster saw him, his eyes nearly leaped out of his head and his chest was twitching hard. He looked petrified, like he'd seen someone step out of a coffin, fully dressed in a suit and tie. His fear had paralyzed him. He couldn't move an inch. It was like he was wearing a pair of cement shoes. With the blood splattered on his cornrows, face and clothes, Wicked looked like Jack Nicholson in *The Shining,* a fucking psychopath. He licked the blood from off of the bladed tool laughing and then pointed it at the juvenile. He then went charging after him, raising his killing utensil above his head. He ran right out into the middle of the intersection and that was his undoing.

Boomp!

Wicked went flying over the windshield, looking like a rag doll before settling down in the middle of the street. Te'Qui's eyes bulged further and his jaw dropped open. He studied his aggressor as he lay in the street bloody, broken, and twitching. His hand held firm to the Instrument of Death as he clung to life. His head fell to the left, locking eyes with the boy he'd planned to slice and dice. His face twisted with anger and he attempted to move.

Urrrrrrrk!

Boomp!

Wicked's head splattered like a rotten watermelon as a second car that was tailing the first car bent the corner. His gold grill tumbled forward and stopped, a gleam swept across the length of it.

Te'Qui lay where he was wide-eyed and slack jawed. He was in shock. Although he had seen quite a bit growing up in the hood, but never anything like this.

"Oh my God, are you alright?" A light-skinned girl with her individual braids pulled back in a bun asked him.

"Yeah...yeah." He eyes stayed on the mess that was once Wicked as he swallowed his spit, nodding.

He couldn't believe how close he was to death. It was a close call.

***

"Wat da fuck was dat?" Uduka asked, reloading his brother's .45 automatic.

"I hit someone back dere." Uche answered, gripping the steering wheel firmly, a face of determination. "I may have keeled 'em, but fuck 'em. Only thin' dat mattas is avengin' Boxy."

"Right." He chambered a live round into the handgun and passed it to his brother. He took it.

Don Juan and Uche drove side by side, looking from one another to their windshields.

Bunk! Bunk! Urrrk! Bunk!

Uche slammed into the side of his Porsche repeatedly, wearing a scowl. He hoisted up his gun and pointed out of the window, still looking back and forth.

"Dis is a gift from Boxy!" The oldest of The Eme Brother's growled, letting his gun talk.

Poc! Poc! Poc!

Don Juan ducked down, but kept a firm hold on the steering wheel. He narrowed his eyes, looking back and forth between the street and Uche, trying his best not to get his top blown off. He clenched his tool tighter, waited his chance and came back up, letting that thang go.

Splock! Splock! Splock!

His brows furrowed when he saw Uche had vanished. It dawned on him to look over his shoulder. When he did he caught one in it.

"Ahhh!" He bit down on his bottom lip to fight back the fire in his shoulder. Uche drifted alongside him toward the rear of his truck, giving him hell with his .45 automatic.

Poc! Poc! Poc! Poc!

Don Juan slumped down to avoid the fire that was sent his way. He floored the gas pedal and the vehicle zoomed forward. He peeked over the dashboard and a big ass Mac truck was about to collide with him.

Buuuunk! Buuuunk!

The driver of the mammoth size vehicle blew its horn.

"Oh fuck!" Don Juan threw the steering wheel to the right, cutting through lanes. Seeing that he was about to crash into a nearby parked car, he whipped the Porsche back around and lost control of it. The SUV fishtailed and slammed up against a light pole, wrapping around it. The impact dislodged Don Juan from the driver seat. The windshield exploded as he went flying through it along with broken glass. He hit the ground with the shards rolling like he was on fire. Coming to a stop, he slowly scrambled upon his feet, slicing up his palms and forearms on the broken glass.

Hearing the screeching tires of a car coming upon him, his head snapped in its direction. He narrowed his eyes as blood from a gash in his forehead slid down his face. He was a little dizzy and discombobulated from the crash, so he couldn't tell who was upon him. He held a hand over his brows and saw a silhouette hopping out of the car and moving in his direction. That's when it came back to him that it was the Africans. In a hurried panic, his bloody fingers reached for his gun amid the shards. He pulled it from the loose glass and went to turn around just as the silhouette was advancing in his direction lifting something. Before he could get off, fire exploded in his hip and he howled like an old wounded dog, hobbling about. He dropped his banger and jumped forward on one leg like he was playing hopscotch.

Hearing police car sirens, Uduka's head snapped all around trying to see exactly where they were approaching from. He was starting to get worried now. The heat was on and it was starting to get hotter.

"Uche, we must go," he called out. "Dee authorities will be heah shortly."

Uche didn't pay any mind to his baby brother. That nigga was too far gone. His mental was warped. He was consumed with murking out Don Juan. He and his prey were all that existed in the world in that hour. He'd allowed him to get a good distance from him. Looking on, Uduka thought that he was letting him get away, but that couldn't be farther away from the truth. Uche was toying with him, sort of like a cat playing with a mouse before devouring it. The Nigerian slowly walked behind his intended victim, letting him get only so far before putting slugs in different body parts. He wasn't concerned with killing him just yet. Nah, he wanted him to feel pain before he took him out.

"Ucheeee!"

Poc!

Fire ripped through Don Juan's side. His eyes bulged and his mouth opened so wide that you could see that little pink thing at the back of his throat. He crashed to the ground on his side, breathing hard, vision going black and then coming back. He was exhausted. If this was to be his end then he was ready. He was about to see if there was a heaven for a G.

Urrrrrk!

The first police cruiser pulled upon the scene.

A bullet whizzed through Don Juan's forearm and he clenched his teeth, fighting back the excruciation. He was determined to pull the small caliber pistol from his ankle holster. He heard the driver side door of the police cruiser open and booted feet hopping out. His eyes shot up and Uche was there. The murky blue sky was the background to his silhouette. He couldn't see his eyes, but he knew that he was staring down at him with contempt.

"Drop it! Drop it now!" He heard the cop bellow, his voice sounding slow and demonic the more he talked.

Several more police cruisers skidded to a halt on the scene.

"Ucheeee!" Uduka shrilled so hard and loud that veins formed across his forehead and neck.

Uche was so thirsty for Don Juan's blood, that he wasn't aware of anything going on around him. It was like he was possessed. The only thing that mattered to him was his vengeance, even if it meant his life. Don Juan snatched the pistol loose from the holster on his ankle, lifting his weapon as the Nigerian pointed the .45 down at his face.

A surge of gunfire filled the night's air and with it came Uduka's grief. He shut his eyes and his hot tears spilled down his cheeks. He sucked his lips inward and bowed his head, crossing his heart in the sign of the crucifix then jumped back behind the wheel of the G-ride and peeled off. As soon as he left, Bianca pulled up beside Don Juan's wrecked Porsche. She looked on, watching the police handle the suspect that they had left. The Spanish vixen was about to drive away, when she heard a baby crying.

"Waa! Waa! Waa! Waa!"

Bianca frowned, hearing the wailing baby. She realized that it was coming from the mangled truck and jumped out of her whip. Keeping an eye on the police, she crept over to the SUV and peeked into the backseat. Her face took on a look of surprise when she saw little DJ in the backseat. After popping the locks through the broken driver side window, she pulled open the backdoor and recovered the child.

"Shhhh! Shhhh!" She hushed him as she took a hold of the car seat and slipped his diaper bag over her shoulder. With a watchful eye, she moved back to her ride and strapped the car seat into the passenger seat. Next, she ran over to the driver side and hopped in, firing that big bastard up.

"Aye, stop!" a police officer shouted, as he and a couple of others ran in her direction. It was too late though, because Bianca was already peeling out of there.

***

The light-skinned girl with the individual braids pulled Te'Qui to his feet. She took off her jacket and draped it over his shoulders.

"I'm going to call 9-1-1, okay?"

"Okay." He nodded, slowly getting to his feet as he stared at Wicked's mutilated body, which a crowd was forming around.

The girl had just dialed the number and pressed the cellular to her ear when she heard the squealing of a car's tires.

Urrrrrk! A black Caprice came to a halt in his line of vision and the driver side door flew open. His eyes got as big as saucers when he saw his mother, breaking into a plaque covered toothy smile from his days of captivity.

It was as if the world stopped spinning in that moment they laid eyes on one another. All of the things they went through in the time they were apart lead them to believe they'd never see each other again. But here it was. That miracle they'd both prayed for. It was unfolding right before their very eyes and if they could they'd freeze this moment in time and admire it for as long as they lived.

"Te'Qui, my baby!" She hopped out, smiling and crying all at once. Her hands cupping her mouth as she jumped up and down.

"Momma." Te'Qui's eyes became glassy. The youngster couldn't contain his joy. He took off toward his mother. She took off right after him, hurrying in his direction. He jumped into his mother's arm and she caught him, spinning around. Chevy and her son cried in each another's arms. She kissed him on the cheek and along the side of his face.

"My God, my baby, my lil' man." She ran her hand up and down his back, feeling him shudder as he sobbed against her. "I missed you so much, Te'Qui. I thought I'd never see you again."

"I...I miss you too, momma, and I love you so, so much."

"I love you so much too, baby, and I promise I'm never gonna let chu go again. You hear me? Never." She sniffled, looking into his eyes and wiping the tears from off his cheeks. He nodded and she kissed his forehead, hugging him tighter.

At long last mother and son were reunited.

Chapter Fourteen
Hours Later

Bianca drove up the freeway tickling little DJ's chin and making him giggle. The baby wore a jovial expression as he flailed his arms and kicked his legs. Seeing the little guy this happy, caused her to smile. It made her think back to the unborn child she'd lost, which was the reason she'd snatched him in the first place.

"Him a happy baby, huh?" she cooed. "Yes, he is. Oh, yes he is." She passed him a bottle and he held it, sucking on its nipple.

"I was thinking since I'm your new mom now, that you should have a new name. What chu think about that?" She looked to the baby boy and he smiled with the nipple in his mouth. "Okaaay, I was thinking we'd name you after your daddy that died. How does Cameron sound?" She glanced over and little DJ was swinging an arm excitedly. "I thought you'd love it. Okay, your name is Cameron Jr. and your nickname will be Young Threat."

Bianca cranked up the volume on Beyonce's *Drunk In Love* and mashed the gas pedal, zipping the rental up the highway. "Las Vegas, Nevada, here we come. Whooo!" She sounded like a drunk ass sorority sister, holding her fist out of the window while gripping the steering wheel, tearing up the freeway lane.

The baby was the silver lining that came out of all of the madness those past few days. She wasn't the least bit concerned about kidnapping charges, even though the police had spotted her leaving the scene with Little DJ. She couldn't care less. This was another shot at motherhood and love for her. And she was thankful.

A couple days later

The day was one of the hottest it had been in some time. The enormous ember in the sky shined, casting a blinding light over the vast land that was Nigeria. She rung out her wet clothes until they were somewhat damp then flapped them out aggressively before hanging them out on the line. Her eyes narrowed as she went to pin up a sheet, the intense rays of the sun irritating her pupils. She winced, but finished her task, wiping the beads of sweat from her forehead when she was done.

When she slid her hand from off of her brows, she saw a silhouette moving in her direction. It was about her youngest son's height and size. Smiling, she jumped to her feet and ran toward him, her ebony skin glistening from her perspiration. She ran with everything she had, quickly closing the distance between them. Having gotten a few feet away from him, she noticed the grief written across his young face. This slowed her running to a jog, until she eventually stopped, looking upon him. Her chest rose and fell rapidly as she breathed hard, studying her baby boy's expression.

He stopped where he was looking down at his fidgeting fingers, and occasionally glancing up at the woman that had given birth to him. His eyes were pink and had red webs on them, his cheeks streaked wet from crying. In a panic, her eyebrows raised and she looked to both sides of him. The lines across her forehead defined themselves. Her curiosity made itself present on her lips.

"Where's your...where's ya brudda?"

Finally, Uduka stopped fidgeting with his fingers and locked eyes with his mother. He didn't have to say a thing, his eyes told her the entire story.

Uma's eyes widened and she staggered back with her hand to her chest, choked up, devastated. Suddenly, she fell to the ground. Her eyes accumulated tears in them and her bottom lip trembled uncontrollably. A cache of emotions hit her all at once. Her head snapped up and she looked up into the sky.

"Nooooo!" she screamed, veins rippling through her forehead and up her neck. "Nooooo!" The sound left her voice, but then came back, she shook her head fast. "Gawd, notta 'nudda one of ma baybees. Lord, wat have I done? What have I done to deserve dis?" Uduka dropped to the ground beside his mother and wrapped his arms around her, allowing her to bawl against his chest.

***

The morgue was scarcely lit. Several lifeless forms lay on metal tables with sheets draped over them. Every single one of them wore a tag on their toe, like they were some kind of shirt inside of a department store. A pathologist stood over the corpse of a tall dark-skinned man whose complexion was food stamp blue. His body was riddled with holes, having been shot several times. He was swollen, really swollen. If it hadn't been for the rest of him being slender one would have mistaken that he was a muscular man, but that definitely wasn't the case.

At the very center of him was a large Y where he'd been cut open. It was held together by stitches. This was due to the autopsy that had been performed on him. The huge letter like scar looked like the symbol a super hero would have on his chest. It put a person in the mind of a black Superman.

The pathologist scribbled something down on a clipboard, draped the sheet over the dead man's body, and slipped a tag around his big toe.

***

He made his way down the tier, holding the items he received when he walked through the gates of the place that was considered hell on earth. Prison. His head was on a swivel as he mad dogged all of the hardened criminals that were glaring at him like they wanted to put a sharp piece of steel through him. He looked one buff ass nigga up and down like *'What's up? You don't want none of this, homeboy'* when he passed him. Focusing his attention straight ahead, he moved toward his cell's door where he walked right in and sat his items down on the bottom bunk. He was glad he had the house to himself, but knew that it wouldn't last for long. Someone would be occupying the space sooner or later with him. So, he figured he'd enjoy his alone time while it lasted. After he closed the door shut, he laid back on the bed and pressed a piece of gum on the wall. Afterwards he pressed a picture of his family against it. It was a happier time for him and his family. He clasped his hands behind his head and stared up at the bottom of the bunk above him. Next, he took a deep breath and exhaled, closing his eyes shut.

"Rest in peace, Boxy." Uche whispered, not regretting sacrificing his freedom in order to get the man that murdered his brother. He'd make the same choice a thousand times if given the option.

That night he had the drop on Don Juan in the middle of the street, but when the police ordered him to drop his weapon, he complied at the last minute. His adversary saw this as his chance to body him and tried to shoot him. This action led to the police unloading everything that they had on him.

Epilogue
A Few Days Later

Tiaz was bussed from the courthouse to the County jail. After going through all of the bullshit they put a person through when he first came through that shithole, he made his way to the telephone, slapping hands with the cats he knew and mad dogging others. He was surprised at how his name was ringing off behind the walls. Dudes were talking about how he was putting it down and giving it up in the streets. Although he got some love, he knew he'd also feel the hate. The two coincided with one another. It wouldn't be long before he had to set a mothafucka straight so they'd know that he wasn't one for the bullshit.

Tiaz pushed the thought of having to check a nigga to the back of his mental. Right now, he was focused on getting in touch with someone on the outside so they could get his money and hire him a decent lawyer.

Tiaz stepped to the payphone and reached for the receiver. Before his hand could grasp it, a bony one grabbed it. His eyes followed the bony hand, up its arm and over to the face of the body it belonged to. It was in the possession of a dark-skinned man with nappy hair and some serious acne. His face looked like plastic bubble wrap and his eyes were as yellow as lemons. His uniform was two sizes too small so his limbs looked like tree branches coming out of his sleeves and pants. He sized the thug up, studying him as if he was the tallest stack of shit he'd ever laid eyes on.

"My man, now I know you aren't tryna use my phone without asking?" dark-skinned asked.

"Your phone?" Tiaz frowned. "I don't see your name on the mothafucka."

"The hell you don't." Dark-skinned pointed to the name on the phone.

"Your name is Pacific Bell?" He raised an eyebrow.

"Ya damn skippy, now pay up." Dark-skinned rubbed his thumb and index finger together. "What chu got, money? Commissary?"

"How about an ass whopping?" Tiaz punched him in the mouth with all of his might. The force behind the punch was so great that it caused him to bump the back of his head on the wall and slide down to the floor. The dark-skinned man's bottom jaw split straight down the middle and his grill quickly filled with blood as he tried to push the separated halves back together. The pain was so intense that it brought tears to his eyes. Tiaz went to work on him, kicking and stomping him as he held his arms up trying to shield his face.

Tiaz was so occupied with giving the man the business that he neglected to watch his back. A look of surprise came over him when he felt sharp metal puncturing his back and ribcage. He swung around with his full strength, bringing his balled fist across the jaw of a stockier, muscular cat. The blow caught the man off guard and caused him to stagger to the side, but he held tight to his shank. He righted himself before he could fall and wiped his bleeding mouth with the back of his hand.

His eyes took on a frightening glint and a satanic grin emerged on his face. The sight of blood seemed to entice him. He charged at Tiaz. The thug sidestepped him, grabbed the back on his neck and gripped his wrist. He twisted his wrist so hard and fast that a sharp pain shot through it. It was the equivalent of piercing the skin with a hot needle and it made the man drop his shank. The man's mind was quickly taken off of his wrist when his face smashed into the wall and his forehead split open like a coconut. The man fell to the floor in a heap, groaning in pain. He slowly made to get up when the cats Tiaz knew from the hood finally rushed in and mopped him and the dark-skinned man up. All he could do was watch before collapsing to the floor from blood loss. An alarm blared inside of his ears. The last thing he saw were the C.O.s suited and booted in riot gear rushing in to restore order.

A couple days later

Tiaz' eyelids fluttered open. His vision was blurry, but it came back into focus after a while. He sat up in bed and looked around. The room he was inside was dimly lit. There were hospital beds lined up on both sides of him. Some of them were occupied by inmates. A nurse was checking one of the inmates' vitals. He also saw a doctor standing in an open door jotting something down on a clipboard. That's when it dawned on him that he was in the infirmary. He looked down at his torso and saw that it was wrapped in a bandage.

Tiaz brought both his hands down his face and blew hard. He realized that he passed out from loss of blood, but he didn't know how long he had been out. The nurse walked inside of the room that the doctor was in. As soon as she went through the door, two inmates arose from their beds, slammed the door closed behind her and pushed a file cabinet down in front of it. A C.O. came running towards the two inmates. He radioed for help through his walkie-talkie and suddenly an inmate pulled a pillowcase over his head tightly and rammed his head into the wall until blood smeared the inside of it and he passed out. As soon as the C.O. hit the floor, the inmate along with a few others, barricaded the rest of the entrances into the infirmary.

They then moved in on Tiaz. The dim light in the room bounced off the metal of their shanks and caused them to glint.

Danger! Danger! Danger! The alarm inside of Tiaz' head blared like the dismissal bell for after school detention.

"Arrrr!" He grabbed his side, his moving too fast caused pain to shoot through his ribcage like bolts of lightning. He shuddered, feeling groggy and weakened from his wounds, but forced his eyelids back open. These niggaz wanted blood, his blood. And he wasn't giving up a drop of it without a fight.

Swiftly, he pulled the IV from his arm and hopped out of bed. He wrapped his left hand up in a sheet and unscrewed the top half of the IV pole beside his bed. He held tightly to the lower half of the IV pole, planning to use it as a spear. He then backed himself up against the wall. His head was on a swivel as he surveyed his surroundings, searching for the first man looking to claim his life.

The shank wielding inmates formed a circle around him. He looked around at all of their ice grills wondering why they hadn't attacked. That's when the circle parted and a man came waltzing through. His face was partially hidden by the darkness of the room, so he had to peer closely to I.D. him. When recognition ripped through his brain, he had to blink a few times to make sure who he was seeing was actually standing before him.

"Sa...Sa..." Tiaz stammered.

"Savon, alive and in the mothafucking flesh," the man spoke.

Tiaz was speechless, he couldn't believe it. Chevy's brother was standing right before his eyes.

"You done my niggaz up real nasty, but they were throwaways. I got plenty more hittas where they came from." He swept a hand around to all of the men surrounding them. "Are you ready to die, nigga?" He pulled a sharp metal shank from the small of his back. It was about seven inches in length and had fabric wrapped around its lower half for grip. Tiaz readied himself for the fight for his life once he saw the weapon come into play. "You set me up, pussy. Left me to rot in this shithole, put cho mothafucking hands on my sister, got my nephew out here pushing poison in the streets! Ah, nigga, you gots ta go off of GP! What chu did was a violation punishable by death! And yo' sentencing has come, bitch-nigga!"

"You ain't saying shit, let's dance!" Tiaz shot back with a hard face. His heart was beating fast, but it didn't pump Kool-Aid, it pumped Gangsta Juice.

A flicker of movement at his left brought his eyes around. One of the inmates was tossing him a metal shank identical to Savon's. He threw the IV pole down and pulled the blade down from the air. As the alarm blared in their ears and the inmates cheered them on, the two men circled one another, looking for flaws in the other's defense. The thug's eyes were trained on his opposition's left side. He knew vital organs were on this side and attacking the right spot could kill a man.

With movements that looked like blurs, Savon thrust his hand forth trying to stab him in the heart. Tiaz knocked his hand aside with the hand that was wrapped in the sheet and stabbed him in the cheek, drawing a howl of pain out of him. Savon backed up and touched his cheek, his fingertips came away with blood. He avoided his rival's next few attempts at assaulting him, moving with the agility and grace of a ballroom dancer. He was good on his feet until a slip-up cost him a bleeding shoulder.

The fight went on to the point where both men were bleeding something awful. Their faces were coated in sweat and their hearts were slamming up against the interior of their chests. Their uniforms looked like they had been hit with splashes of red wine. Droplets of blood and sweat covered the floor of the infirmary. The doors of the entrances to the infirmary rattled as the riot squad of the County jail facility tried to force their way in.

One of the men moved in for the kill, thrusting his shank forward. The other man smacked his hand away with such a force that it sent his shank flying across the room. He then delivered an upper cut that lifted him off his feet and dropped him on his back. The man bumped his head and was nearly knocked unconscious. He lay on his back looking through narrowed slits and groaning in pain. The other man straddled him and gripped his throat, squeezing it and lessening the oxygen flowing into his lungs. The man beneath him squirmed and punched at his torso, but his opponent clenched his jaws and took the blows without complaint. He then slammed his seven inch metal blade into the man's armpit down to its handle. The blade pierced the man's heart, killing him instantly.

His eyes bugged and his mouth dropped open. He took his last breath and his arms dropped limply beside him. At that moment the infirmary went deathly quiet as the inmates stared at the man that was victorious. All that could be heard was the blaring alarm and the rattling of the entrance doors. The victorious man lay over his dead opponent, breathing heavily and bleeding from everywhere. He felt relieved having been the one that came out on top. No one could tell him that he wasn't completely justified. He did what he had to do to survive, so whatever punishment came for his actions, he was willing to face. It was survival of the fittest.

Boom! Boom! Boom!

The doors came flying open and the riot squad came pouring inside of the infirmary.

Years later

The C.O. opened the cell's door and he came waltzing out. He moved down the hallway toward his death as confidently as he could with his wrists and ankles in shackles. A host of correctional officers and a priest crowded around him walking with him as he moved down the mustard yellow corridor.

"Dead man walking! Dead man walking!"

He flinched hearing the officer's voice sting his eardrums. He glanced over his shoulder with a scowl and twisted lips.

"Damn, homie, you all in my ear and shit," he complained, heatedly.

Continuing on his way, he threw his head back at the other inmates on Death Row like *'What's up?'* Never breaking his stride. His face was one chiseled out of stone, void of expression and emotion. It was like he was taking an evening stroll through his neighborhood, taking in the sunshine and mingling with the people of his community.

"Alright now, hold yo' head, bro!" A prisoner called out from his left.

"No doubt!" he responded.

"That's the realest nigga to have ever walked the earth right there!" Another prisoner called out from his right.

"Balls of steel." A third prisoner called out.

He locked eyes with him and said, "You mothafucking right."

He knew the life he led would lead to either death or the penitentiary and it led to both. Cold world. But what the fuck could the nigga do? The streets were all that he knew. He played the hand he was dealt and came up short. He wasn't about to bawl and cry about the shit though. He had a reputation to keep. He knew the streets would keep his legacy alive. Once he finally closed his eyes his name would be mentioned with some of the most gangster niggaz in history, he was sure of it. No one could tell him otherwise.

He was led to the room where his life was to end. He stared at the dark green leather cushioned gurney with all of the straps on it as one of the correctional officer's unlocked the shackles around his wrists, waist, and ankles. After the C.O. removed the chains and shackles, he passed them off to the other officer who hoisted them over his shoulder. The officer then told the prisoner to lay down on the gurney. He obliged.

His head snapped to all of the areas of his body that the correctional officers strapped down. They made sure that the thick leather brown belts were pulled good and tight to ensure that their prisoner wouldn't escape. Once the officers finished strapping him down to the gurney, they stepped back to allow the doctor through. He was a tall, white man with thinning hair. He wore glasses and a lab coat. He tied a tourniquet around the thug's arm, cleaned it with a swab moistened in alcohol and tapped it until a ripe, juicy vein was visible. Once he did this, he inserted the IV then removed the length of rubber. He repeated this same routine with the other arm, as well. He then opened his patient's shirt and attached the patches that would monitor his heart. This was done so that the time of his death could be recorded and confirmed.

When the doctor turned around walking off and pushing his specs back upon his face, he noticed a machine that housed three large syringes containing three concoctions. The first one was sodium thiopental, an anesthetic agent that would be used to render him unconscious. The second one was pancuronium bromide, a non-depolarizing muscle relaxant that would cause sustained paralysis to the skeletal striated muscles. The last one was called potassium chloride which would stop his heart, thus causing death by cardiac arrest.

Thump! Thump! Thump! Thump!

His heart was beating fast now because he knew that death was looming around him like a foul stench. But he wasn't afraid of dying. Hell mothafucking nah, he embraced it, welcomed it even. The next thing he knew the curtains were pulled open from over the large windows surrounding the diagnostics room, leaving a host of people looking in on him. They sort of resembled the audience at a talk show like Jerry Springer or Wendy Williams.

One face stood out among them all though. He'd come to love it like he loved breathing. She was beautiful, but at that time her appearance was less than flattering. Chevy's eyes were red webbed and pink. Her cheeks were slickened wet, making her face shiny. She swallowed the lump of hurt that had formed in her throat, her nostrils expanding and shrinking as she breathed angrily. He didn't know if she was mad at him for what had happened or not. One thing for sure was that he didn't care. Nah, he had other matters that had his attention, like all of the hoes he was going to get at once he got to heaven or wherever he was going.

He looked from her and took in all of the faces behind the thick glass. He figured that this was what an animal caged up at the zoo must have felt like. Most of the people in the audience wore solemn expressions. Some looked like they felt sorry for him, while others were crying. Not crying because they felt for him, but because they were happy that justice was being served for the murder of their loved ones. He cracked a wicked smile at them and they went ham, jumping to their feet and hurling chairs which deflected off of the glass. They talked shit and some of them even tried to rush out of the room to get to him. He chuckled and threw up his hood the best way he could with his arms being in restraints. It was his last *fuck you* to them.

After a couple of armed guards ushered the unruly guests out, kicking and screaming, the priest approached the prisoner with an opened Bible. He began reading off a passage when he shouted at him.

"Father, I don't wanna hear that shit, God gave up on niggaz like me a long time ago!"

The priest closed the Holy Book and cleared his throat with a fist to his mouth. "Very well, may the Lord bless your soul, my son."

"Yeah, whatever, nigga." His head whipped around to the warden, looking him up and down like *'Fuck you doing here?'*

"Can I help you?"

"Any last words, Savon?" he asked. The room had a PA system, so everyone outside of the glass could hear what he had to say.

"Once y'all done killing me, and it's time to lay me to rest, y'all just make sure they bury me a G!" He said aloud, taking in all of the faces of the people in the audience, making sure he had everyone's attention. "You hear me? Bury me a G, bury me a mothafucking G!"

To Be Continued...
Bury Me a G 4
Coming Soon

Submission Guideline

Submit the first three chapters of your completed manuscript to ldpsubmissions@gmail.com, subject line: Your book's title. The manuscript must be in a .doc file and sent as an attachment. Document should be in Times New Roman, double spaced and in size 12 font. Also, provide your synopsis and full contact information. If sending multiple submissions, they must each be in a separate email.

Have a story but no way to send it electronically? You can still submit to LDP/Ca$h Presents. Send in the first three chapters, written or typed, of your completed manuscript to:

LDP: Submissions Dept
Po Box 870494
Mesquite, Tx 75187

DO NOT send original manuscript. Must be a duplicate.

Provide your synopsis and a cover letter containing your full contact information.

Thanks for considering LDP and Ca$h Presents.

Coming Soon from Lock Down Publications/Ca$h Presents

BOW DOWN TO MY GANGSTA

By **Ca$h**

TORN BETWEEN TWO

By **Coffee**

BLOOD STAINS OF A SHOTTA **III**

By **Jamaica**

STEADY MOBBIN **III**

By **Marcellus Allen**

BLOOD OF A BOSS **V**

By **Askari**

LOYAL TO THE GAME **IV**

LIFE OF SIN II

By **T.J. & Jelissa**

A DOPEBOY'S PRAYER **II**

By **Eddie "Wolf" Lee**

IF LOVING YOU IS WRONG... **III**

LOVE ME EVEN WHEN IT HURTS **II**

By **Jelissa**

TRUE SAVAGE **VII**

By **Chris Green**

BLAST FOR ME **III**

A BRONX TALE III

DUFFLE BAG CARTEL

By **Ghost**

ADDICTIED TO THE DRAMA **III**

By **Jamila Mathis**

LIPSTICK KILLAH **III**

WHAT BAD BITCHES DO **III**

KILL ZONE **II**

By **Aryanna**

THE COST OF LOYALTY **II**

By **Kweli**

SHE FELL IN LOVE WITH A REAL ONE **II**

By **Tamara Butler**

RENEGADE BOYS **III**

By **Meesha**

CORRUPTED BY A GANGSTA **IV**

By **Destiny Skai**

A GANGSTER'S CODE **III**

By **J-Blunt**

KING OF NEW YORK IV

RISE TO POWER II

By **T.J. Edwards**

GORILLAS IN THE BAY II

De'Kari

THE STREETS ARE CALLING II

Duquie Wilson

KINGPIN KILLAZ III

Hood Rich

STEADY MOBBIN' **III**

Marcellus Allen

SINS OF A HUSTLA II

ASAD

CASH MONEY HOES

Nicole Goosby

TRIGGADALE II

Elijah R. Freeman

MARRIED TO A BOSS 2...

By Destiny Skai & Chris Green

KINGS OF THE GAME II

Playa Ray

Available Now

RESTRAINING ORDER **I & II**

By **CA$H & Coffee**

LOVE KNOWS NO BOUNDARIES **I II & III**

By **Coffee**

RAISED AS A GOON I, II, III & IV

BRED BY THE SLUMS I, II, III

BLAST FOR ME I & II

ROTTEN TO THE CORE I III

A BRONX TALE I, II

By **Ghost**

LAY IT DOWN **I & II**

LAST OF A DYING BREED

BLOOD STAINS OF A SHOTTA I & II

By **Jamaica**

LOYAL TO THE GAME

LOYAL TO THE GAME II

LOYAL TO THE GAME III

LIFE OF SIN

By **TJ & Jelissa**

BLOODY COMMAS I & II

SKI MASK CARTEL I II & III

KING OF NEW YORK I II,III

RISE TO POWER

By **T.J. Edwards**

IF LOVING HIM IS WRONG…I & II

LOVE ME EVEN WHEN IT HURTS

By **Jelissa**

WHEN THE STREETS CLAP BACK I & II III

By **Jibril Williams**

A DISTINGUISHED THUG STOLE MY HEART I II & III

LOVE SHOULDN'T HURT I II III

RENEGADE BOYS I & II

By **Meesha**

A GANGSTER'S CODE I & II

By **J-Blunt**

PUSH IT TO THE LIMIT

By **Bre' Hayes**

BLOOD OF A BOSS **I, II, III & IV**

By **Askari**

THE STREETS BLEED MURDER **I, II & III**

THE HEART OF A GANGSTA I II& III

Tranay Adams

By **Jerry Jackson**
<u>CUM FOR ME</u>
<u>CUM FOR ME 2</u>
<u>CUM FOR ME 3</u>
<u>CUM FOR ME 4</u>
An **LDP Erotica Collaboration**
<u>BRIDE OF A HUSTLA</u> **I II & II**
<u>THE FETTI GIRLS</u> **I, II& III**
<u>CORRUPTED BY A GANGSTA I, II & III</u>
By **Destiny Skai**
<u>WHEN A GOOD GIRL GOES BAD</u>
By **Adrienne**
<u>A GANGSTER'S REVENGE</u> **I II III & IV**
<u>THE BOSS MAN'S DAUGHTERS</u>
<u>THE BOSS MAN'S DAUGHTERS II</u>
<u>THE BOSSMAN'S DAUGHTERS III</u>
<u>THE BOSSMAN'S DAUGHTERS IV</u>
<u>THE BOSS MAN'S DAUGHTERS</u> **V**
<u>A SAVAGE LOVE I & II</u>
<u>BAE BELONGS TO ME</u>
<u>A HUSTLER'S DECEIT I, II</u>
<u>WHAT BAD BITCHES DO I, II</u>
By **Aryanna**
<u>A KINGPIN'S AMBITON</u>
<u>A KINGPIN'S AMBITION</u> **II**
<u>I MURDER FOR THE DOUGH</u>
By **Ambitious**

TRUE SAVAGE

TRUE SAVAGE II

TRUE SAVAGE **III**

TRUE SAVAGE **IV**

TRUE SAVAGE **V**

TRUE SAVAGE **VI**

By **Chris Green**

A DOPEBOY'S PRAYER

By **Eddie "Wolf" Lee**

THE KING CARTEL **I, II & III**

By **Frank Gresham**

THESE NIGGAS AIN'T LOYAL **I, II & III**

By **Nikki Tee**

GANGSTA SHYT **I II &III**

By **CATO**

THE ULTIMATE BETRAYAL

By **Phoenix**

BOSS'N UP **I , II & III**

By **Royal Nicole**

I LOVE YOU TO DEATH

By **Destiny J**

I RIDE FOR MY HITTA

I STILL RIDE FOR MY HITTA

By **Misty Holt**

LOVE & CHASIN' PAPER

By **Qay Crockett**

TO DIE IN VAIN

SINS OF A HUSTLA

By **ASAD**

BROOKLYN HUSTLAZ

By **Boogsy Morina**

BROOKLYN ON LOCK I & II

By **Sonovia**

GANGSTA CITY

By **Teddy Duke**

A DRUG KING AND HIS DIAMOND I & II III

A DOPEMAN'S RICHES

HER MAN, MINE'S TOO I, II

By Nicole Goosby

TRAPHOUSE KING **I II & III**

KINGPIN KILLAZ

By **Hood Rich**

LIPSTICK KILLAH **I, II**

CRIME OF PASSION I & II

By **Mimi**

STEADY MOBBN' **I, II**

By **Marcellus Allen**

WHO SHOT YA **I, II**

Renta

GORILLAZ IN THE BAY

DE'KARI

TRIGGADALE

Elijah R. Freeman

GOD BLESS THE TRAPPERS I, II, III

THESE SCANDALOUS STREETS I, II, III
FEAR MY GANGSTA I, II, III
THESE STREETS DON'T LOVE NOBODY I, II
Tranay Adams
THE STREETS ARE CALLING
Duquie Wilson
MARRIED TO A BOSS...
By Destiny Skai & Chris Green
KINGS OF THE GAME II
Playa Ray

BOOKS BY LDP'S CEO, CA$H

TRUST IN NO MAN

TRUST IN NO MAN 2

TRUST IN NO MAN 3

BONDED BY BLOOD

SHORTY GOT A THUG

THUGS CRY

THUGS CRY 2

THUGS CRY 3

TRUST NO BITCH

TRUST NO BITCH 2

TRUST NO BITCH 3

TIL MY CASKET DROPS

RESTRAINING ORDER

RESTRAINING ORDER 2

IN LOVE WITH A CONVICT

Coming Soon

BONDED BY BLOOD 2

BOW DOWN TO MY GANGSTA

Bury Me a G 3